THE
UNNAMED
COUNTRY

THE UNNAMED COUNTRY

JEFFREY THOMAS

WORD HORDE
PETALUMA, CA

Publication credits:
"The Uninvited Grave" first appeared on the Patreon website *Jeffrey Thomas is Creating Weird Fiction*, 2015.
"The Unicorn Farm" first appeared on the Patreon website *Jeffrey Thomas is Creating Weird Fiction*, 2015.
"Motherboard" first appeared in the publication *Interzone*, issue #263, 2016.
"Distinguished Mole" first appeared in the publication *Black Static*, issue #48, 2015.
All other stories are original to this collection.

First Edition

ISBN: 978-1-939905-54-3

A Word Horde Book
www.wordhorde.com

TABLE OF CONTENTS

CHOLUKAN AND THE GODS

The Ten Jeweled Gods themselves could not walk among mortals to observe their ways. They only appeared in visions, usually before individuals but sometimes before crowds, and their presence was so overwhelming that humans invariably cast themselves to their knees and bent their foreheads to the dirt. Humans in such a state and position could not be appreciated for their normal manner of existence. And so the Gods decided to send an agent to walk and live among mortals, who would report back what he observed, so that the Gods might experience vicariously the life of mortals from an earthly rather than heavenly perspective. This knowledge was to them both educational and vastly entertaining.

The task of creating this agent was accepted by the goddess, the Ruby Empress. She made a decision that rather surprised the other Gods, and some of them protested until she explained her reasoning. She intended to change her beloved pet monkey into their proposed holy scribe. She had taken this mortal beast to Heaven as her pet because, to her mind, monkeys represented a mid-point between the dust of nothingness from which all life was created, and the pinnacle of life, which was the human. Thus, a balance between Heaven and Earth.

The Ruby Empress wept as she cradled her pet monkey, knowing that his time of innocence as a mere beast was over. Her tears were drops of blood, which fell to her chest and crystallized as rubies. One drop fell into the sleeping monkey's ear, and he awakened then, transformed into an entity that was no longer merely an earthly creature, and yet not quite divine.

The Ruby Empress had never given the tailless, yellow-furred macaque a name, but now she dubbed him Cholukan, which meant "Awakened to Emptiness," in the sense that he was now an empty vessel waiting to be filled with the wonders he would experience on the earthly plane…and which, as the scribe of the Gods, he would report back to them.

Now dressed in blue silk and ready to depart to the Earth, Cholukan laid his head in the Ruby Empress's lap, and she stroked his yellow-furred head, saying, "Beware, my dear little companion, of the mortals you will meet. You are a tricky creature, but they are trickier still. We know that much about them already…all too well. They will mock you. They will hurt you. Because they will not understand you."

"All of them, mistress?" Cholukan asked. For now he had the power of speech.

"Not all. But too many." She lifted his chin so she might look into his eyes, and fresh tears of blood rose in the corners of her own eyes. She had once been a beautiful young goddess, but vast stretches of time can weather even the Gods, and her contributions to the creation of all life on Earth had further aged her. Yet her eyes remained lovely and compassionate. "You must go now, my child. Bring us back your stories. And you will find, too, that you have a story of your own to be written."

B-2

It had been ten years since the wildly popular serial *B-2* had first appeared on TV, but it was still watched on reruns and video disc, with little of its audience's enthusiasm diminished, no matter how many times they viewed it. The series, a romantic drama consisting of fifty one-hour episodes, centered around several turbulent, passionate, and beautiful couples living in the capital city of Haikan, in an apartment complex called B-2. Though it would seem identical to countless other serialized dramas—depending greatly on implausible plot turns and coincidence, as many love stories do—the drama became a small phenomenon, in the unplanned and inexplicable way such things occur, unmatched even by a pseudo-sequel and other soap operas pairing up some of the same actors.

Fans were so obsessed with the program that they took to stenciling B-2 on the doors of their apartments, the fronts of their houses. Many ordered formal plaques bearing B-2 in gold letters. There was now even an actual apartment tower in Haikan that sported B-2 near its summit in huge metal characters.

These ubiquitous tributes to the much-loved TV program were not without their complications. Postmen had to learn to disregard such address designations, and memorize people's actual locations instead, though Western tourists remained mystified when the addresses displayed for certain restaurants, shops, and hotels proved to be at odds with the fold-out maps in their travel guides.

The nightclub where Kwen worked was named *B-2*—the pairing of a single letter and single number stood out in looping blue neon on the front of the block-like building—but one night in the dressing room, while her fellow performers discussed one of the drama's complex plotlines, she admitted that she had never watched *B-2* herself.

"*What?*" Twee screeched, reaching out from her stool in front of the wall-length mirror to swat at Kwen's leg with a rolled up fashion magazine. "Have you been living on another world? How can you not have ever seen *B-2?*"

"It's ten years old," Kwen replied self-consciously, the stares and gasps of her friends now making her sorry for her admission. "It came out when I was only nine years old. I watch all the newer series."

"No new series is as good as *B-2*," Phep told her. At thirty-two, Phep was the oldest of the troupe, still severely beautiful, her face bleached white by chemicals and her thick eyebrows tattooed in bluish-black.

"It doesn't matter that it's ten years old," Twee admonished her. "It's never stopped being on TV! It's *immortal!*"

"That's it," said Chok firmly, "I have the discs at home. I'm bringing in the whole set tomorrow and you had better watch them, or I'll never talk to you again."

"None of us will!" Twee chimed in. She fanned herself with her magazine and fluttered her eyes as if she were growing faint. "Good gods…you poor, ignorant, uncultured child."

"All right, all right," Kwen told them, "I'll watch Chok's discs, okay?"

Ko, their short and burly manager and the right-hand man

of the club's owner, burst into their dressing room with bulging eyes and said, "Phep, didn't you hear me announce you? You're on!"

The seasoned veteran rose from her stool with a proud sneer. "I know it's my time—you don't have to tell me, you little ape." She strutted past Ko regally, washing him in a wake of overpowering perfume, and the rest of them in the dressing room heard the throb of electronic music grow louder, the applause and drunken cheers of the club's patrons, at her appearance on stage.

"Ko," Twee said to their boss, "can you believe Kwen has never seen *B-2?*"

Ko turned to Kwen with his eyes gone protuberant again. "*What?* Never? Not a single episode?"

"Like anyone could, or should, watch only one episode!" Twee said.

"Chok is lending me her discs tomorrow," Kwen replied, embarrassed all over again.

"You had better watch it," Ko commanded, as if it were a condition of her continued employment. He pointed at her sternly. "I'm going to quiz you on it, to make sure you do!"

"Good idea," Twee said.

"And don't forget," Ko further ordered Kwen—the youngest and newest of his dancers—just before withdrawing from the dressing room, "you're on after Phep."

***

When Gil had last been in this country, almost twenty years earlier, he had been a sergeant in the army stationed in a neighboring country, on a three-day leave with a group of his men. His memory of that leave was a single blur of too-loud music, too much drink, and preternaturally smooth gold-brown flesh.

Though in the midst of that blur, like a lustrous pearl enfolded in an oyster's cloudy flesh, something more profound had endured...a memory within the memory.

Back then, automobiles hadn't been prevalent, bicycles had abounded, and the swarms of motorbikes had been cheap and dusty. Now, on the long drive from the airport he'd found the cars had multiplied, the bicycles had all but disappeared, and the motorbikes that still proliferated in a buzzing chaos were mostly slick, modern, more colorful models. And everyone, no matter how impoverished looking, seemed to own a cell phone.

One thing that hadn't changed, except for their more Western attire, was the women. As diminutive and slender as children, as if they defied aging, as if these might be the very same women he had hungered after back then. That shimmering black hair which seemed to define them. Eyes that seized his guts, whether they were hard or warm. Smiles that made his heart trip, whether they were carnal or shy. And those endearing crooked teeth, like fangs to rend his very soul.

"First time to our beautiful country, sir?" asked a bellhop attired in a smart maroon uniform, with epaulets and matching cap, as he unloaded Gil's bags from the taxi. It had pulled up in front of the 777 Hotel, where he would be staying alone—no fellow soldiers with him this time, and he had lost track of those men in the intervening years—through the duration of his business trip. It was because he had been to this country before, and knew a little of the language, that his company had agreed to send him when he'd volunteered for the project.

"It's been a long time," Gil told the bellhop, without getting into particulars.

"Welcome back!" the young man said, grinning. He himself had the same striking dark eyes, high cheekbones, and crooked bright teeth as the women.

***

"Laiki is going to do her laundry for the first time in her new apartment building, and carrying her basket, when she realizes the elevator isn't working. So she has to go down the stairs from the fifth floor to the basement. A handsome young man meets her coming up the stairs and he offers to carry her basket down to the laundry room for her. He introduces himself as Tendu, and he lives on the sixth floor. In the basement, which is kind of dark and spooky, he helps throw her clothing into the washing machine, but when he picks up a pair of her panties she snatches it from him shyly. They like each other right away, but while they're talking Tendu gets a call and he says he has run; he has to go meet someone at the airport. Laiki is sorry to see him go."

In the dressing room, the four of them—Kwen and her audience: Twee, Chok, and Phep—perched on their stools in a circle, eating from styrofoam takeout boxes, their dinner brought to them by Ko. The older dancers listened respectfully; one might even say raptly. It was as though they hadn't heard this story before…as though they didn't know it by heart. Even Ko had listened approvingly for a bit, from the doorway, before retreating to tend to other matters.

Kwen went on.

"One day Laiki is trying to catch a cab to work, because she only has a bicycle and it's raining badly. She has no luck, but she sees Tendu getting into a car nearby. She waves to him, smiling, but he drives right by her like he doesn't see her, and splashes her. She's soaked from head to feet. When she meets Tendu on the stairs again later that evening, he tries to talk to her but she's angry and ignores him…"

"You skipped the scene between Moop and Din!" Twee protested, cutting in. "At the swimming pool on the building's roof!"

"I'm not as interested in their story," Kwen replied.

"You can't just edit out a whole other storyline! *B-2* isn't just about Laiki and Tendu!"

"They're the characters I like most," Kwen said insistently. "The point was, you wanted to be sure I've begun watching *B-2*. I have! And I like it! Don't you see that?"

"Shh," Chok told Twee. "Let her go on…don't interrupt."

"But Moop and Din are my favorite couple in *B-2!*" Twee persisted.

"Shh!" Phep, the senior dancer, weighed in.

Twee snicked her tongue and bent over her noodles sulkily, allowing Kwen to continue.

"In the basement doing her laundry again, Laiki sees Tendu come in carrying his own clothes. He looks more rough than he did before, unshaven, and he's smoking a cigarette. He ignores her totally. She's angry and blows up at him. He's surprised by her behavior and accuses her of being crazy. Laiki is close to tears and turns to run from the room…and collides with Tendu in the doorway. Tendu looks as handsome and well-groomed as ever. Laiki looks between the two identical men in confusion, as if she's losing her mind, until Tendu says, 'Laiki, I'm happy to see you again. And let me introduce you to my brother, Zo. He's come to live with me for a while.' Laiki looks at Zo and understands now that it was this man, not Tendu, who splashed her with his car. She nods at him politely, and Zo winks at her, smirking around his cigarette as he finishes loading his clothes in the washer."

"Zo seems like a bastard at first," Twee said, enthused about the unfolding plot developments, "but later when he starts flirting with Laiki you can tell he really likes her. Then she gets to feeling torn between the two of them. Zo the sexy bad boy, and Tendu so sweet and straight."

"Ha!" Chok said. "So it seems at first! Before Laiki finds out about the gangsters, and—"

"Stop!" Kwen cut Chok off. "Don't give away what happens… I'm only done with the first episode!"

"Sorry," Chok admitted, "we're getting ahead of ourselves."

"You'd better watch the next one tonight," Twee told Kwen. "We want to hear about it tomorrow."

"I promise," Kwen told them. And frankly, she couldn't wait to get home from work tonight to her little apartment and view the next installment. She was happy her friends had goaded her into watching the old soap opera. She was hooked already.

***

Gil shielded his eyes against the sun's blaze as he stepped from the taxi to the sidewalk. The general neighborhood looked much as it had almost two decades earlier: sultry and sleazy, dingy and run-down in the day, but no doubt colorfully transformed at night, like a corpse made up for a wake. The street smelled much the same, too: a dizzying brew of garbage and incense, sewerage and smoky street food. But the building he stood in front of was no longer called *The Love Army* (a rather blatant bid to the foreign soldiers who had once frequented the establishment when on leave). Instead, for whatever reason, the new name in a scrawl of blue neon was *B-2*.

Gil ducked inside quickly, as if afraid to be spotted by someone he knew, which he understood was irrational. No one else from his company was in the country…nor were his wife and two teenaged children.

He was grateful for the adequate air conditioning and dark

interior, though the latter briefly disoriented him. When after a few beats he felt more grounded, he spotted a familiar sight: the same taxidermied monkey in a glass showcase, set back in a little niche at the base of the front counter. Deposited in front of the monkey were offerings in the form of a cup of rice wine, a bottle of beer, and a bowl into which customers dropped loose cigarettes or coins for good luck. Maybe the monkey was more moth-eaten than he had been so many years ago, but he still had two red glass spheres like marbles jammed into his eye sockets. Gil had never asked why the red glass eyes. Long ago he had come to expect the mysterious, the unexplainable, from this country. From *any* country other than his own. That was just the way of things. And here he was, come back to reacquaint himself with the unfathomable.

The striking hostess behind the counter greeted him with a perfect smile and mannerisms, like an automatonic figure at a Western theme park, and summoned a waitress who could speak his language sufficiently well. The waitress was leggy in towering stilettos, and unnaturally tall for someone of her nationality, encased in a sparkling mini-dress so tight that second skin didn't quite capture it. She smiled at Gil soullessly. He didn't care. She escorted him to a seat right at the edge of the dance floor's raised platform, which was currently unoccupied, and took his order for a beer imported from his own country, whereas back in the day he and his men had had to make do with the local brews.

While he nursed his beer, waiting for the live entertainment to begin, he swept his gaze around the nightclub's interior. Until, at the bar, he saw her, and his bottle stopped dead in the air on the way to his lips.

She was sitting with three other women, all of them drinking coffee or soft drinks, and leaning their heads close to hear each other over the incessant, bass-heavy background music. All four of these women were stunning, in his eyes, even the one who was plainly overcompensating for her age with her too-white face and too-black eyebrows, but the youngest of them seized him in such a way that he went breathless.

The girl was the spitting image of Nai. His Nai. The love of his life, even if that love had only lasted three days. A love confined not only to three days, but to this very room and the bedroom where she lived on the second floor, just above. The love of his life…whom he wasn't sure had loved him back. But why should she have? Another Western soldier passing through. How many might she have known? Had any of them ever married her, finally, sponsored her to come live in his own country? All Gil knew was that *he* hadn't married her. But how he had fantasized, over the years, what it would have been like. How he had regretted, all these years, that he had ultimately returned to his fiancée when his foreign stint was over, and married her instead.

Did Nai even remember him today, wherever she was? And why had he fallen in love with her at all? Only lust, he told himself. It had only been the desperate hunger of desire, the need to *possess*…akin to a sudden and overwhelming madness. It was… unfathomable. Yet he felt that madness wash through him again as he stared at this young woman across the smoky room. He told himself he was superimposing. Maybe the women in this country looked too much the same to his foreign eyes. But no… no…that wasn't true. The truth was that the resemblance was uncanny. She was like Nai reincarnated.

Gil summoned his waitress, gestured toward the young girl at the bar, and ordered a fresh drink be brought to her. He considered being polite and ordering drinks for her friends, too, but didn't want his message to be muddled.

When the waitress handed the young girl a new glass of soda, she turned on her bar stool to smile at Gil across the room, and his heartbeat leaped up to match the rhythm of the pounding music.

***

Before the Westerner across the room had sent a drink to her, obligating Kwen to get up and go sit with him at his table, she had been encapsulating the fourth, fifth, and sixth episodes of *B-2* for Twee, Chok, and Phep. She had stayed up too late last night, watching three hours of the program in one sitting.

"Laiki is coming out of the elevator, which the repairman just finished working on, and is carrying her laundry basket into the basement when she passes the foot of the staircase and almost trips over a body lying on the floor. She didn't see it at first because of her basket, but when she puts the basket down and rolls the body over, she realizes it's Tendu."

(Did Twee actually gasp, as if learning this revelation for the first time?)

"His forehead is bruised and his head rolls limply, so we know his neck is broken. Laiki looks up the stairs, knowing that Tendu has tumbled down them, and then she bursts into wild sobbing and lifts his head onto her lap. She says his name over and over. 'Tendu! *Tenduuu!*'" Kwen imitated the actress's anguished tone. She had come to embrace her role of storyteller in the past few days. "In recent weeks she's come to love this man, and now just like that he's been taken out of her life...out of this world."

Kwen's voice broke and she had to stop, on the pretense of sipping her soda, before she outright broke into tears like Laiki herself. She noticed that Twee was dabbing at the corner of one of her own heavily made-up eyes.

When Kwen had taken a few moments to get her voice under control, she resumed, "Other of the building's tenants hear

Laiki screaming and come down to the basement to investigate, including the elevator repairman and Din, who Laiki has begun talking to whenever she visits the swimming pool on the roof. When an ambulance comes she finally lets herself be torn away from Tendu's body. After they take him away, still weeping, she gathers up all his clothing that spilled down the stairs when he tripped and fell. She loads up a machine with his laundry, as if she might wash it for him and later give it to the man she loved."

It was at this point that the tall waitress in the short, glittery sheath brought Kwen a fresh soft drink and indicated the foreigner sitting at the base of the long dance platform. Kwen put on a gracious smile for the man, and her friends teased her with whispered comments as she slid her bottom off the bar stool and walked across the room toward her new admirer.

***

She wasn't a clone of Nai, now that he saw her up close. Nai's feline eyes, though just as wide-spaced, had been more slanted in appearance. This girl's eyes were wider, with double rather than single eyelids, giving her a look of youthful innocence. Nai's nose had been shorter and flatter, though this girl didn't appear to have had surgery to render a more Western-looking nose, as many women did in this country. Nai's skin tone had been a shade or two darker. And, markedly, Nai had been almost flat-chested, whereas this girl's T-shirt bulged improbably considering her slight frame. Yet despite these touches, the overall resemblance remained strong. The same wide but rounded jaw line, the same full lips that when not smiling warmly held a haughty, sneering kind of pout. He remembered kissing Nai…sucking her succulent lower lip between his teeth…as he had done with the lips between her legs as well.

"I'm sorry to be so forward," Gil told Kwen, "but I just…I had to…you're so beautiful I just wanted to…"

She smiled and clinked her glass of soda against his bottle of beer, mercifully cutting short his stammering. "Cheers," she chirped, taking a swallow. Then she said, "Thank you for saying that. You're very handsome yourself."

"Oh, come on," Gil said, looking away. He knew he was by no means handsome. Maybe almost handsome, two decades past.

"I love your hair color. Red. Women in my country would kill for that color. And your white skin, especially."

Nai had said almost those exact words. Nai had teased him about his pretty pink nipples, too; said she with her dark brown nipples envied him.

He looked back to Kwen—afraid and desperate, both, to gaze directly into her huge dark eyes. Twin black holes, sucking him in without chance of escape. Fathomless and unfathomable eyes. "You speak my language so well."

"Thank you. I studied it in school. But then, most students are required to study your language these days."

"But I bet they're not all as adept at it as you are."

"Adept?"

"Good at it, I mean."

"Oh. Thank you."

"I'm Gil." He extended his hand, even though he knew it was considered too intimate to shake hands with a woman in this country. At least, that was the tradition when he'd last been here. But she accepted his hand without hesitation. Her own was small and warm as a child's. He was reluctant to let go of it.

"I'm Kwen," she said.

"Kwen," he repeated aloud, her name like a lover's secretions on his tongue. "I thought that was a boy's name," he teased.

"It is one of the names that can be used for either a male or a female," Kwen informed him, taking on a more serious expression.

"Ahh." He drew in a deep breath. "When I told you...when I said you're beautiful," he started stammering again, "that doesn't begin to do you justice. You have a kind of *magic*."

"You are so kind." She cocked her head, grinning. Was that grin sincere, or well practiced?

"You remind me so much of a woman I got involved with when I came here the first time."

"Oh? When was that?"

"Almost twenty years ago. I was a soldier then, and I came to this city on a three-day pass."

"Only three days? So you didn't know this woman long."

"No, I didn't." He was about to tell Kwen that the woman had been a dancer in this very club, back when it had been known as *The Love Army*, but stopped himself lest she think he was in the habit of picking up women for brief meaningless flings. Or paying prostitutes for sex, which—though he didn't like to dwell on that—was what it had been between him and Nai. *All* it had been for her, perhaps...nothing more. Despite her gentle words, gentle caresses, gentle kisses. Probably just a lie. The pearl he had clutched in his mind all these years merely artificial, after all.

"Are you here on vacation from the army again?"

"Oh no...no...God, I left the service shortly after that. No, I'm on a business trip now."

"Alone?"

"Yes, alone." He tensed up inside, waiting for her to ask if he had a wife at home, but she probably knew better than to bring that up.

After taking a fortifying slug of his beer, he noticed that Kwen was noticing her friends at the bar, giggling as they watched the two of them as if enjoying a TV program. When Kwen noticed he had noticed her noticing, she apologized. "Speaking of love stories, my friends and I were just discussing a TV series they insisted I should watch. It's very romantic. Very sad, too."

"That makes sense. Romantic and sad go hand-in-hand."

"Do you think so?"

"Sure. If we get what we want…the person we're pursuing… we become jaded. We don't want them anymore. In *real* love, I mean the lovesick kind of love, you usually don't get the person you want. That's what makes the feeling so intense. That longing for what you can't have. Don't you think so?"

"I don't know. I've never really had a serious relationship, happy or sad."

"You never cared to?"

"No one else cared to."

"Huh? Come on…I find it hard to believe no one would care to have a serious relationship with you."

"Maybe they didn't understand me enough," Kwen said, showing him a small smile that might have been wistful, or bitter, or merely fatalistic. "Or maybe they understood me too much."

"I think any man would be incredibly lucky to be involved with you."

"How can you say that?" she challenged him softly, tilting her chin up. "You don't know me. Am I worth so much just because you think I look beautiful?"

"It's a start," he said, "a first impression. But I can tell you're very sweet, and gentle, and smart." He realized he was saying the same words, pretty much, that he had said to win over Nai—to win her mind, her *soul*, and not just her body, which was a cheap prize in this country—right here in this same room those many years ago. So who was acting out a practiced routine, now?

"You remind me of a character named Din in the TV series I'm watching," Kwen told him. "He has a wife named Moop, and they were married only a few months before, but it was a marriage arranged by their parents. A girl named Laiki moves into the apartment building, and one day Laiki goes swimming in the pool on the roof where Din likes to sit writing his novel…"

"He writes his novel in the swimming pool?" Gil teased.

"No, in a chair beside the pool." Kwen slapped his wrist lightly. "Anyway, when Din sees Laiki he immediately falls in love with her. He goes *crazy* over her. He starts writing love poems for her and sliding them under her door, but she doesn't know yet who's been sending them."

"Does she end up falling in love with him?" Gil asked hopefully, since Kwen had compared him to the writer character and hence must be equating herself with Laiki.

"I don't know; I haven't seen past episode seven yet. There are fifty episodes."

"Oh wow!"

"Right now Laiki is in love with Tendu. At least, she *was* in love with him…but he died. He fell down a flight of stairs. At the end of episode seven, Tendu's twin brother Zo embraced her and comforted her, and she held him tight and cried against his chest."

"Ahh," Gil said. "Twin brother, huh? That final scene would seem to indicate that this girl…Laiki…is going to fall in love with the brother next, because he reminds her of her boyfriend."

"It looks that way. I will find out soon, when I watch the next episode."

Just then, striding toward them purposefully from across the room came a short, muscular man in a tight polo shirt. At first Gil thought he had done something to anger the man—a jealous husband, despite Kwen's avowals of never having known a real relationship?—but as he came near and Gil tried to summon his dusty old fighting training to the fore of his mind, the man smiled apologetically and said, "Excuse me, sir, very sorry to interrupt, but Kwen is our first dancer tonight and she must begin very soon."

"Dancer?" Gil echoed, looking quickly to Kwen.

She stood up from her chair, smoothing the tail of her T-shirt over her jeans. "You didn't know, Gil?"

"No, I'm sorry...I didn't realize."

"Please stay to watch her dance," Ko said in his heavy accent, placing a hand on Gil's shoulder.

"Of course," Gil told the man, and then he turned to repeat to Kwen, "Of course."

He found he was trembling. A dancer. Like Nai. He was dismayed and excited at the same time, and he watched her walk away, watched her small bottom rocking in her tight jeans, and she glanced back over her shoulder at him and wiggled her fingers.

***

His waitress left Gil a fresh bottle of beer, and he watched her totter away on her high heels. Over a microphone somewhere came loud garbled talk in the native language—that bull-like man who had approached his table earlier—and when Gil looked back to the stage he saw Kwen mounting the steps on its far side. Her jeans had been exchanged for a pair of low-slung, frayed denim cutoffs, cut off at the very top of her thighs, legs as slim and hairless as a twelve-year-old's. The white T-shirt had been replaced with a lacy black bra, exposing the upper curves of breasts that surely had been surgically enhanced. Her belly was a long flat expanse, black navel like a secret keyhole.

She took hold of the metal stripper pole with one hand and

held onto it as she swayed and rolled her hips with a slow, sensual laziness to the thumping electronic beat. Gil waited for her dance to really kick in, but she stuck to this routine, simply walking around the pole once in a while to reposition herself, altering the view for the men scattered around the base of the stage (though the customers weren't many at this early hour). The go-go dancers Gil remembered from his visits to *The Love Army* had danced up a storm, punishing the air with their gyrations, so that he had almost worried they'd drop dead from exhaustion, their bodies dipped in sweat. And in his own country, the muscular strippers worked their pole like gymnasts, wrapping their legs around the metal phallus, hanging upside-down from it as if they were trapeze artists. Those go-go dancers (and he couldn't picture them in their forties today) hadn't removed all their clothing—it hadn't been permitted in this country—but the strippers in his own country took everything off, baring their shaved pudenda, and one time he had summoned the courage to put a bill between his teeth and stand at the foot of the stage. The busty blonde had come over to him, leaned down and squashed his face between her own enhanced breasts, suffocating him in her powdery perfume, a scent that lingered in the grooves of his brain to this day. He had been afraid his wife would smell that perfume on his face when he returned late from work, and a little drunk, but she hadn't noticed. Or hadn't cared.

Yet Kwen continued to mostly stand in place, her body rippling like that of a swimming mermaid. He wasn't complaining, though, because despite the other patrons ogling her she kept her eyes on his most of the time. Smiling a secret little smile. Or so he wanted to believe. A smile just for him.

Would she remove all her clothing? Had her country loosened up, that way, in the intervening years? He started to become

anxious as he heard other men, all of them locals, hoot and
call out lascivious remarks. She was seeming less like a dancer
and more like a piece of merchandise on display, on an auction
block, waiting for a bidder.

Without consciously deciding to do so, he held up a bill for
her to see. They had no qualms about accepting his nation's cur-
rency in this country, but did dancers allow customers to slip
bills into their bras or waistbands? Kwen immediately looked
away from him, and he lowered the money, feeling embarrassed
and hoping her boss hadn't seen, lest he'd stepped over some line
of etiquette. And sure enough, here came the stocky little man
now. Gil turned to him, ready to apologize. The man bent down
close to Gil, a hand on his shoulder again, and spoke loudly in
his ear over the throb of music.

"Do you want a special dance, sir? In a private room?"

Nai hadn't taken off her clothes while dancing. Her sequined
and long-fringed bra, her glittery hot pants, as she pumped the
air and smiled glassily as though in a religious frenzy. But upstairs, as if they could shut out the rules and restrictions of her
country, shut out the rest of the world, she had taken off everything. And his everything, too. Was that what this man meant
by a private room? Was it that very same bedroom upstairs?

"Yes," Gil told him, without reservation. "Yes…I do."

***

The ground floor private rooms doubled as storage rooms. This
one had a small fridge in one corner and stacked cases of 777
brand beer cans. There was also a cot in another corner. The
table was circular, intended as a patio table with an umbrella
pole set into its center, but there was no umbrella and the top
of the pole was affixed to the ceiling. Kwen's one-man audience

was already seated at the table, his eyes so nervous you might think he was awaiting a surgical procedure.

Kwen smiled at him as she crossed the room, but she was already reconfiguring her mindset, passing through the boarding gate in preparation for travel to a faraway place. It was what she did when she performed on the stage, or in bed.

She mounted the table, and began her slow, sensuous gyrations anew, clinging to the makeshift stripper's pole. The Westerner gazed up at her like a reverent worshipper before the idol of a goddess come to life before his eyes. Whereas she saw beyond him now. In her self-induced trance, she reflected on the latest episodes she had watched of *B-2*. She could even hear its distinctive mournful theme music (which insinuated itself into the drama perhaps every fifteen minutes of its fifty-hour cumulative length) instead of the muffled thud of music from the main room, where Chok was now performing. It was the *B-2* music in her head that Kwen danced to.

She had been interrupted earlier, before joining Gil at his table, before she could relate the concluding moments of the last episode she had seen (though of course the others would know very well what transpired just then). Standing in the doorway behind Laiki, as she wept and did Tendu's laundry, was Zo secretly watching her. But then Kwen had shivered, when she realized that Zo's head was cocked oddly to one side, a pronounced bruise on his forehead. It wasn't Zo, after all, but Tendu himself. Tendu's ghost.

Kwen hadn't realized that *B-2* was going to go in this kind of direction. It wasn't truly surprising, though. Her people believed in ghosts like they believed in the land and the sea, the cycle of day and night, of life and death. They lived with ghosts as they lived with family and friends. As they lived with themselves.

But Kwen had been quite unsettled by this development,

because of her own particular ghost. She had never seen her mother's spirit while awake, only in dreams, but she believed completely that these visitations were not simply figments of her sleeping mind. Rather, that this was the manner in which her mother's ghost was able to contact her.

Her mother had died of breast cancer five years ago, when Kwen was fourteen. Since then, she had appeared to Kwen vividly in her dreams on perhaps a dozen occasions. The last time had been only last week. Her mother had been wearing a pristine white gown, with long sleeves and high collar, and she had been holding two green melons—typical funeral offerings—in front of her chest as if in imitation of Kwen's disproportionate virtues. Smiling gently, still beautiful despite the years and her illness, her mother had said, "They are for us, my beloved child. One for you…and one for me."

The melons had terrified Kwen, though, reminding her of a cruel prank a fellow student had played on her back when she had been much younger, which she didn't care to think about now.

Her father had been devastated by the loss of his wife, despite their daily ferocious bickering. Kwen had envied their love, before and after her mother's death. She hadn't lied to the foreigner: she had never shared romantic love with another person. Oh, she had had crushes, sometimes heartbreaking crushes bordering on obsession, and she supposed there had been those who had crushes on her as well, but there had never been a reciprocal *connection* with another soul. Then again, she didn't really seek one, nor await one. Her sole driving motivation was to provide for her family the best she could. At her insistence, even when they tried to refuse it, she gave nearly all her money to her widowed father, her curmudgeonly uncle Depo, her cousins and her father's lifelong neighbors. She donated to the neighborhood temple. She gave money to dirty children selling lottery tickets and gum in the streets. She felt as though she were sinning so as to afford to pay penance for her sins.

She wanted to be like the mother she had so loved. That she so missed. Wanted to be like her so much that she strove to duplicate her, *embody* her. And maybe that was why her mother appeared to her in her mind, *inside* her, as opposed to an external manifestation. Perhaps her mother's spirit possessed her. But if so, she invited that possession.

Kwen became conscious of having drifted from thoughts of *B-2* to thoughts of her mother, and hoped that her face didn't reflect the sadness that had suffused her while her body went about its mechanized movements. She focused on the foreigner, Gil, and didn't see a change in his glaze-eyed, appreciative upturned face.

She switched back to thoughts of *B-2*, as she reached behind and unclasped her black bra. She leaned down and draped it over Gil's shoulder. His grin flickered at the ends as though he were suppressing a spasm. Stepping back from him but still bent forward a bit, she cupped her bared breasts and squeezed them together as if to align her nipples with his eyes.

Swaying her hips, she unsnapped the front of her blue jean cutoffs, unzipped them, wriggled them down her legs. She tossed them toward Gil, and they dropped off the edge of the table onto his lap. He put both hands on them instantly as if grateful that they now covered *his* crotch.

Just black bikini panties now, and she turned her back to him and pulled the edges up over the curves of her cheeks, exposing one small buttock and then the other, drawing the rear of the panties into the divide of her bottom like a thong. When she sashayed around to face him again, she hooked her thumbs into the elastic and worked the panties down past her straight, sparse pubic hair and her small, dark-skinned, uncircumcised penis.

Her penis was flaccid, but she had set her mind to work on a fantasy. This scenario involved her and Tendu, from *B-2*. She imagined it was him, not this overweight aging john, staring at her so longingly. (And this was *Tendu*, not the actor who played Tendu.) While she danced, she cupped her testicles in one hand, closed her eyes and tilted her head back as if in mounting pleasure. She imagined it was Tendu squeezing her testicles so tenderly in his hand. Imagined Tendu's lips trailing whispered kisses down her belly from her navel, into her musky hair. Tendu's warm mouth taking her in whole.

She stroked herself almost fully erect. The glossy turtle head of her glans cleared its hood. With her cock thrusting out of her little fist, she rubbed it back and forth across the metal pole as if that were Tendu's cock.

But the coolness of the pole made her think of Tendu's broken corpse at the foot of the basement steps. Made her think of Tendu's faintly bluish-skinned apparition, spying on Laiki unseen behind her back. Startling herself, she flashed her eyes open, breaking her own spell…and saw that Gil was walking toward the private room's door. He let himself out without even looking back.

No longer dancing, but still holding the metal pole in one hand and her already drooping penis in the other, Kwen watched as the man shut the door behind him. She was not hurt, because she certainly didn't love him, and she wasn't even insulted, because she had grown a thick skin when it came to men, who might as readily mock her as hunger for her (as if the mockery relieved the discomfort of their hunger). She felt only a numbness, mildly curious at best. That was how she felt about the world in general, anyway.

***

He sat on the edge of his bed in boxers and T-shirt, cupping the hotel room's phone to his ear, and was just about to leave a message when someone finally picked up on the other end. But instead of his wife, it was his son Kenneth. "Hey, Dad," the fifteen-year-old said. "How's it going over there?"

"Good...good," Gil told him. "Is your mom there?"

"She took Wendy to the mall for something." Wendy was his sister. She and Kenneth were fraternal twins.

"Okay...well, I was just checking in to say hi."

"You must be up late, Dad," Kenneth observed. There was a twelve-hour difference between the two countries, like some kind of time warp separating them. "It's three in the afternoon here. Can't you sleep?"

"Soon," Gil assured him. "Anyway, uh...I miss you guys. Tell your mom and Wendy I love them. I'll call again."

"Okay, Dad. See ya."

"See ya, Ken," Gil said. Somewhere along the line, he and his son had found it too awkward to say they loved each other.

Gil set the phone in its cradle and turned to stare at his hotel room window, the blackness of night beyond, as though if he looked long enough he would discern a blue neon sign out there, like a star singled out in the night's constellations.

***

"Laiki has been spending more time on the roof, by the pool, and so she's been seeing more of Din as he sits up there working on his novel. She explains to Din that she needs brightness and sunshine in her life right now, but she doesn't go into the real reason for that. The reason is, Tendu's ghost has begun appearing to her openly now. The first time was on the stairs where he carried her basket for her when she first met him. She was terrified and almost fell, but at the last second she caught herself. The next time it was in the hallway outside her apartment, then in the elevator. Finally right in her bedroom. That time she screamed at the ghost, asking him what he wants, but he only stares at her blankly each time and doesn't speak. Maybe he can't speak because his neck was broken? Anyway, she's afraid to go down into the basement to do her laundry now so she let her dirty clothes pile up, until she finally takes them to a crowded downtown laundromat.

"Meanwhile, Zo has been coming to check in on her a lot. He seems much sweeter than he appeared at first, very concerned about her, and they start going out to cafés and restaurants to talk. One night when they're walking home from dinner, a man with scar tissue in place of one eye stops them in the street and talks in a menacing way to Zo. He says, '*Gods*...you do look just like that brother of yours, don't you? Lucky for Tendu he had that accident of his before my friends got their hands on him. He owed us a lot of money...a *lot* of money. I don't suppose you would know where he left that money? With you, perhaps?'

"Zo says to the one-eyed man, 'If he had any money, I don't know whether he spent it, or hid it, or swallowed it and took it with him to the afterlife. Sorry I can't help you. Now if you'll please excuse me.' And he walks past the scary man, pulling Laiki along by the arm.

"Laiki looks back and asks, 'Zo, what was that all about?'

"Zo says, 'I hate to tell you this, because I know you had feelings for him, but my brother Tendu was in a lot of trouble with some very bad people. He borrowed money from them to cover massive gambling debts.'

"'Tendu? Gambling debts? That doesn't sound like him!'

"'Tendu hid his true face from people, Laiki. You didn't know the real Tendu.'"

"She *still* doesn't," Twee snickered.

"Shh!" Chok hissed.

"Anyway," Kwen continued patiently, "Zo says that's why he came to live with Tendu, to try to help him with his problems. But he just didn't have the money to pay Tendu's debts.

"You can tell Laiki is confused by her feelings. She opens up to Din about the brothers, and tells him she still aches for Tendu, but is also feeling attracted to Zo. She still doesn't talk about the ghost, though…and I think it's the ghost reaching out to her that prevents Laiki from forgetting her love for Tendu and moving on. You might even say, as frightened as she is by it, she *wants* the ghost to haunt her.

"But I think it's plain that she's drawing closer to Din, too, and it's even more obvious how lovesick he is for her. Now he doesn't go up to the roof to write his novel so much as he goes up there in the hopes of seeing Laiki every day. I'm sure he feels for her what he doesn't feel for his new wife, Moop. But Laiki still doesn't know Din writes the love poems that appear under her door—she thinks Tendu's ghost is writing them, because he's mute."

"Laiki is a little slow," Twee broke in.

"One afternoon Laiki asks Din to describe his novel-in-the-works to her, so he tells her all about it. He says he's writing an updated version of the story of the Holy Monkey, Cholukan, in which Cholukan is a modern man, who instead of having eyes of red glass wears sunglasses with red lenses. Whereas in legend Cholukan is the scribe to the gods, who comes among men to write down what he sees and report back to his masters, Din's Cholukan is a newspaper reporter who dreams of being a novelist himself. Instead of facing off against the golden dragon, he'll confront a

powerful gangster chief in a gold lamé business suit, who Cholukan has angered with his newspaper reports. The chapter Din's
working on now is when Cholukan goes into Hell to rescue the
virgin from the demon hags who want to steal her beauty. In Din's
novel, the hags will be nasty old women who run a beauty salon,
and have been badly mistreating a beautiful young girl who works
for them. The modern-day Cholukan will rescue her from them."

"Ooh," Chok said, "I really want to read Din's book! I wish it
was real. Why hasn't anyone thought to write it?"

"I've never seen you read a book," Phep scoffed, filing her
nails. "I don't think you could read your own name."

"Hmph!" Chok said.

Twee sighed and said, "I love that part of Cholukan's adventures best of all. It's so romantic, even though it turns out so
sad." She spun on her dressing room stool to face Chok. "Do
you think you could go down into Hell to rescue someone?"

"Are you worried about your future, Twee?" Phep asked. "You
know you're no virgin, but we'll have Ko go rescue you, okay?
We put that man through hell every day, anyway."

As if on cue, their manager slipped into the dressing room
with his eyes immediately locking onto Kwen. He hooked a finger, and she dropped off her stool to go to him.

"He's back," Ko said in a low voice, as if there were any secrets
between the four dancers.

"Him? You mean…Gil?"

"Yes. He wants to see you again."

"I thought I scared him off." She cupped her crotch through
her jeans. "With this."

"Looks like lust has won over phobia. He wants to take you
out to lunch, he said."

"Aah!" Twee called. "That translates into, 'take you to his hotel
room.'"

"I told him you'd go," Ko said. "So…you'd best get going. He's waiting for you at the bar."

***

At the bar with an untouched beer in front of him, Gil fidgeted while he watched a TV on a bracket near the ceiling. He couldn't hear it over the club's music, though at this early hour no one was currently dancing, and anyway he didn't think sound would make the program any more comprehensible to him. It was some kind of costume fantasy, featuring an actor made up in barely competent simian makeup, apparently with red glass balls for eyes in the style of that moth-eaten monkey in the glass case at the front counter. Dressed all in blue silk, one minute the ape-man was laughing at the clumsy befuddlement of the human characters around him, and the next—via terrible special effects—he was soaring through the sky shooting red lightning bolts from his eyes at a rubber and papier-mâché spider monster with bat wings.

Walking up behind Gil, Kwen saw the TV and recognized Cholukan. It was funny, as they had been discussing him only a minute ago in the dressing room (in regard to the modern version of the Holy Monkey's adventures as written by the fictitious Din). Coincidence, in her culture, meant the gods were at work weaving their mysterious webs for their unknown purposes. So what, she wondered, did this coincidence portend for her? Then again, this thirty-episode program, older than *B-2*, was immensely popular with adults and children alike and was never absent from the airwaves.

Gil looked around with a start as Kwen boosted herself onto the stool beside him. "Hello," she said, smiling. "I'm sorry…did you grow bored with me two days ago? Maybe you remembered an appointment? Or your wife called you?" She knew it wasn't proper etiquette to tease a customer, but she hoped he realized she wasn't hurt. She could see how uncomfortable he was, and thought she might as well break the ice. If it only made him more uncomfortable...well...there would always be more customers.

"I'm so sorry," Gil told her, squirming again on his bar stool. "I, ah...no, I'll be honest...I was surprised. At first. I mean..."

"You didn't know *B-2* is a ladyboy club?"

"I had no idea, no. It wasn't that way back when it was *The Love Army*. So, um...all of you are...like that? The other dancers, too?"

"Yes. My friends, too."

"No wonder the taxi driver was grinning at me so much."

"I think in my country we're more relaxed about these things than in your country," Kwen suggested. "Well, men are considered more important than women in my culture, and a man always hopes his wife will give him strong sons, so a gay man here is seen as weak. He's thought of as...what's that word?... defective. But if the gay man tries to look like a woman, and live like a woman, then he is accepted as an 'accidental woman.' A woman accidentally born in a man's body."

"Hm. That doesn't really sound all that accepting to me. But like you said, we can be pretty puritanical in my country, too, no matter how modern-thinking we like to think we are." Gil looked away from her uneasily, watching that monkey-faced man stand over the corpse of the spider monster, hands on his hips and head thrown back as he laughed uproariously. "But I'm not...I've never been...I'm not attracted to men."

"Do I look like a man?"

"In one important way."

"So why did you come back?"

He'd been asking himself that. Why he would want to come back. Why he wanted that so *badly*. Yesterday he had engrossed himself in work related to his trip, as best he could, hoping the hunger would pass if ignored, but it would not be ignored. Was it that she still reminded him of Nai, even now? If so, it only proved Nai haunted him to such an extent that next he'd be superimposing her over...over...over that monkey superhero on the TV. No, he thought this was becoming something other than his decades-long obsession with Nai. This was the attraction of the alien, the exotic, with the dial turned to volume 11. He was alone in a foreign land, unmoored and drifting straight into the jungle swamps of *otherness*. And it felt liberating and frightening...exhilarating and dizzying. It was the potency of taboo, and after two decades of subverting his raw desires—moving along the grooves his society, but also he himself, had laid for him—he hungered to lose himself in the madness of it.

And yet, awkwardly he lied, "I just wanted to apologize for the rude way I acted, walking out on you like that. I thought maybe I'd invite you to lunch to make up for it, if you're interested."

"Sure, Gil. You don't have to apologize, but I'd like to have lunch with you"

"Thanks. Um...there's a nice little restaurant right inside the hotel where I'm staying," he managed to get out in his creaking voice, creaking like the deck of that boat sailing into uncharted waters. "The 777 Hotel—I'm sure you know it?"

Kwen thought of Twee teasing her only a few minutes ago, and smiled to herself. "Of course," she said, patting Gil on his thigh, bared by the khaki shorts he was wearing. The first touch of his skin; another ice-breaker. She knew how to put a customer at ease and at the same time stoke his fires. As she did so, she noticed an inflamed pimple with a white head of pus on his leg. "What's this?"

"I found a big spider in my bed yesterday," Gil explained. "I think the bastard bit me while I was asleep."

"Oh!" Kwen said, still staring at the tiny imminent volcano, remembering the spider monster she had just seen on TV and thinking again of the gods and their playful coincidences.

***

Moaning softly, Gil stroked Kwen's long hair, which curtained and concealed her face, and spilled across his thighs in rivulets like ink. When he reached a certain intensity of pleasure, he couldn't bear his passive position on his back any longer and reached down to pull at her hot sticky shoulders. He whispered, as if his hotel room might be bugged by his company, by his wife, "Turn your body around...up here...I want to kiss you, too."

She pivoted without interrupting her ministrations, and he helped pull her body around like the arm of a clock until she lay atop him, yin to his yang. He spread her cheeks open with his hands, widening her deep black hole, which many would shun as an opening to foulness, but which to him was more like a chink in a wall beyond which any and all mystery might dwell. He pressed his face into her crease and probed his tongue to taste the unknown.

After that, the last shreds of his inhibitions dissipated. He threw away his compass, willingly lost his bearings, gave himself over to a kind of disorder. As if to accentuate the sensation, as if to test his commitment to this new insanity, his hotel room's phone rang. Who else could it be on a weekend but his wife, rather than someone from the company, returning his call? But he ignored the rings until they ceased.

Next he took her in his mouth, and she was fully hard, at

least physically aroused, though he wondered what was going through her mind. Maybe she was only watching the muted soap opera that played on his room's TV. Maybe she was only communing telepathically with that gecko pasted to one wall near the ceiling. It, too, had nowhere better to be.

When it came time, ultimately, for her to brace herself on hands and knees and present herself for entry, he first rolled a condom onto his own straining member, so erect it actually hurt him. He hated condoms, but knew STDs were very prevalent in this country. He had never used them in his marriage, but had used them with Nai. They had been a cheap local brand, and he recalled his horror (and her great amusement) when after one feverish bout of lovemaking he had withdrawn from Nai's body only to find that at some point the condom had burst like a balloon, leaving only a rubber ring around the base of his member.

He held Kwen's waist as he pumped into her, and she moaned wonderfully but he almost wished she wouldn't, because he couldn't be certain of her sincerity. From behind, with her face and the marker of her biological gender hidden from him, he could again imagine he was making love to Nai, his enigmatic Nai. Though he now knew this person was fundamentally different from Nai, the core of the attraction was the same. He understood he hadn't known Nai any much more than he knew this woman...this man...but that was why the obsession had endured: because mystery promoted idolization much more readily than the mundane and familiar did. He was fond of his wife, but she would never be his goddess. She grounded him... but he didn't *want* to be grounded anymore. At least, not for now.

He held back his climax. He was in no hurry to end this fever-dream. He flipped her onto her back, bent back her legs in his hands and entered her again, but this time he could see everything, *needed* to see everything, and she clenched her eyes shut and clenched her teeth in a grimace and worked her own phallus in her fist frantically until she cast her pearls on her ribs. The sight of her pleasure sent him over the edge and he could restrain himself no longer. He launched his sperm into the condom's tiny receptacle, dashing themselves like lemmings to die on unfertile ground...and though his spewed cells didn't enter Kwen's body, it felt to him as though they did, vanishing forever like tears of inexpressible loss into the bottomless well of her bottom, the mysterious void of infinity that her ambiguous flesh embodied.

***

They lay side-by-side, oiled in sweat, heaving with gasps. Kwen opened her lids and smiled at him...despite the fact that with her eyes open she could see he was a paunchy, red-headed Western businessman and not the gentle, romantic, and ethereal Tendu.

Now that Gil was satiated, it was as though he couldn't bring himself to touch her again. He smiled at her sheepishly, considered asking if he'd hurt her in his wild abandon, but didn't. Fumbling for something to say, he asked, "So your friends...the other girls, um, dancers...have any of them had the full deal, surgically?" His bedmate contorted her face, confused, so he clarified, "Have they had an operation to change them all the way into a woman?" As if such an operation existed, he thought.

"Oh," Kwen said. "No. I haven't met many ladyboys who've done that. We just take hormones...maybe get our breasts done. But we don't usually get our things removed. If our customers wanted that, they'd get a real woman. How about you? If doctors took my thing off, and made me like a woman down there, would you like me more?"

No, Gil wanted to admit. If that were the case, as she herself said, then he might as well have a woman. The fever today, the exhilaration, had been in the fear. Diverting the topic, he instead asked, "Did your family give you a hard time when you decided to…to live this way?"

"No, they didn't. They accepted me. As I say, in my country you're forgiven if you're an 'accidental woman.' My mother died of cancer before I started taking hormones and became a dancer, but she could tell what I was. And my father's love has never changed. Actually, my father is really my stepfather. But he always treated me like his own son. And later, as his own daughter. He took care of me all through my childhood, and these days I do my best to take care of him."

"That's so nice," Gil said, without relating that he had two teenage children of his own back home.

Kwen propped herself up on one elbow, looking down at Gil's cooling body. "Come on…let's take a shower. I'll help clean you."

"Um…okay," he said. He felt self conscious, lumpy and grotesque, exposed beside her beauty.

Kwen frowned, lightly touching his inflamed spider bite. "This looks infected. Let me take you to a clinic near here so they can look at it. I can go back to the club and get my bike, if you're not afraid to ride on the back."

"Riding with you sounds fun, but I'm so tired right now. I think I'm too tired at the moment to even take a shower. I just want to sleep."

"Do you want me to go now?" she asked, interpreting this as a cue. He probably couldn't sustain his lust in the face of phobia any longer.

"I don't want you to go," Gil replied. "I'm not saying that. You can sleep here with me. I'd like that. I'll pay you for your time, don't worry."

Kwen smiled again, rolled onto her side and pressed her back and bottom against his front. And finally the foreigner overcame the return of his inhibitions, and draped his heavy arm across her.

It was a comforting feeling, quite pleasurable actually, and Kwen soon drifted into slumber.

***

Her mother stepped through a theater curtain of velvet blackness, onto the stage of Kwen's dream.

For a long time she stood there in silence, gazing at Kwen sadly and lovingly, a little smile on her full lips, a faint breeze stirring her straight black hair, wearing her long white gown with its high collar and long sheer sleeves. Again in her arms, against her chest, she held the funerary offering of two identical green melons. Kwen thought she saw a spider scamper across the surface of one of the melons, but either she had imagined it or it had crawled away onto her mother's body.

"You aren't the son I thought I'd brought to the world," her mother spoke at last.

"I'm sorry, Mother," said Kwen to the dream-ghost. "Please forgive me. I didn't mean to betray you."

"Oh, you don't need my forgiveness, my child. Children often surprise their parents."

"And mothers often resent their daughters," Kwen said, "because they fear being replaced by them."

"No, no, my darling…my beloved daughter…I never feared that you would replace me."

"But I so want to *be* you," Kwen said, breaking into tears. "Not to replace you—it's true—but to keep you alive!"

"And so you have," the ghost said. "For you and I are one."

As she said this, the beautiful apparition pushed the two green melons against each other. They flowed together, merging, and within moments they had become one smooth sphere like the reverse of a cell dividing. Then the ghost raised this single orb and extended it to Kwen in both hands. Instead of a mourner's offering to the dead, a gift from the dead to the living.

Kwen awoke with a tiny gasp. Golden afternoon light poured into the hotel room. She hoped the man pressed to her back hadn't heard her...hoped she could sneak out of bed and leave... but he had heard her, because he rose on one elbow and turned her face gently by the chin. When he saw that her cheeks were wet, he said softly, "Oh...what is it? What's wrong?"

"Just a dream," she told him. She pulled his arm around her again. "Will you hold me?"

He did. He held her tight. And he whispered with his lips touching her ear, through her screen of hair, "It's all right, baby...it's all right."

She expected his greedy cock to grow hard against her bottom, waited for that disappointment, but it didn't happen. She was grateful for that, and clung to his thick arm like a child to its mother's leg.

***

"Laiki goes up to the roof seeking out Din, maybe because he gives her some balance in all her confusion, but he isn't there, so she falls asleep by the pool waiting for him. Then we see Din and Moop in their apartment, arguing. Moop has been seeing her old school sweetheart, Oc, and Din came home today to find Oc visiting. Oc was only sitting at the kitchen table, but he excused himself and left in a hurry. Din isn't really jealous, because he doesn't love Moop that way, but he feels insulted by her disrespect. Moop cries hysterically, like a child, and tells him she only invited Oc over to get Din's attention, because she says he neglects her. Din storms out and goes up to the roof.

"Meanwhile, Laiki wakes up, and realizes it's become night-time. She looks nervous; these days she's afraid of anyplace dark. When she sits up in her chair and looks into the swimming pool, standing on the floor of the pool is the ghost of Tendu, glowing in the dark water and looking up at her. Laiki screams, and hearing her, Din bursts onto the roof and comes to her side. He grabs Laiki in his arms. The ghost has vanished and Laiki lies to Din, telling him she has just woken from a bad dream. Din still holds her in his arms, the two of them staring into each other's eyes...and then they kiss."

"Mm," Twee sighed, fanning herself with a sticky menu, "my favorite kiss in the whole series."

"But Moop has followed Din out of the apartment, up to the roof, and she sees her husband kissing Laiki. She shrieks like a madwoman and runs to the edge of the roof to throw herself off, but Din and Laiki rush over and grab her, and pull her back to safety..."

A cell phone's ringtone interrupted Kwen's story. It was her own phone, and she had changed its ringtone to the roman-tic, melancholy theme music of *B-2*. While she answered the call, her coworkers sucked the juice from green coconuts with the tops hacked off, at an outdoors café where the palm trees were interlaced with tiny colored lights, and where a succession of amateur singers ranging from the impressive to the dreadful would soon be coming onstage. A plump rat darted between their legs under the table but they barely noticed.

Kwen saw the call was from Gil's hotel. She had given him her number. "Hello?" she said, trying to sound cheery, but shy about the proximity of her friends.

"Hi. It's Gil. You said there was a clinic you could take me to for my leg?"

"Yes, but it's late, now. I can take you in the morning…would that be okay?"

"I'd appreciate it…thanks. My leg's gone all swollen and red. I'm getting kind of nervous, here." He chuckled, as if to make light of a silly problem, but she could hear the worry underneath that.

"I'll pick you up on my bike, early in the morning. Okay, Gil?"

"Thanks, baby." A few empty beats, and then he said, "I miss you."

She was going to reiterate she'd see him tomorrow, then disconnect, but at the last moment on impulse she murmured, "Do you want me to come see you tonight?"

"Can you? I know it's late, like you said…"

"I'm finished with work. I just stopped for a drink with my friends. I'll be there soon—okay?"

"Thanks, baby," he said.

The second she tucked her phone away, the others started in on her. "Ooh…do you have yourself a boyfriend, *baby?*" Chok asked her.

"Just be careful," Phep warned in a more serious tone. "Don't give your heart to this foreigner, Kwen. He can't sponsor you to his country. It wouldn't be allowed…not for a girl who's really a boy. And he won't even love you, let alone marry you. You have to know that, of course. He's just drunk on you. It will pass—believe me." The barest flicker of pain rippled beneath her proud, porcelain mask. "I've been hurt by his kind before."

"I'll be careful," Kwen assured them all. She sucked her coconut empty and rose from her scraping metal chair. "It's just for the money, anyway."

But she wasn't so sure she believed that, herself. It was also about the feeling of his heavy arm around her when they had slept together, as if to shield her from ghosts. And the way he called her "baby."

***

Gil could tell when the doctor tsk-tsked that things weren't good. But it wasn't a surprise, in any case. By morning his leg had become as fat, tight, and red as a gigantic sausage, hot to the touch with infection. Not that that had stopped him from making love with Kwen when she had arrived at his hotel room late last night.

The chief physician's examination desk was situated outside, in a central area of the little clinic, like a courtyard in a temple. The man wore a gold wristwatch, a jeweled ring, and cheap plastic sandals. At least he wore sandals; Gil had spotted one doctor who was casually barefoot.

Kwen translated the chief physician's pronouncement. "He's going to have a nurse give you an injection of antibiotics, and he's going to prescribe you some more antibiotics to take with you. He wants you to come back tomorrow so he can see how you're doing." The doctor spoke further, and Kwen continued, "But right now he wants to cut into your leg and drain out the infection."

"Cut?" Gil said. *Cut?* In this place? There were families lined up on benches just behind him in the outdoors waiting area, looking to him like plague victims, children coughing as if to eject their lungs. To his eyes, it was like the waiting room for hell.

Yet what was he to do? Trusting Kwen in this more than he did the doctor, he consented, and was taken to a tiny side office with one wall open to the courtyard, though the doctor discreetly pulled a curtain. There were actually dribbles of drying blood on the floor from an earlier patient, and a metal pan rested on the floor filled with medical instruments soaking in what appeared to be nothing more than tap water. Gil lay back on a cot with Kwen holding his hand. He wanted to be manly and strong about this, and the initial incision with a scalpel at the site where the spider had injected its poison wasn't too bad, but when the doctor pressed down on his leg with both palms, putting all his weight into it, to squeeze blood-streaked pus out through the hole he had made, Gil almost crushed Kwen's hand in his and clamped his jaws together. Fixing his eyes on the ceiling, he was suddenly intent on working out how many tiles composed it. (Count along one side… count along the other side…multiply…) He believed many men would have already given up more than just their name, rank, and serial number to this torturer, and yet he was still determined not to appear weak to Kwen. And so he didn't let out the slightest moan, even when the doctor next used a long pair of forceps to insert a wad of gauze into the cavity that had formerly been filled with pus. He pushed the wad in tightly, until it was soaked, then pulled it out and and accepted a fresh pad from the young nurse assisting him. After several more pads, the doctor packed the cavity with a last square of gauze, left it there inside, and bandaged and taped the wound.

Kwen helped Gil sit upright. He gave her a brave, nauseous smile. She helped him count out money for the doctor, who grinned and pumped Gil's hand. "Thank you, sir," the doctor said, to show off what little he knew of Gil's language. "See you next time, sir!"

"Yep…tomorrow," Gil said. "I can't wait."

They picked up his prescription of oral antibiotics before

leaving, at the clinic's tiny pharmacy. The woman at the counter, handing Gil a sandwich bag of variously-colored pills and gel capsules, smiled flirtatiously and said something to Kwen in their native tongue. Kwen related to Gil, "She says you need to eat shrimp. It will help you heal."

"She prescribes shrimp, huh? Okay." Gil smiled back at the woman and said, "A shrimp a day keeps the doctor away."

He waved to the woman as they turned away. He walked with a bit of a limp, Kwen holding onto his arm with both hands as if to support an old man.

Last night, while waiting for Kwen to join him, he had lain in bed envisioning himself dying of fever brought on by the spider's poison, in this country half a world away from his wife and children. Now, he envisioned himself dying of infection brought on by dirty surgical implements, shivering in bed and counting the tiles in his hotel room's ceiling, too. But as he rode away from the clinic on the back of Kwen's little motorbike, squeezed up tight against her back, her long hair spilling out from under her helmet and snapping at his face, it wasn't feverish shivers that shook him but the vibrations of the bike's motor and the trembling of his heart.

"I love you," he said as she drove him through the streets of the city, Kwen looking for a restaurant where she could order shrimp for him. He knew she couldn't hear him above the mad cacophony of traffic, and through her helmet, but he just wanted to taste the words on his own tongue. He found himself smiling into the exhaust-filled hot breeze, and he held her tighter, smelling her cheap perfume and the faint hint of underarm odor that only made her all the more real and human to him. He hadn't felt so deliriously and savagely *alive*, so illogically *happy*, in almost twenty years.

***

"Laiki feels guilty that Moop saw her kissing Din, so she stops going up to meet him on the roof. Din takes care of Moop to calm her down, and she promises she'll stop seeing her old sweetheart Oc, but you can tell Din misses Laiki so much. And now Laiki is more upset than ever. Zo visits her and he can see she's depressed, so he invites her into his apartment and gives her a glass of wine. He gets close with her on the sofa, and they start kissing gently, but Zo becomes more excited and tries to unbutton her shirt. Laiki pushes him away and runs back to her own apartment crying. When she turns the lights on, Tendu is standing there waiting for her..."

"You mean the ghost?" Gil said.

They lay in his hotel room's bed together. They had both had a busy day. Kwen had taken Gil to the clinic again this morning so he could have fresh gauze packed into his wound and another shot of antibiotic, then he had addressed some of the work he was in this country to perform. Meanwhile, Kwen had gone on to the club *B-2*. Somewhere between the clinic and her job, Kwen had caught two more episodes of the soap opera *B-2*.

"Yes," she replied. "Tendu's ghost still can't speak, but he is doing this—" Kwen waved her right arm back and forth, holding up her index finger "—as if to tell Laiki, 'No...no.' She talks to Tendu, crying, and tells him he can't be jealous—he is dead but she is still alive. She pleads with him to move on and let her live her life now. He disappears, but she doesn't know if he is obeying her wishes or if he will come back to haunt her again."

"Ghosts are stubborn by nature," Gil remarked.

"They are," Kwen said thoughtfully. "They are. But maybe they're just lonely."

"Oh, no doubt. Ghosts are lonely by nature, too."

"Do you believe in ghosts?"

"Well, not literally. I don't think so. I meant in their fictitious sense. Do *you* believe in ghosts?"

"Of course," Kwen said, looking away. "I believe in ghosts more than I believe in the living."

"More than you believe in me?"

She didn't reply. Didn't want to hurt him. But as a kind of compromise she noted, "You'll be leaving soon. Going back to your own country. I'm sure you have a wife waiting for you."

Now it was his turn to withhold an answer, not so much to avoid hurting her as to avoid admission of his selfishness, which he was fully aware of. Not that he didn't feel badly about it. Very badly. He wasn't looking forward to going home to his wife. He wanted this madness to go on and on.

"I'm like the girl you loved when you came here a long time ago," she went on, her tone not bitter and accusing, but sadly accepting. "The one you only loved for a short time."

Not a short time, he thought; he still loved Nai. But again, he couldn't respond to that. Instead, as if by way of consolation, he picked up one of Kwen's feet, lifted it to his lips and kissed her tough, wrinkled sole. He noted that she had recently painted her toes a pretty red. How easy the accoutrements of gender could be; a thin shellac.

"I think Tendu's ghost is trying to warn Laiki about something," Gil told her, still holding her foot, to change the subject.

"Warn her about what?"

"Who knows? There are still a lot more episodes, you said, right? Ghosts by nature also like to warn people about stuff."

Kwen thought of her mother. What was *that* ghost trying to warn her about, then?

An uneasy silence passed. He stroked her foot in his lap, like a cat. "Did you kill people as a soldier?" Kwen asked at last, as if to get a better measure of the harm he was capable of.

"Do you mean, have I made any ghosts myself? No...there wasn't a war going on when I was in the service. At least, not where I was stationed."

She wanted to ask him what the neighboring country where he'd been stationed was like, she who had never been beyond the borders of her own country and never even very far from this city of Haikan, but instead she found herself speaking of her own land. "Do you know what the name of this country means, in our language?"

"Your country? No, I don't."

"Other countries have conquered us over our long history, and sometimes they changed our name. Hundreds of years ago, our Emperor Tho tried to think of ways to protect his country from being attacked again, after he managed to drive out the last invaders. And he knew he had to change the name his enemies had given to his country. Then Tho had an idea...a way to keep other people from wanting to come here and steal his empire. He would hide it from their eyes, and their minds, and the eyes and minds of any demon lords who might try to bring more bad luck to his empire. So he gave our land the name it has to this day."

"And what name is that?"

"The Unnamed Country."

Gil grinned. "For real? That sounds more like a fable than history."

"That's what it means," Kwen insisted quite solemnly.

He nodded, adopting more respect for her story. "But it really hasn't stayed hidden from the rest of the world, has it?"

"You can't hide something forever," she conceded.

***

When Kwen came into work the next day—after having taken Gil to the clinic again and then having returned him to his hotel—Ko was waiting in the narrow hallway outside the dressing room as if to ambush her, blocking the way. He pointed a stubby finger at the center of her chest. "Hey you," he said, "this foreigner of yours; are you taking his money behind my back? Keeping it all to yourself, are you?"

"I haven't taken any money behind your back," Kwen said, and it was true.

"So you're giving it to him for free now?"

She hesitated. "A few times."

"Then he's your boyfriend, like the girls say?"

She didn't answer.

He narrowed his eyes at her, and poked her chest again but not hard enough to hurt her. "Don't be stupid. Don't give it away for free."

"What I do in my free time is my business. As long as I'm not hiding money from you, which I'm not. That's all you need to know."

"If I ever find out that you are working on your own, you'll be out of here, you understand me? Then how will you support your stepfather and the rest? Huh? Keep that in mind. Your boyfriend won't support them, will he? He'll just go back home to his family."

Ko squeezed past her roughly and swaggered away down the hall. Kwen sneered at his back, but without much resentment. Ko was better than a lot of other men would have been in his position. He threatened Twee and Chok, too, when they got carried away with the drugs they spent much of their own earnings on, but he'd never hit any of them. His warning about Gil forgetting about her wasn't anything Phep hadn't already cautioned her about…or that she didn't know all too well on her own.

Gil had told her he would be busy all day today, meeting with the local factory that would be entering into a collaborative effort with Gil's company back in his country. He'd said he needed to better concentrate on his assignment here in the next few days, as he only had another week left in her country. Kwen found herself regretting that their time together would be more limited now. Gil working mostly in the day, herself working mostly at night. But he had said he would take a taxi to the club tonight, catch her act, and then they could ride her bike back to his hotel when she finished.

She didn't love him, she insisted to herself. There was no reason to. And what was there to love about him? Did a man's lies and hunger take on more glamour wrapped in a white skin? But if she didn't love him, then she wondered why she wanted to be by his side.

It was a mystery to her. Unless, of course, he had made her realize that she was more incomplete than she had even realized, or at least admitted to herself. Her mother had left a chasm in her life that she had thought no one else could fill…except herself, in a living personification of her mother. But now she was finding she needed more than that.

Anyway, he would leave soon, and maybe that was a good thing. The mystery would end…the confusion. Back to business as usual. It was easier that way. Safer that way. The self-induced trance, the mechanical dancing, the mechanical fucking, without having to think too much. Without having to feel too much. A pretty mannequin, a scarecrow of makeup and silicone, of hormones and nail polish; the artifice that inhabited her, instead of the other way around.

But whatever Gil felt for her, right now it made her feel more than the sum of her painted and enhanced parts. It made her feel desired and valued. If she was only destined to enjoy that sensation for another week—like the limited run of a soap opera, after which its passionate characters ceased to exist—then she would take that brief gift, whether either of them cared to call it love or not.

***

The owners of the factory wanted to take Gil out that night, to dinner and then to a fancy nightclub in one of the city's five-star hotels, so he couldn't refuse. He still hoped to catch Kwen before her shift ended at *B-2*. But a few of the factory's managers lingered long at the club, calling for one drink after another, and then one of them insisted on arranging a "date" for Gil that night. Gil wanted to beg out of the offer, yet he was afraid to offend the man. And when the date that the manager had phoned arrived, and Gil saw how beautiful and poised she was, he gave in. But on the pretense of using the restroom, he took leave of his increasingly boisterous table to duck out into the hotel lobby and borrow a phone at the counter, calling Kwen to make up some excuse as to why he wouldn't be seeing her tonight.

He only got her voice mail. She must be on stage at that very moment. He was relieved he wouldn't have to lie to her in real time, and left her a rambling, half-drunken message. He promised he'd call her again tomorrow. To soothe any hurt feelings, he said he wanted to take her to the city's Ruby Mall and buy her a nice handbag or pair of shoes.

Gil returned to the table, to his noisy new friends and his elegant robotic date. And that night, though he was drunk and afraid he might not be able to perform, he and the date fucked in a luxurious room in the five-star hotel. She was gorgeous, with silicone-enhanced breasts, but that sensual deceit was her only similarity to Kwen. She was a woman.

He was certainly aroused. The variety excited him. And yet he still found himself regretting that he was not in bed with Kwen instead.

***

The glassy and modern Ruby Mall actually struck Gil as being more of a multi-leveled department store. On one floor they ate at a fried chicken fast food restaurant, one of the few Western franchises Gil had spotted in this country. He supposed more would come in time. His role as liaison between his company and the local factory demonstrated that this formerly closed-off country—the once secretive Unnamed Country—was opening itself more to the world beyond. For better or worse. Personally, he hoped it would never lose its own unique, mystifying character.

While they ate, and now while they strolled through the so-called mall's bright, clean levels—stocked with expensive merchandise geared toward the wealthy and tourists like himself—Kwen had remained withdrawn and sullen. He tried to engage her with jokes. He took her hand, and she let him, but her fingers were limp. He might have been too shy to be seen with her in respectable surroundings like this, let alone holding hands with her, had she not been so thoroughly convincing as a woman, even dressed casually as she was in T-shirt and jeans. He wondered, though, if her fellow citizens could spot the truth more readily than he had.

Before coming to the mall she had brought him to the clinic as was their routine. This time the doctor had told them that Gil's infection was fading away nicely, and the tiny aperture of his incised wound was on the way to closing and healing. He should keep it covered, but he would not need to return. Kwen had translated all of this in a chilly way, as if merely performing a job.

Now, in the sprawling department store, they came upon a section selling skimpy underwear and sheer lingerie. Gil nudged Kwen and said, "Hey, let's buy you some of this stuff, huh?"

She dragged him away by the hand, saying sharply, "Why bother? You won't be here to see me in it."

So they browsed elsewhere, in silence again, until Gil started to become depressed about the tension between them. It was as if she could smell on him the woman he had been with last night. A real woman, which she could never be. Suddenly he realized just how much he had betrayed all of them. His wife. Kwen. He had even been unfaithful to the memory of his Nai.

"Have you been watching that show *B-2* any more?" he asked awkwardly, in another attempt to draw her out. "Anything new with Laiki and her ghost lover?"

"I watched a few more episodes," she admitted, without looking at him. "Last night, when you didn't come."

"And?"

She drew in a long breath through her nostrils, as if reluctant to elaborate, but when she'd filled her lungs she said, "The show is focusing more now on Moop and her old boyfriend, Oc. I don't really like either of them. Anyway, Moop promised Din she'd stop seeing Oc, but she can't help herself. And that gangster with one eye is coming around again, threatening Zo. He still thinks Zo might be holding some or all of the money that Tendu owed to the gangsters."

"Yikes," Gil said. "Sounds like dangers are brewing."

They had arrived at a long glass counter filled with imported perfumes. He pulled Kwen to a stop in front of it, and pointed at one of the bottles, something expensive. "Ooh," he said, "that perfume is very nice. Let me buy it for you, honey." He squeezed her hand, and whispered, "I want to smell it on your skin and your hair."

"Is that the perfume your lover used twenty years ago?" she asked icily. "Do you want me to smell like her? So you can pretend that's who I am? Instead of a *man?*"

She said "man" too loudly. The young woman behind the counter was pretending to ignore them, but Gil could tell she'd heard. Hopefully she didn't understand his language.

In a hushed voice, he said to Kwen, "You don't have to be jealous of her, do you? I haven't seen Nai in two decades, and I'm sure I never will again."

Kwen looked up at him, her expression going from hostile to something less defined. "Nai? That was your lover's name?"

"Yes." He remembered he hadn't got into the particulars before. Hadn't wanted to. "Her name was Nai."

"That was my mother's name," Kwen said.

"Oh yeah?" Gil said. "Oh…wow. Well, I guess it's a common name, isn't it?"

Kwen stared at his face for a few moments without speaking, and then said, "When you realized *B-2* is a ladyboy club, you said it wasn't that way back when it was called *The Love Army.*"

"Right."

She hadn't thought about that casual statement before, but it came back to her now. "Your lover…your Nai…was she a dancer? Was she a dancer in *The Love Army?*"

Gil started to admit what he had avoided telling her before… that his lover in that long-ago time had been a dancer at the very same nightclub, yes. But the words died off in his throat. When he reformed them, even though they were the same, they carried a whole new weight behind them. "Yes. Nai was a dancer in *The Love Army.*"

Kwen nodded, chewing her lower lip, perhaps to keep it from quivering. "My mother was a dancer in that club twenty years ago." Tears spread over her eyes. "It was my mother you loved."

"You look like her," Gil said, his own voice starting to quaver. "You...look like her."

Kwen slipped her hand out of his. He didn't try to prevent it. He didn't call after her, even as she spun on her heel and darted away, racing off into the mall to becoming lost in the throngs of this country's countless dark-haired beauties. Through Gil's own rising tears, they might all blur and appear to him to have Nai's face.

Kwen had told him her mother had died of cancer.

***

Gil called his company's office and apologized that he needed to come home prematurely. He'd been bitten by a spider some days ago and had been receiving treatments for infection, but was still struggling to recover. He assured his superiors that he had laid sufficient groundwork for the collaboration between the two countries, enough to be built on henceforth. He even suggested he might be willing to return to this country later to follow up. Once he had healed.

When his request was granted and promises made that his travel arrangements would be adjusted for him, he called home to tell his wife the news. His wife wasn't there, however; he got his fifteen-year-old daughter Wendy instead. As he told her he'd be coming home almost a week early, he choked up and started sobbing hard. Wendy cried out to him across the great distance, "Dad, what's wrong? Dad, are you okay?"

"I'm okay," he wept. "I just...I just miss you. I miss my family."

Once he was alone in his hotel room, having returned by taxi instead of on Kwen's bike, he had become assaulted by memories, swirling around him in a tight vortex. As if a raging ghost occupied the same space as his body.

One of the memories was of his own cock, glistening with their combined juices as he withdrew it from Nai's body. A yellowish rubber ring around its base, like a joking caricature of a wedding ring. He remembered his dismay to find the condom had burst, and remembered how Nai had laughed and laughed.

***

At the dressing room's long counter, mascara brush in hand, Kwen stared into her doppelganger's face. Her friends had always complimented her on her naturally long, curled lashes. Normally women of her country had straight eyelashes, like the hair on their heads, like their pubic hair.

It was split, too, how many women in her country had mono eyelids as opposed to double eyelids, such as all Western women possessed. Many women, and even some young men nowadays, paid for surgical procedures to emulate the Western double eyelids. But Kwen had hers naturally. *Genetically*, she now understood.

But whether mono or double eyelids, all her people had that tiny bit of skin, called the epicanthus, at the inner corner of the eye. That tiny bit of skin that had made her race easier for Westerners to kill, in times of war, as something other than themselves, something alien. Yet it had also made the women of her race something to be coveted, if only as a brief taste of the exotic. That damnable little piece of skin. Like the bit of skin between her legs.

It was a bitter train of thought this analysis of herself had led to, but it was part of digesting the deduction that she was not only a blend of two sexes, but a blend of two races.

"This is what you wanted me to know," she said to the mirror. "Isn't it, Mother?"

Kwen watched fresh tears form, and trickle down her cheeks. She was alone in the dressing room, at the moment, so she didn't bother wiping them away.

"I'm sorry," she told her mother. "Forgive me." She started to sob outright. "Come to my dreams tonight, Mother! Come to me, please! I need to hear if you forgive me! I need to hear you say it!"

But her mother's ghost would never appear to her in dreams again. She didn't need to, Kwen would come to understand. The two of them were now fully one.

***

Gil sat in the taxi, which idled at the curb, staring through its window at the block-like building, its stark ugliness not redeemed by the flowing blue neon that spelled out *B-2*. His luggage was in the trunk.

He had tried calling her cell phone from his hotel room over the past two days, but she had never picked up or called back. He had left voice mail messages, telling her he wanted to see her. They *needed* to see each other. In his last message he had promised to send her money every month, even if he had to explain it to his wife. Though of course he couldn't explain everything. But in the message, he had said he didn't want Kwen to live the way she did.

"I'm sorry," he had said, in his final message. "Please forgive me, baby." That last word slipped out on its own. But he supposed it still applied in another context.

He considered getting out of the taxi and going inside...he still had time...he even had his hand on the door latch...but at last, in a dead voice, he said to the driver, "Okay...let's go to the airport."

"Yes, sir!" the driver chirped, and eased the car into the dense crawl of traffic, mostly a congestion of motorbikes. Out his window, Gil watched women riding behind their boyfriends or husbands, arms hugging their waists, long hair streaming like the black blood of life from beneath their helmets.

It would be a long, long flight back to his country. Several layovers. And because this part of the world was twelve hours ahead, it would also be like a journey back in time, as he raced home to his wife and his son Kwen's twin siblings.

***

"Din's novel about Cholukan is an immediate success, but he still isn't happy. He's not sad that Moop has run away with Oc, now that Oc broke up with the one-eyed gangster's girlfriend, after Oc figured out the girlfriend baited him into fighting her jealous boyfriend up on the roof—where Oc ended up shooting the gangster with his own gun. No...Din is sad because Laiki still won't let herself see how much he loves her. She still doesn't realize the beautiful notes he passes under her door are from him. She thinks they're from Tendu's ghost. She believes this is the only way Tendu's ghost, with his broken neck, can communicate with her. So she starts leaving blank sheets of paper, and a pen, around in the places she has seen the ghost. On the staircase. In the elevator. On top of one of the washers in the basement.

"After she leaves the paper on the washer and goes back upstairs, we see the pen lift in the air by itself and the tip start writing on the sheet of paper..."

"This is it!" hissed Twee, leaning forward in great suspense.

"Shh!" Phep scolded her.

"Laiki is getting ready for bed when she sees a piece of paper sliding under her apartment's door. She throws the door open but no one is there. She reads the paper and her eyes bulge, but as yet we can't see what's written on the page. Laiki runs to the stairs, up to the sixth floor where she bangs on the door of the apartment the brothers Tendu and Zo shared.

"Zo answers the door, and he smiles when he sees it's Laiki, but she pushes the paper into his hands and demands an explanation. The camera finally shows us the paper, and in a shaky scribble are the words:

"I am Zo. Tendu is not dead. He is Tendu. Zo is dead.

"Zo tries to babble an explanation, but he doesn't really have one. Laiki starts crying, and she screams at him, 'Why didn't I figure it out before, you monster? It *was* true...Tendu *was* the bad brother. Tendu's gambling did lead him to borrow money from the gangsters. Didn't it...*Tendu?* Your brother Zo came here to try to help you, yes! But he didn't realize you saw him as a way out of your troubles! You murdered your own brother— you murdered Zo! You pushed him down the basement stairs, or maybe you even broke his neck first before you did it! And then you took on Zo's identity, so the gangsters would think Tendu was dead and you could start over again! But you didn't count on your brother's ghost returning, did you, Tendu? It is Zo's spirit I've been in love with, not you, and I only realize that now!'

"Of course, Tendu knows that Laiki is onto him now, and even though Oc has already killed the one-eyed gangster, Tendu can't have Laiki running to tell his crimes to the police. So he grabs Laiki and covers her mouth and drags her over to the balcony.

He slides the door open so he can throw her off and kill her and make it look like an accident...just as he did with his brother.

"But Din has decided enough is enough: now that Moop has gone off with her true love, tonight he is going to come right out and announce his love for Laiki, unafraid. He starts toward her apartment, but in the stairwell he hears Laiki yelling at Tendu on the floor above, with all her accusations. So he starts running up the stairs. He bursts into Tendu's apartment just as he is about to throw Laiki over the railing..."

"Yes!" cried Chok.

"Din rushes over to them and pulls Laiki away. Then as Tendu spins around, Din punches him in the face. Tendu flies backward, hits the railing, and falls over it. He screams all the way down to the street.

"Din embraces Laiki, and she sobs against his chest. Din tells her, 'I love you, Laiki. I have loved you since the moment I laid eyes on you. And now, I will be with you forever.'"

Kwen had to stop for a moment as her voice fractured. Understanding this had to do with more than just the concluding moments of the serial *B-2*, Twee and Chok both reached out and held one of her hands. Even Phep's proud face was softened with sympathy. But Kwen hitched up her composure, and finished:

"The camera pulls back from the embracing couple, out into the hallway, and standing there unseen by them is the ghost of Zo. He looks sad, because we know he will love Laiki through eternity...but he is also smiling, because now all the mysteries are understood." With her friends holding her hands, Kwen had to wipe her tears off on her own shoulder. She repeated, "Now all the mysteries are understood."

THE UNINVITED GRAVE

"**F**uck my mother!" Depo Ep cried out when he saw the new tombstone in the precise center of his field of corn seedlings.

By tradition, the dead were to be buried in the town or city in which they had been born, not necessarily that in which they had lived—even if they had never lived long in their place of birth, and even if their place of birth was quite distant at the time of their death. Therefore, the families of the deceased often did not own a cemetery plot or any piece of property where they could inter a coffin and raise a monument.

It was thus a custom for relatives to purchase a plot of land from someone, perhaps an old friend or casual contact but usually a perfect stranger, in the city of the deceased's birth. This might be a corner of their front yard, the periphery of a field if they owned one, but it might also be a spot within their very house (in the case of an above-ground sarcophagus). The conditions of such a contract were that the relatives could look in on their loved one's resting place at any time without formal request. The contract did allow, though, because of their bulk, for an above-ground tomb to be respectfully utilized by the homeowners, who might very well use it as a coffee table, place quilts on its flat upper surface so that they might sit upon it to watch

TV (unless they placed the TV on it), or even stretch out upon those quilts at night to use it as a bed.

But it was also an old tradition that, because of the often crippling expense of purchasing a grave plot and of possibly having to travel from afar to inter the deceased, that a family might simply claim a spot of someone else's property without paying for it. This was permissible so long as it was done when the landowner was not present at the time of the burial or tomb erection, so that no violence would be instigated by either forceful relatives or landowners defending their property. So, a gravestone or above-ground tomb resting in one's front yard or at the periphery of a field might spring up unexpectedly, and custom was—as reinforced by law—that the property owner could not in any way deface the burial site or deny the family the right to visit it. Such an unexpected tomb might even show up in the center of one's living room, if one forgot to lock their door when they went to work.

The granite headstone on Depo Ep's property, however, had not been politely tucked away at the border of his corn field, but planted dead smack in its center.

"Fuck my mother!" he cried out again, even louder this time.

He looked around wildly, as if he might find the culprits still lurking nearby, catching their breath after their labors. After all, he hadn't really been gone that long. He'd ridden into town on his motorbike for a haircut, where his unruly graying eyebrows had also been trimmed and the wax excavated from his ears, all three aspects of maintenance long overdue. And what greater pleasure was there than to have a pretty young thing dig the wax out of one's ears with her delicate little probes, leaning her breasts against his arm? From there he had run a few errands and ended his excursion with a trip to the little graveyard in the neighborhood where his wife had grown up, to leave a monthly offering at her gravestone: a pair of perfectly spherical green melons (representing the two of them, still symbolically united) and burning some incense sticks he slotted into the little holes in the base of her lichen-splotched headstone. He'd hated the stubby little bitch. When she was harboring bitterness, which was always, she would purposely probe too far when digging the wax out of his ears, turning the sensuous to the torturous. But, tradition was tradition. The gods were always watching. A man who didn't honor his dead wife might very well, upon his own death, find himself called to the court of the Ten Demon Lords of Hell.

Depo didn't spy anyone lingering nearby to gauge his reaction, so he turned his attention back to the invading gravestone and read its new, clean-edged inscription aloud, lighting a 777 brand cigarette with hands trembling with rage as he did so.

"Ecco Bin Bin," he said in a mocking, disgusted tone, as if this were some absurd foreign name instead of one quite common in his country. "'Beloved husband, revered father, reverent servant of the gods, faithful citizen of his nation, productive worker, lucky gambler.' Pah! Would that I could engrave more words here, you pompous old goat's scrotum! And that is what I would engrave: 'Pompous old goat's scrotum'!" But Depo knew all too well he couldn't so much as spit on this tombstone, lest some police officer witness his offense. Or worse…the gods.

So he left his field (ah, but it was all right to deface his *field*, wasn't it?) and stormed back to his little farmhouse with its darkly mildew-stained cement walls, and rusted corrugated metal roof, and the misleading address B-2 stenciled over the door by his deceased wife—who had been more faithful to her precious TV than to the gods—growling curses all the way. He felt violated, and yet he felt impotent to address that violation. Tradition was a kind of glue that held a country and its people together, but it could also be a glue to stick one's hands together helplessly.

Still—except when it came to his domineering wife, may the Ten Lords of Hell feast on her heart through eternity—Depo Ep had never been a man to countenance helplessness.

***

Depo collected long stalks that grew from the swampy troughs at the sides of the dirt road running past the front of his property, but only those stalks that had gone yellow and hard from baking in the sun, and dragged bundles of them to the workshop at the rear of his humble little house. There, he separated the stalks into smaller bundles and with wire bound them into the limbs and long torsos of scarecrows. He had fashioned scarecrows in the past, to frighten birds from his corn field, before he had simply taken to shooting at them with an old bolt-action army carbine instead (oh, by the gods, if shooting were only an option now!), but these new scarecrows would be of another order altogether.

He tore to shreds some articles of his wife's clothing he'd uncovered, faded from rough laundering, and wound the strips around the scarecrows' arms in dangling tatters that would stir in the breeze. And upon the fronts of their roughly ball-like woven heads, he painted features. Fearsome, grimacing features with bulging eyes and wolfish tongues, his own tongue pushing past his teeth as he carefully rendered these details in black paint. These monstrous visages were the most important component of all.

His labors took him through the night, but he was driven first by his rage and then gradually by a gratified sense of purpose that grew into exhilaration, a bright aggressive pleasure.

The sun set, and rose again to find him in his field, where he had dragged his brood of scarecrows, each one a head taller than himself. There, he propped the scarecrows in a ring around the tombstone of Ecco Bin Bin, facing inward as if to pay the dead man tribute. But the congregation of scarecrows were effigies of the Ten Demon Lords of Hell.

Standing back to admire the finished composition like a true artist, clapping his callused palms together, Depo Ep let out a little snort of satisfaction. Then, he turned back to his house to allow himself, finally, a well-earned sleep. Though he was utterly exhausted and basting in sweat, never had his work in this field felt so rewarding.

***

He awoke with a start, his heart nearly firing itself through his chest like a cannonball. Disoriented, he thought for a moment that he was standing in a courtroom surrounded by ten towering figures with hideous faces. The Demon Lords were chanting. The solemn chants were his sentence, condemning him to an eternity of torture. Hideous old crones, leaning their withered breasts against his arms, would insert metal probes into his ears and tease out his brains bit by bit, only for the tissue to regenerate to be teased out again…

But as his heartbeat came more under control, he realized that the chanting was continuing even with his dream having dissipated. And the chanting was coming from somewhere nearby, just outside his house.

Depo threw himself from his mattress laid on the cement floor and went to a small barred window without any glass, drawing back a lace curtain stained yellow from decades of 777 smoke.

Night had descended again, weighing black upon his field,

but at its center—its exact center—burned a circle of torches. Incense smoke wafted on the warm night breeze. So did the chanting.

Before bursting outside, Depo Ep reached for the old bolt-action carbine leaning in a corner of his kitchen, but with an effort of will he withdrew his hand.

He tramped through his field unmindful of the delicate green seedlings he crushed beneath his sandals, not even bothering to walk in the rows between.

At the center of his field he found three mourners. One was a stubby old woman who, gods forbid, might have been a fleshly apparition of his own wife. But he knew whose wife she really was. Ecco Bin Bin's widow was accompanied by two adult sons, short and stout like overgrown babies, their heads still shaven bald from their father's funeral rites back in their own town, wherever that might be.

Joss sticks jutted from the holes drilled into the base of their father's clean new monument. Four bright green melons rested at the headstone's base, as well. The three of them at least had had the decency or respect—but of course, only out of fear— not to knock down the ten leering scarecrows. They knew the precepts of tradition as well as he. But they had stabbed a torch into the ground in front of each scarecrow to ward off their powers, and they had placed offerings at the feet of each of the Ten Demon Lords to placate them. Ten bottles of 777 brand whiskey, cartons of cigarettes, cellophane-wrapped packages of dried squid treats, and wads of colorful faux money. Everyone knew demons loved such things. Demons, like police officials, were easily bought.

Depo choked on an aborted exclamation. He was going to bellow at this trio to get off his land, and take their litter with them (though on second thought, it would be preferable if they left those ten bottles of 777 whiskey), but he knew that it was within the family's rights to pay tribute to their fallen loved one whenever they saw fit. They ignored him utterly as if he were an invisible spirit, knowing that he knew these rules. There was nothing really he could say. He could not even disparage the man's memory in front of them.

All he could utter, as a hiss under his breath, was, "Fuck my mother!"

But wait until they returned to their own town or city, as sooner or later they must. He would erect effigies of the entire Ten Legions of the Demon Lords' infernal army if he must, to surround and glare at the presumptuous tombstone of Ecco Bin Bin. Even if he had to sacrifice every inch of his field to do so.

With a renewed sense of purpose energizing him—or at least allowing him the saving of face—Depo Ep turned on his heel and marched back to his house, slamming its blistered old door behind him.

***

Depo Ep couldn't return to sleep that night, and paced his small house like a caged animal, wracking his brains for a means of exacting revenge against Ecco Bin Bin and his family in a way that wouldn't overtly violate the codes of the law, and of the gods.

He thought of drilling holes in the earth over Ecco Bin Bin's grave, and pouring in termites to eat through his coffin, no doubt a cheap wooden one, not nearly as pretentious and presumptuous as his thick granite headstone. Then, with the termites having paved the way, Depo would pour in a horde of hungry grubs or maggots or—yes!—the corpse-eating beetles of the type that the monks of the Va Tung Va temple bred and used to strip their dead brothers down to their bare bones, so that their denuded heads could be added to the walls of skulls that lined the catacombs beneath their temple. Depo didn't care if the termites or larvae or ravenous beetles went on to eat every last seedling in his field. His pride couldn't be bought for a corn field that spanned the entire surface of the world.

But then he considered that even if the beetles made their way into the coffin and chewed Ecco Bin Bin to the bones—so what? His family wouldn't see him that way, wouldn't even know it (however much Depo enjoyed the image of swarming blue-black beetles covering every inch of that goat scrotum's body, feasting on his face, his eyes). And wouldn't his family expect, anyway, that insects would one day whittle their loved one down to his inner architecture? Depo's method would only hasten that outcome. Again: so what? No...this idea wouldn't do.

Anyway, the gods might still view this as a direct attack against the deceased. Better to keep his revenge focused on *proximity* to the gravestone, rather than any kind of action directly against it or the arrogant old gambler planted beneath it, like a giant seed from which no profit would ever sprout. And how much corn would that tombstone displace, in the future? How much lighter would Depo's pockets be for that loss, as the years went on and on and that shiny gravestone became spotted with lichen and spattered with bird shit? Depo Ep shouted curses as he paced, just thinking of Ecco Bin Bin down there grinning with his eyes closed in serene satisfaction. The thief! He might as well have wads of Depo's future earnings clutched in his gnarled fingers, right now.

Depo considered that he could dump a huge pile of manure right next to the grave. Or better yet, he himself could shit in a bucket and dump *that* in front of the grave every day. Not touching the plot or its grave marker, oh no, not a single brown dot on that lovely grainy stone, and Depo could always defend himself by saying that he liked to produce his own fertilizer. He had always been frugal!

But even this idea didn't seem sufficient. Maybe it just wasn't… creative enough. To properly answer this outrage called for the strategy of a master general, the brushstrokes of a brilliant artist.

He returned to his idea of an army of scarecrows (let them put a bottle of 777 whiskey at the feet of a hundred soldiers!), but that idea was a bit…exhausting, now that he revisited it. Yet thoughts of demons led to thoughts of ghosts, and thoughts of ghosts reminded him of his dear nephew Kwen when he was only a child of seven. His brother's stepson Kwen was one of the few members of his family he had ever really loved; only a demon wouldn't have loved that child's sad eyes and sweet smile, his respectful and gentle ways. And—truth be told, if only to himself—what man with blood in his veins wouldn't have been heartsick in love with Kwen when she had changed herself into a woman, her eyes still sad and smile still sweet (or was it the other way around)?

In any case, one night a bullying schoolmate, perhaps responding to Kwen's femininity, had placed a ghost melon on the window sill of Kwen's bedroom while he slept. Kwen awoke to this frightful vision in a panic. For days afterward he refused to sleep in his own room, and as an adult woman she had once confided to her Uncle Depo that she still had the occasional nightmare about the ghost melon on her window sill.

(Depo had found out about the story from his brother, also a vengeful sort, who had enlisted Depo's aid in passing a dozen large but harmless snakes through the bullying schoolmate's own bedroom window while he slept.)

A ghost melon…of course. No sane fruit seller, whether tending a market stall or peddling their wares from a much-laden bicycle or motorbike, would attempt to sell a ghost melon, though they were said to be as edible as green melons. But Depo knew just where to find one. Not all that far from his property was a boggy area, once a rice paddy, where there grew in profusion tall stalks like those from which he had fashioned the Ten Demon Lords of Hell. In this marshy stretch, visible from the narrow dirt road, were scattered ghost melons...seeming to bob in the shallow water like the tops of the heads of a dozen drowned men.

And so, with the pink of dawn spreading, charged with another burst of inspiration, Depo Ep set out again on his dusty old motorbike.

But first, walking his bike toward the road, he glanced back toward his field, where a mist lay heavily like a cloud that had descended wearily from the sky. Because his was a newly-planted crop of corn, on the tail of the last harvested crop, the only things in the field that poked up from the blanket of fog were the dark hump of the tombstone and the circle of silhouetted scarecrows. No sign of the bereaved, though; they'd even removed their ring of tall torches. Depo was both relieved and disappointed to see them gone. So now they wouldn't see the ghost melon, after all? Or were they crouched in the bushes at the edge of the field, waiting to spring forth at the slightest offense against their loved one, as had seemingly been the case before? If they were indeed gone, back to their home, so be it. He'd put a new ghost melon in his yard, at the foot of the grave plot, each time the last one rotted, from now until eternity if he had to, until Ecco Bin Bin's family returned to pay their respects.

When he'd arrived at the bog, Depo rested his sandals on the seat of his motorbike, rolled up the legs of his trousers, then waded into the dark water. Mud and probably the things that lived in mud oozed between his toes, but he ignored this as he reached the first melon, tethered like a buoy by its vine underwater. He cut the vine free with his knife, washed the melon off in the water, then held it up at face level for inspection. Ah! It was perfectly spherical, like the green melons he had left at his wife's tomb, but its smooth skin was a pale grayish-blue. Tucking this fine specimen under his arm like a severed head, he turned toward his bike leaning at the edge of the road. But it was not back toward his home that he steered. Oh no, not yet. First, another visit to the little neighborhood graveyard where his wife was ensconced.

***

Depo Ep sat cross-legged in the matted grass beside his wife's grave plot, upon which he had set down the ghost melon as if it were an offering. But it was not an offering. It was a temporary vessel.

When ghost melons moldered, their smooth bluish skins became mottled with gray and black patches. In these patterns of decay, words were sometimes discerned. The word might be nonsensical or cryptic, though it could be something significant like a person's name. Depo had a neighbor who swore he had once seen a ghost melon bearing the words, *"Death! Death! Bloody Death!"* He had asked Depo how someone could dismiss something that extensive as merely a trick of the eye. (Though his neighbor had been drunk at the time he related the story, and had most likely been drunk when he came upon that particularly wordy ghost melon.)

Often it wasn't words that the rot formed, but faces. Usually these were vague like faces drawn by children, open to interpretation, though many people claimed to have witnessed the face of a furious demon...or the face of the ghost that resided for a time in the melon.

A ghost, because it was believed that if a person were to place a blue melon upon a grave, the hungry soul would be lured forth to feast on the succulent fruit and become trapped inside its skin. Only when the fruit rotted away would the spirit be freed to return to its resting place. That was why his beloved nephew Kwen had so feared the ghost melon he had seen in his window, looking in at him like a skull without features. Because, even though it had not yet become splotchy and thus bore no ghastly countenance, it was always feared that an egg-like ghost melon carried an angry spirit inside it.

"I know you hated me, you old bitch," Depo spoke to the gravestone beside him, "as much as I hated you. Ours was an arranged marriage and I know you never stopped pining for that rascal guitar-player Zwoon. But if you ever loved your little home, where you watched your stupid soap operas and talked all day on the phone to your bitch mother and your bitch sister and your bitch sister-in-laws, instead of fucking me and giving me a few sons, then you need to help me now. It's too late to protect our home from these parasites, but we can strike back in vengeance. Do you hear me? Come eat now, you fat old sow. Come eat the sweet thing I brought for you."

***

Three days passed without the family showing up in his field again; at least, not that Depo witnessed, and he made sure to stick close to home, peeking out his windows often. Closer in-spections of the grave site proved that no new joss sticks had been burned, no new green melons added to replace the four that were now rotting, caved in on themselves like battered skulls and attracting hordes of flies. His own single ghost melon, a few discreet inches away from the foot of the fresh dirt plot, had also begun its process of decay. Gray-black blotches had appeared here and there on its skin, which was beginning to lose its glossy tautness.

It was possible the last few days of heavy rain had discouraged the family from revisiting the grave, though they might still be visiting some old friends or relatives in town, but it was much more likely they had returned to their own town by now.

"That's fine," Depo Ep said to Ecco Bin Bin. "I'll keep bringing new melons when this one has decayed. I'll grow them in my field instead of corn if I have to, to keep myself supplied with them. I like that—yes! I'll flood this field and grow ghost melons! I don't care if my neighbors don't like it, if the police come here to chastise me. I'll do it, I tell you! One day your family will see a ghost melon waiting here, with my wife's horrid soul bottled in one after another, and they'll be terrified that the ghost inside will escape from her shell to sink down there to keep you company. Believe me, I'd be terrified too, if I were you, if my wife crawled down there for a visit."

Depo laughed happily as he strutted back toward his house. There was no denying that this challenge had given spark to his life. It was a sport, a game. In fact, he'd even go so far as to admit he hadn't felt this alive in a long time.

***

On the fourth day since having placed the ghost melon at Ecco Bin Bin's feet, Depo still found no new incense sticks or green melons to replace those turned to muck. There was one very striking development, though. It should not have shocked Depo Ep, after the stories he had heard since his childhood, but nevertheless he was quite shaken when he knelt down to inspect the withering surface of his ghost melon, and upon its rind—facing

Ecco Bin Bin's tombstone—discovered a remarkable, unmistakable representation of his deceased wife's face, rendered in inky blotches of black and gray. She looked so filled with fury he had at first mistaken her face for that of a demon—just like when she'd been alive.

After a few moments of stunned terror, Depo actually laughed with delight, and exclaimed, "Good job, bitch! *Glare* at him! Make that old goat shiver in his box with no escape from your ugly face! The gods know I suffered that fate for too long a time, myself."

His wife seemed to be glaring at him, though, the longer he studied the ghost melon. So, feeling uneasy again, Depo rose and retreated to the shelter of his home.

***

"No," Depo Ep moaned in his sleep. "Nooo…"

They stood in a ring around him, looming a head taller than he. Depo wheeled around desperately, at the exact center of that circle, with no avenue of escape. The baleful red eyes of the Ten Demon Lords of Hell blazed with harsh judgment, as if shooting fiery rays into his very core. The demons were oblivious to the field of dancing orange flames in which they stood, but those flames were cooking Depo in his own skin. Hotter every second…*hotter*…

He jolted awake. Smelled the smoke flowing in through his windows. Heard the crackling of the flames outside. Felt the intense heat against his skin. Depo leapt from his mattress and scrambled to the nearest window.

"Fuck my mother!" he cried out in horror.

His field was a sea of lapping flame. He saw that all but two of the ten scarecrows had already fallen and been consumed, but he failed to recognize the pole-like remnants of several tall torches. To his mind, the family of Ecco Bin Bin—still in the vicinity all this time, after all—had set his field on fire purposely, but it had in fact been an accident. One of the new torches they had erected as protection against the ghost glowering from the blue melon had accidentally tilted during the night, and set the nearest scarecrow alight. From there, the flames had spread. The family had already left well before then, expecting the torches to burn themselves out harmlessly after a few hours.

Depo bolted from the window to the door, but found the flames had spread to such an extent that they completely surrounded his tiny house. He darted from window to window, choking as more and more black smoke poured into those windows.

At last, knowing he was hopelessly surrounded, Depo sat down at his little kitchen table and lit himself a 777 cigarette defiantly.

"You were the one really behind this, weren't you?" he coughed, as if talking to someone in the empty chair across from him. "You think you're in heaven now, listening to your old boyfriend strum his cheap guitar? Pah!" He took another drag from his cigarette. "See you in Hell, bitch!"

***

Fen Pwee wagged his head in disbelief. How had they managed this outrage? (Whoever *they* had been.) He had only been away in the city—delivering a load of bricks to a work site in his battered old truck—for a few hours. But here it was, as if it had appeared by an act of black magic, nonetheless: a brand new, sharp-edged granite gravestone standing at the head of a fresh dirt plot, right in the middle of his front yard. He turned slowly, as if dazed by a blow, to stare at the road, as though he might actually find the culprits standing there grinning maliciously, waiting for him to discover their surprise. But of course there was no one.

With anger finally flooding into him, rousing him from his stupor, Fen stepped closer to scrutinize the words engraved into the headstone (unbeknownst by him, that stone purchased by the deceased's beloved niece, Kwen).

Fen read aloud: "'Depo Ep. Devoted husband, favorite uncle, faithful servant of the gods, honorable citizen of his nation, productive farmer.'"

Shaking his head again, Fen Pwee added his own verbal addendum to the epitaph:

"Fuck my mother!"

LUCKY TRIPLE SEVEN

The dirt alley that Nolee drove her motorbike down as a shortcut to reach the local lottery office was strewn with small slips of paper like shed cherry blossoms. When she drew close to the building itself, the end of the dirt alley where it met the street was fully carpeted with these little paper slips, which were white on their back sides but brightly colored on their fronts. They were unsold and obsolete lottery tickets, torn and discarded like so many unfulfilled dreams.

The air here was poisoned with the smell of ink from the presses that churned out the tickets. Even these short visits— two a day—gave Nolee an instant headache. She wondered how the workers inside the building could tolerate the chemical atmosphere. It was the overpowering smell of money.

Nolee stopped her bike and dismounted, glancing back at her son Cee as if to reassure him as she approached the lottery office's chief, Bolun Sep. Standing outside to smoke a cigarette, the rest of his many street people having already reported back to him, Sep pointedly glanced at his watch as Nolee quickened her pace to reach him.

Sep said, "Do you come late on purpose, Nolee, to avoid a line? Or do you like to see me alone because you're in love with me?"

Nolee smiled at his joke nervously, but stammered because his face was not good natured. "I'm sorry, Bolun…forgive me." Lowering her voice, she motioned with her head back toward her bike. "It's my poor son, you know that. Getting him in and out of the sidecar is difficult."

"Don't try to wring pity from me, Nolee; that may work on your customers, but not on me. If it takes time to put the boy back in the sidecar, then you should start here earlier. You know the cut-off point is three. It is now three twenty."

Nolee extended a stack of lottery tickets bound with a rubber band. In her other hand, she proffered a thick wad of faded, grubby bills also held together with an elastic. "Please, Bolun… I'll be more careful next time. Look, I sold sixty of one hundred tickets. Isn't that good?"

The lottery chief snatched both bundles from her. He snapped the band from the money and began counting it, muttering around the cigarette in his mouth, "If you're late like this again I'll make you pay me for the cost of every unsold ticket…you hear me? You know that's the way it works. After three, unsold tickets are yours."

"I understand, Bolun. Never again."

"Never again until the next time, eh? How many times have you taken advantage of me this way?" From the wad of money he extracted the dirtiest, most crumpled bills and shoved them at her. Ten percent of the money she had collected.

Nolee bowed to him as she accepted her day's wage. "You are kind, Bolun."

"Huh!" he snorted. "Take that poor monster home now and make him some dinner. Or do you starve him on purpose to make him look more frightful?"

"It is hard with no husband to help me feed him. I do what I can alone."

She knew if she were as pretty as she had been when she was young, Sep might take this as a cue to proposition her. And if her situation then had been as lamentable as it was now, she might even have accepted his proposition. But he had younger ticket sellers to seduce, so he only said, "Huh!" again, and into her hand slapped a batch of one hundred new tickets for tomorrow's drawing. The tickets were almost hot to the touch and reeked of ink.

Then Sep turned and went back inside the lottery office to wait for the four o'clock radio broadcast, and the stream of winners who would descend on the office to collect their winnings. But before he passed through the door, he pulled the rubber band from the forty unsold tickets Nolee had handed him, tore them in half, and tossed them back over his shoulder. They fluttered in the air like butterflies, scattering in the street and adding to the carpet at Nolee's feet.

She felt like running up behind him and stabbing him in the back for what he had said about her son. "Monster," eh? But she hadn't a knife. And hadn't the nerve. And if she killed everyone who said insulting things about her son, then she'd have to kill many a citizen of her town indeed. If she were to kill even one of them, then what good would she be to Cee in front of a police firing squad? Who would take care of him then?

So she turned back to him. All this time, she knew, his eyes had been roving across his surroundings and the sky without direction. Though he didn't acknowledge her, Nolee smiled at him as she straddled her dusty bike again. "Home now, my ruby," she told him.

It was what her husband had once called her—"my ruby"—back when she had been young and pretty. Long before he had met that young and pretty little street food vendor, whom he slept beside now.

As if in response, Cee rolled his head, twitched his bent and useless arms, and grunted something. It sounded like garbled words, but if they were Nolee couldn't make them out.

***

Nolee, her husband, and Cee had lived with her husband's three brothers and their families, all in one good-sized two-story house. But now that her husband had gone off to live with his sly little whore, Nolee had moved herself and Cee in with her cousin, Maik, and Maik's husband and two small children. It was an uncomfortable arrangement. Nolee knew Maik's husband didn't want them there, even though Nolee paid for her expenses. More than once she had overheard Maik's husband, when he'd been drinking, refer to Cee as "unlucky." The blighted creature would bring misfortune to all of them. Just look at him. Cursed. No wonder Nolee's husband had wanted to be rid of them.

In fact, Nolee's husband himself had often mourned his bad luck in having a deformed monstrosity as his only child. What an heir! What must this town think of him for siring such an abomination? He wasn't a drinker and had said these things while sober.

It was the fear of the mutant, her cousin Maik had told Nolee. (Maik had always been a smart one in school, a reader.) Maik apologized for her husband and Nolee's husband both, explaining their prejudice was an instinctual kind of reaction. Reject the tainted…shun the bad genes. Keep the lineage pure. An animal instinct. It had nothing to do with luck. Modern-minded, rebuffing superstition, Maik didn't believe in luck. At least, not in the sense of blessings and curses. To her, luck was only arbitrary, random, senseless.

The problem was: Nolee did believe in luck. Both good and bad. Luck as a cosmic, celestial force. Luck was, after all, her trade.

But she had found, since going to work for Bolun Sep and the local branch of the government lottery, that Cee didn't hamper her work selling tickets in the streets. Cee didn't bring her bad luck. On the contrary, once she had started bringing him with her on her daily rounds, she had found herself selling many more tickets. Because people pitied Cee...pitied *her*. By buying their lottery tickets from her instead of some other street dealer, they were showing charity that the gods themselves might take note of. In a way, they were buying more than a stab at winning a large sum of money. They were investing in the good fortune of their eternal souls.

Nolee had staked as her primary territory a long string of outdoors cafés and restaurants pressed right up to the bank of the sluggish green river that flanked the town. She went out with Cee twice every day: once from ten till two, and again after dinner from six to ten. (In the morning and afternoon, selling tickets for that day's drawing...and at night, beginning the sale of the next bundle of tickets for tomorrow's drawing.)

Nolee preferred selling at night. It was cooler. At night, the colorful strings of lights decorating the open-air cafés and restaurants shone in the river, now as black and wide as the sky above it. And at night, men drank beer and rice wine and were looser with their earnings. They became gallant, sometimes buying a can of soft drink for Cee, which Nolee would hold for him, as he sucked sloppily from a straw.

Whether day or night, she would leave her bike at home and go on her rounds on foot, pushing Cee in a pink plastic stroller she had hoisted him into. The stroller, shaped like a cute-faced rabbit with its back gouged out, was intended for a much younger child than her malformed son. Sometimes when she pushed him along and the stroller jostled over a rock or a broken section of sidewalk he would laugh. His laugh was deep, barking, did not sound human.

Tonight Nolee wheeled her boy amongst the tables of the Banyan Café. The owner never gave her any trouble, as long as she didn't press customers who weren't interested. And why should he protest? Gambling was as natural as eating, in her country where belief in luck was as natural as belief in fickle gods.

All the strings of lights in the Banyan Café were green, flashing like hordes of fireflies, making the trees seem preternaturally alive, irradiated with life. The thick, ropy trees rose like columns between the little tables, supporting the glowing green canopy. Nolee wheeled Cee to one of these tables, where three men in their thirties sat smoking, drinking, and admiring the model-pretty waitresses in their miniskirts and high heels. Green lasers strobed, and painfully loud disco music pounded but no one danced to it; her shy countrymen were not dancers.

One of these men had motioned Nolee to come over, smiling at her. She knew him. His name was Uhi. Uhi as always wore his uniform of dark blue shirt and trousers. He was a funeral man. He collected the dead in the back of his truck (even their motorbikes if they'd been in an accident) and brought them to their homes, for several days of rites and feasting, after which he would return to drive their cheap coffins to be cremated. He was very good looking, and polite, and a regular customer, so Nolee liked him.

"Hey, boy," Uhi said to Cee, reaching out to take hold of one of the child's gnarled hands. "Keeping your mother company like a good son, are you?" Uhi was in the good humors of drink. Still holding Cee's useless paw, he grinned up at Nolee and asked, "How old is your boy now?"

"Seven," Nolee said. With a touch of pride she elaborated,

"And he just had his birthday a few weeks ago. He was born on the seventh day of the seventh month."

"Ah!" Uhi exclaimed, widening his eyes and switching his grin back to Cee. Everyone knew that seven was an exceptionally lucky number. Any year of one's life with seven in it (beginning with age 7, of course, and continuing to 17, 27, and so on) was supposed to be especially auspicious. "Triple seven! This is a special year for you, boy! Mark my words! So are you going to share your luck with me tonight...hm? Will you help me pick a good set of numbers?"

Uhi reached a hand out to Nolee, and she handed over her entire stack of tickets for him to sift through in search of a promising group of numbers (each ticket printed with a string of seven numbers). As he flipped through the tickets, he leaned in close to Cee...put his ear right to Cee's mouth. "Tell me a good number, boy!"

Uhi's two friends laughed, but they also looked repulsed. Nolee recognized the look by now. Cee's body was tiny, monkey-like, shriveled, his limbs atrophied and stiff. His head, on the other hand, was disproportionately large, which was why it lolled and bobbed so on his skinny neck. It was shaped like an inverted triangle, and he had a harelip besides, his skin also too dark as if it had been burned leather-brown in the sun. His eyes were impossibly far-spaced. And yet they were beautiful in themselves, Nolee felt, in their form and shape and brightness. Maik had said it, too, though maybe only agreeing with her to make her feel better.

Over the throb of music, Nolee thought she heard Cee gurgle softly in the funeral man's ear.

She saw Uhi's eyes grow large. He sat back and said to Cee, "Really?" Then he studied the tickets in his hands more carefully, shuffling through them until he found a series of numbers that obviously agreed with him, because he said, "Aha!"

His two friends laughed again. One of them said, "Told you the winning number, did he? Are you going to match all seven tomorrow?"

"He didn't tell me all seven," Uhi said, "but he told me three, and three is enough to win a nice sum."

"So what numbers did he say?" chuckled the other friend dubiously.

"Ha! As if I would tell you, so you'd search for another ticket with those same three numbers in a row! Get your own good luck charm!"

"I'll ask him for different numbers, then," said this man, and he scraped his metal chair closer to Cee and overcame his revulsion to bend down close to him as Uhi had. "Okay, little wise man, give me some lucky numbers, too."

Nolee watched, and heard her son quietly gurgle again. What could he be saying? Nothing…that was what…because she had put her own ear to his mouth on numerous occasions when she'd thought he was trying to wrestle out a word or two. Oh, how even a single word would have made her soul soar! "Water." "Cookie." "Mama." But nothing. Never anything. Not a word.

With the music so loud, and the drink in their ears, they were hearing things…first Uhi, and now this one, for he too sat back with a surprised grin and clapped his hands for Nolee to pass him her tickets. Like Uhi, he flipped through them until he apparently found a row of seven red printed numbers that in whole or in part agreed with what he believed Cee had just said to him.

***

In the next room, Cee sat on blankets spread on the floor, positioned in front of the flat-screen TV mounted on the wall. A

Western cartoon played, a cat chasing a mouse. Sometimes they heard Cee's braying laughter.

In Maik's kitchen, Nolee and Maik and several older neighbor women sat cross-legged on the tiled floor, playing a game with tiny glossy cards and betting with small denomination bills worn thin as tissue. They were waiting for the four o'clock radio broadcast, which was imminent, Maik with notebook and pen ready because she was the educated one. She kept a record of every day's winning numbers, to study later for trends in lucky numbers, which she swore turned up again in some kind of cycle or formula that she one day hoped to crack, like a pioneering mathematician. Up until recently the winning numbers had been selected from a fan-driven air mix machine, in the form of plastic balls, but now the government proudly utilized a modern computer system that selected randomly generated numbers. Nolee was suspicious of this new process, since she knew nothing of computers; plastic balls with numbers printed on them had been a much more tangible concept.

Maik's husband arrived home from work, and as he stepped through the kitchen's open wall from the dusty courtyard he sneered at the circle of women. "Gambling my earnings as always, woman?" he said to Maik—though he had many times joined in their games, and for more serious stakes. He passed around the women to check on his dinner boiling on the stove top.

Spreading her colorful miniature cards in a fan, Nolee glanced into the next room when there came a particularly loud burst of laughter from Cee. She heard a commercial playing; had he laughed at that, or was it some mysterious thought in his mind? She stared in at him for a long moment, and then said to Maik seated beside her, "Who will care for him when I am gone, cousin? He may not outlive me, but what if he does...by many years?

Will he be thrown into a hospital like a prison, to be beaten and neglected? If I were truly a good mother, I would kill him now and myself, too, so we could go on to the afterlife together."

"Hush!" Maik slapped Nolee's leg. "I will begin teaching my young ones to feed him, do small things for him, to prepare them…so that one day they will see to his needs."

"Oh!" cried Maik's husband Teng, leaning beside the sink to watch the card game and wait for the government radio broadcast. "Of course! Burden my children! How can they work and lead normal lives if they have to care for that sorry soul?"

Maik glared up at her husband. "Cee is our blood."

"*Your* blood."

"Your *children's* blood."

Nolee lowered her head, seemingly examining her cards but on the verge of tears, sick inside with anger. It was not an alien state. When, she wondered, would she come to peace with the cruelty of people, and of fate? Seven years and it was like a freshly bleeding wound. She ached for numbness. If not death, at least a kind of living death.

"Shh," said one of the neighbor women to the bickering husband and wife, pulling the radio closer and turning up the volume until the air in the kitchen crackled and sizzled. "It's time!"

Maik snatched up her notebook and opened it, her pen poised as the broadcast began. It sounded sandy with static, the woman announcer's expressionless voice echoing strangely as it always did, as if she sat in a tiny metal room. Maik had once said to Teng and Nolee that the daily broadcasts of eighteen winning number combinations sounded like the mysterious coded readings one could hear on shortwave, known as "number stations," transmitted from around the world, but the others hadn't known what she was talking about.

The announcer began to recite the eighteen winning number

combinations. After each string of numbers, a male voice repeated it. His voice was also a monotone, and echoed as if he were
crowded in the same tiny metal room with the woman. Their
voices were so cold, hard, and dead. Was this how the gods would
sound if mortals could hear them, dealing out their fates?

Every one of the women, but for the furiously scribbling Maik,
stared hard at her own lottery ticket as if willing the numbers to
favor her. Nolee herself had bought one from the stack she had
sold last night along the riverside, and this morning and afternoon among the neighborhoods. Today she had made sure to
return the unsold tickets to Bolun Sep well before three.

But when all the numbers had been announced, not a single
one of the women had won anything.

Teng laughed and said, "And so the government pigs grow
fatter! Better luck next time, ladies. Back to your card game,
then…maybe you'll find your fortune there!"

In the next room, Cee shouted out a loud laugh. All of them
turned their heads to look in at him.

***

After dinner, Nolee and Cee set out onto the streets again, this
time in the vicinity of the river. The sky had already gone purple, with a few dragon tails of orange.

She had been pushing her son in his pink rabbit cart along the
sidewalk, passing big shade trees that grew through the pavement. The center of the sidewalk consisted of individual cement
plates, any of which could be lifted away to get at the water
pipes in their trough beneath. At night, huge cockroaches came
swarming up from beneath these plates and scurried to and fro.
Nolee barely noticed them, but sometimes Cee looked down at
them and laughed.

Nolee had stopped now to sell tickets to two female street vendors who sold sugarcane juice. The sidewalk was heaped with the sugarcane press's crushed pulp. As one of the women prepared a cup of juice for Cee, a motorbike pulled up to a rumbling halt right beside Nolee. She turned, and there was the funeral man Uhi in his blue uniform. Behind him on the bike rode his friend who had also bought a lottery ticket from her last night.

"Sister!" Uhi said to her with cheerful familiarity. "We've been looking all around for you! I need to buy another ticket from your gifted son!"

"Me too!" exclaimed Uhi's friend, dismounting. "We both won last night…from the numbers your son told us!"

"What?" said Nolee, looking to Cee in disbelief. How could that be possible? Surely the two men, with too much drink in them, had only heard what they'd wanted to hear in Cee's inarticulate noises.

"Yes!" Uhi confirmed. Now that it was safe he revealed his numbers. "He gave me 725. He gave Chep 617. We both bought tickets from you that had those numbers in them, and today on the radio our numbers came up in the eighteen! We both won two hundred thousand veng!" Two hundred thousand veng was the equivalent of twenty Western dollars—a nice little sum.

"What's this?" asked one of the two sugarcane vendors, marveling, and maybe a little resentful that Nolee's son had never given *her* a tip before. "Nolee, your son is picking lucky numbers?"

"Yes!" Uhi told the woman, and explained what had occurred. He wiggled his fingers for Nolee's tickets, then bent low beside Cee as he had last night. "Give me more luck, Lucky Triple Seven!"

"If this really worked," Nolee said to the vendor from the corner of her mouth, "then don't you think I myself would be rich by now?"

"He doesn't give you numbers, then?" the vendor asked.

"Cee can't talk!"

Uhi straightened up with a perplexed expression. He said to Nolee, "He only mumbles. I can't hear anything this time."

"Let me try," said Uhi's friend Chep, nudging past him to crouch beside Cee. "Give me some winning numbers, little wise man, just like last night!"

They all heard Cee make some guttural sounds, but this man too eventually stood up looking disappointed and frustrated. "I can't understand him tonight, either."

Uhi beseeched Nolee, "Can you try to talk to him for us, sister?"

Nolee was going to protest that Cee could not speak, no matter what they thought they'd heard, but to humor the men she moved close to Cee and put her ear to his riven lips. "Tell me some numbers for these friends of mine, my ruby. Tell Mama."

Cee burbled, and there was nothing at all in these sounds that Cee could stretch her imagination into interpreting as numbers or words of any kind.

She looked to the two friends and held up her hands. "I'm very sorry."

"A one-time gift," Uhi sighed, contemplating the great mystery that was Nolee's idiot son.

"Let me try this," said the sugarcane vendor, taking Nolee's place beside Cee. "Tell me something, little boy," she coaxed him, as if listening at a keyhole in the door to some unknown world. Did heavenly miracles churn behind that door?

They all watched the woman. Watched her expression become astonished, then delighted...though they, themselves, had only heard more of the same animal sounds. The woman reached to Uhi for Nolee's wad of tickets. "Give those here!" she cried. "He gave me three numbers!"

"What?" Chep cried, looking more disappointed and frustrated than ever.

"You see," said Uhi. "It's like I told you—only a one-time blessing."

"I suppose we should be grateful for what we got," Chep grumbled. "But if I could have won that same amount every day, I'd never have to work again!"

"Here! Here!" The vendor at last pulled a ticket from the stack of tickets, jumping in place as if the numbers had been called on the radio already, to confirm her win. "This ticket has the numbers he told me!"

"I want to try!" said the other sugarcane vendor, shoving past her friend to get at Cee.

A few pedestrians had stopped to watch what was going on with these excited people and the horribly deformed boy.

That night alone, Nolee sold forty-five tickets. And she still had tomorrow morning and afternoon, yet, in which to continue selling this batch.

"My lucky boy," she said to Cee as she pushed him home that night. "My precious ruby." And yet he was already asleep, perhaps exhausted from playing liaison to cosmic forces, his huge head slumped down upon his bony chest.

Nolee was beginning to believe there really was something to this...that some greater power was at work here...for what were the odds that her son would give every one of her customers (except Uhi and Chep) a trio of numbers that appeared in her group of tickets? Even assuming he had the abilities of a savant, he had never even touched her tickets, so how could he memorize them?

It was as though Fate had laid an intricate and unknowable plan...sending those particular red numbers to those little slips of paper, and placing all those particular customers in Cee's path.

And sending this unordinary night's profit—ten percent!—into Nolee's pocket.

Once she had thought her life lay in the shadow of a curse. Now, she thought the opposite situation might be true. Maybe Uhi was right—maybe this sudden burst of luck was due to Cee having reached the age of seven only a few weeks ago. On the seventh day of the seventh month.

Did that mean the gift was only temporary, to last just throughout Cee's seventh year? Or only through this, the seventh month? Whatever the case...she would gladly accept all the luck that fell her way.

When Nolee arrived home, she told Maik what had happened. Maik's husband Teng scoffed and left the room. Maik looked dubious but was, of course, more polite. And though Maik embraced religion only in the context of tradition, as opposed to faith, that night she joined Nolee in kneeling before the family altar and burning incense in thanks to their ancestors, and to the gods.

Nolee especially thanked the Ruby Empress, goddess of benevolence.

***

News of Nolee's little prodigy spread through town, and the next day she sold the remaining fifty-five tickets Bolun Sep had allocated to her. She ran out of tickets by one o'clock. It was the first time since she had begun selling tickets—when her husband had abandoned her—that she had sold all one hundred.

When Nolee arrived a little late at the lottery office, Bolun Sep drew in a deep breath to berate her...until she presented him with an extra-thick wad of bills, and no unsold tickets. Then his face lit up with wonder. But she didn't tell him about the source of this wonder: Cee. In a far more pleasant frame of mind, Sep gave Nolee her one hundred tickets to sell for tomorrow's drawing. "Keep it up!" he told her, then both he and Nolee headed in opposite directions to await the four o'clock radio broadcast.

Straddling her bike, she whispered to Cee in his sidecar, "Now we shall see, my ruby."

***

Nolee had not bought a ticket for herself from her batch. There had been no tickets left from which to pull one. So when the numbers were announced by the dead-voiced radio spirits, there was no immediate indication in Maik's household that any good fortune had favored anyone. And yet, though maybe it was only her imagination, Nolee thought she heard (or was it *felt?*) a distant rising of voices, like when a chorus of agitated dogs barking floats from the distance late at night...when the source of that disturbance is unknown to the listener in her bed.

Soon enough, though, that excited wave descended upon Maik's house, in the form of visitors. One after another in quick succession, like an audience arriving at an appointed time for a performance. Uhi and Chep were among them. A group of about thirty people, and they all wanted the same thing.

"Let me try this one more time!" Uhi begged. "Maybe this time Cee will favor me again."

"He is sleeping," Maik reported sternly, having checked on Cee in the living room, where they had placed him in front of the television.

"Please wake him!" a woman who lived on the next street over pleaded.

"What is all this about?" Teng asked, coming from upstairs. But Nolee hadn't had to ask. She knew. Impossible as this was, she knew.

The neighborhood woman said, "Haven't you heard? It seems that *every* person who bought a ticket from Nolee has won! How can that be, hm? How can it be that every ticket was a three-digit winner? But it's true! It's true!"

"You're right—it's impossible," Teng said. "What are the odds? It has to be an error with the government's stupid computers. I'll be surprised if the lottery office honors these tickets, when the winners all come banging on their door this evening."

"They *must* honor the winning tickets!" protested another neighbor, slapping the back of one hand into the palm of the other. "If you hold a ticket with winning numbers the government must accept that, fair and square! If they didn't, there would be riots!"

"Please, please," begged a young taxi driver Nolee had never seen before, who had parked his little vehicle on the other side of the courtyard. "Bring your son out here! If he has a gift, it was meant to be shared!"

Maik started to argue again that her cousin's child was sleeping, but then they all heard his odd guffaws coming from the next room.

***

More people came to replace those who left, clutching their precious tiny slips of paper. The only people who departed unhappy were Uhi, Chep, and the two sugarcane juice vendors, all of whom had already won two hundred thousand veng over the past two drawings.

"My cousin's son grows weary, don't you see that?" Maik scolded as people continued to arrive at her home. "He has to go to bed now!"

"You can come back tomorrow," Nolee called to the people who her cousin shooed away.

"If any tickets still remain by the time I come back," one man complained gruffly as he returned to his motorbike.

"He's right," Nolee whispered to Maik, showing her only fifteen remaining tickets. "Maybe I should get two hundred tickets from Sep tomorrow, huh? Or even more?"

"Cousin, listen to yourself…you're too giddy. It sounds like you sold one hundred winning tickets yesterday. Whether it was a computer error or not—and it has to be!—how happy do you think Sep is going to be about that?"

"It isn't my fault!" Nolee cried. "Nor Cee's!"

"All I know is the lottery office hates winners. It isn't supposed to work that way."

"Tell that to the gods."

"Don't you see? The gods aren't putting winning numbers in Cee's head. Even if Cee hadn't given anyone a winning number, all they needed to do was select any ticket at random and they would have picked a winner. That stupid funeral man…Cee didn't give him some numbers so he left empty-handed, when all he needed to do was buy one of your tickets."

"Then how does Cee know the winning numbers, when he has never seen the tickets?"

"I thought you said he couldn't possibly be speaking to them."

"I used to believe that, but now…now I think there must be truth in it! How could so many people be deluded, and coincidentally believe they've heard numbers that just so happen to appear on one of the tickets—tickets they haven't yet seen?"

"It's like mass hysteria."

"Mass *what?* Your explanations are no more logical than mine!"

"Cousin! What would you have me believe? That when Cee speaks numbers to someone, the numbers on one of the tickets actually change to conform to that? That he can change the numbers through the force of his mind?"

"Maybe," Nolee said defiantly. "But not through the influence of his mind. Through the influence of the gods!"

"Pah!" said Teng, leaning nearby, lighting a cigarette.

"We can perform an experiment," Nolee said. "When I pick up my tickets from Sep tomorrow, you can write down the numbers from every ticket in your record book. Then we can compare those numbers later, after I've sold them, to the winning numbers announced on the radio to see if any of them were winners...and if so, if Cee changed the numbers somehow."

"Oh cousin, it's nonsense!" Maik groaned. "When they fix the computers your son's magic abilities will be ended."

Another motorbike pulled up in front of the house. Glaring, Maik looked past Nolee and prepared to scare this latest visitor away, but when he strode out of the evening and up into the bright kitchen the cousins recognized him. It was Hiok— Nolee's estranged husband. And he was grinning like a drunk, though the man didn't drink.

"Hallo!" Hiok cried. "Where is this marvelous son of mine? The whole town is chattering about him!"

"He's ready to sleep," Maik snarled. "You aren't to bother him."

"This isn't your affair," Hiok told her, his grin short-lived. "I've come to see my son and I shall see him...I'm his father and you can't stop me."

"So you're his father now?" Nolee said. She had begun trembling all over, within and without, the moment she had recognized him. "*Now* you claim him as your son? But how well I remember your words! 'He can't be my child! You must have fucked some sick man, bitch! You must have fucked someone who uses drugs! Nothing like that could come from my loins!'"

"I spoke from *pain*, woman!" Hiok cried, spreading his arms.

"Pain! Can't you understand that?"

"Oh, I understand pain, Hiok. I understand it only too well."

"I am his father and we both know it. Neither of us understands what affliction caused his condition, and has brought us both such frustration…but I must accept him as my son. In fact, I have decided today that I want him to come live with me. My job brings me more money than yours, and my future bride has her job at the soup stand. We can take the burden from you."

"Oh, what a saint you are!" Nolee laughed, though her trembling had doubled. She was shaking badly, and wild-eyed. "And such a sly saint, too! You turn your back on your son, you don't give me anything to help support him, and now suddenly you hear of his talent and you come here thinking I will just hand him over to you and your whore. I'm sorry: 'future bride.' Well you can forget it, Hiok. You are not taking my son from me."

"I have been considering my decision to take him for some time, to help *you*, and here you insult me!"

"You shameless, selfish liar!"

Hiok hissed through gritted teeth, pointing a finger at her face, "Don't make me bring this to court!"

"Go ahead and do so!"

"I am the man, here—you know they will favor me."

"I tell you, I won't let you have him even if the court orders it. I will run away with him…you'll never find us."

"Bitch!" Hiok cried, and he lunged toward her, cocking his arm across his chest to deliver a backhanded blow to her face.

"Hey!" Teng shouted. They all looked to him, startled: Hiok with his cocked arm, Nolee who had begun to flinch back, and Teng's own wife Maik. Teng held a dirty cleaver in his fist, which he had picked up from inside the sink. "That's enough. If you strike my wife's blood-cousin I will bury this blade in your sorry skull."

Now it was Hiok's turn to flinch. "How dare you threaten me!" he exclaimed. "If I should tell the police, they'll lock you in a hole!"

"You'll have a hard time talking to police," Teng said, raising the cleaver, "with your head hanging from a strip of skin."

Nolee smiled. She had never loved her cousin's husband before today.

"All right, all right!" Hiok cried, backing away. "I won't take him, all right? But you…you can't deny me the right to see him!"

"You can visit him anytime you like," Nolee said. "So long as my cousin's husband is here at the time."

Hiok muttered curses to himself, but then said, "Very well. And he's here now, right?" Sarcastically he waved an arm at Teng, who had lowered but not set down the cleaver. "So let me see my son."

"*If* he's awake," Maik said. "I'll go check."

It was determined Cee was awake still, lying on blankets on the floor and propped up on pillows and a giant stuffed tiger. Watching cartoons, of course. Nolee's husband left his sandals in the kitchen and stepped into the living room, with Nolee, Maik, and Teng trailing close behind.

"Hey, my dear boy!" Hiok said, squatting down beside his child and patting his lumpy head with its sparse, thin hair. "There you are! Can you look at me? Do you remember your dad?" When Cee didn't take his eyes from the screen, Hiok repositioned himself and leaned down directly into the child's view.

Standing a bit apart, Nolee saw Cee's far-spread eyes turn up to take in his father's face, but whether there was recognition there she couldn't tell.

"Dad's going to buy a ticket from your mama tonight. A ticket with numbers you're going to give me…isn't that right, Cee? And not just three numbers like the others: you're going to give me seven, right? Seven lucky numbers, Cee! Then I can win big, and I'll have enough money to give some to your mother." He glanced over at Nolee to be sure she'd heard him. Looking back to Cee, he continued, "I'll help you and your mother…but you must help me first. Give me the numbers, son!" And he brought his ear close to Cee's mouth.

Nolee heard her son's familiar deep gargling sounds. All three of them heard, and later they'd agree they had discerned no words in them. But Hiok jerked back from his son so abruptly, as if he'd received an electric shock, that he lost his balance on the balls of his feet and fell on his bony bottom. He scrambled to his feet and whirled around, showing the adults his long, shocked face. Then he fled toward the doorway breathlessly.

"Wait!" Teng said. He caught Hiok's arm and held him. "What did he say to you?"

Looking into Nolee's face, rather than Teng's, Hiok said in a horrified hush, "He told me I would die. He told me, 'You will die on the sixteenth day of the eighth month.' But he didn't tell me what year. *He didn't say what year!*"

With that, Hiok wrenched himself free of Teng's grip and bolted outside. They heard his motorbike start up, and then rumble away. Nolee and the others trailed after him belatedly into the kitchen, its open wall facing out onto the blackness of deepening night. Nolee looked from Maik to Teng, and then down at the sandals Hiok had forgot to put on again before he fled the house.

"He couldn't have said that," Maik said at last.

"So we said with the winning numbers," Teng mumbled thoughtfully, glancing back toward the living room as if he were afraid to reenter it himself.

Thinking of the future date Hiok had claimed Cee had given him, supposedly the date of his impending death, Nolee turned

her gaze to a calendar mounted on the kitchen wall, with individual daily sheets. Today was the 25th. The 25th day of the
seventh month.

If Hiok had heard correctly, and the prophecy was to come
true, did that mean he would die on the 16th next month? Or
the 16th of the eighth month a year from now? Ten years from
now?

No, Cee couldn't have said that. He could never formulate a
sentence like that. Hiok's mind, expecting wonders—and maybe filled with much suppressed guilt—had played a nasty trick
on him. And all those winning tickets...a computer error, yes,
Maik was the voice of reason. It had to be.

When Nolee returned to the living room, Cee had dozed off.
She muted the volume of the TV, covered him with a blanket,
and then stood staring down at him a long time. In the colorful
flutter of the TV's light, he didn't look human. He resembled
the beings from other worlds one saw in Western movies. But
without familiarity with the word "alien," to Nolee he was more
a misshapen angel. Tears in her eyes, she wagged her head and
murmured, "My ruby."

***

Early the next morning, people started appearing at Maik's
house again, seating themselves at Teng's cement picnic table
to smoke or standing around in the courtyard chatting while
they waited for the occupants to appear. They all looked up and
hushed themselves when Nolee drew back the kitchen's metal
shutter, then stepped out pushing Cee in his bunny cart, with
its huge painted eyes and molded grin.

Once Nolee had determined who had arrived first, she allowed these customers to seemingly genuflect before her son for

his blessing. She sold her remaining fifteen tickets very quickly. Some of those who had waited squabbled about who had come ahead of who, but no serious conflicts broke out.

While she was selling her next to last ticket to an elderly neighbor man, he said, "Very sad about that funeral worker Uhi, eh? The first one to discover your son's gift. His luck did not last him long, did it?"

As she took the old man's money, Nolee seemed to freeze into a statue, but managed to croak, "What do you mean?"

"So you didn't hear? He was killed last night in a motorbike accident, coming home from a café. Well, he'd been drinking too much, hadn't he? Maybe the gods frowned on him for misusing the gift they'd given him."

"Oh my." Nolee put a hand to her chest. A number appeared before her eyes, stark black against white. Was this how the numbers came to her son's inner vision? But instead of three numbers, what she saw were only two: *25.*

The 25th, on the calendar page she remembered staring at in the kitchen last night. The 25th day of this, the seventh month.

And then she *did* see three numbers, after all.

725.

The numbers Uhi had claimed Cee spoke to him. The numbers Uhi had discovered amongst Nolee's tickets. The numbers that had been part of the eighteen strings of seven numbers recited by the impassive, echoing, otherworldly voices on the radio.

"It *is* a curse," Nolee said to herself, as the old man walked away with the ticket he had purchased.

At that point only the final ticket remained, and a woman who worked at a downtown salon called *Superior Nails* wanted it. Nolee tried to tell her she had intended to keep the last ticket for herself, but the woman grew angry and snatched it out of

Nolee's hand. The nails technician said, "I suppose where it's the last one it's a little late to hear what your son has to say, but maybe it won't prove lucky if I don't listen." She stepped beside Cee's cart. "And this way I can see if he says the same numbers that appear on my ticket." Hiding the ticket in the front pocket of her rhinestone-embellished blue jeans, the young woman bent down to Cee and asked for her numbers.

Nolee watched, now understanding the expression with one's heart in one's throat.

The nails technician smiled, nodded, stood erect. "Yes!" she pronounced. "He told me three of the seven numbers that appear on my ticket—in the correct sequence! How do you do this, Mrs. Nolee? What's the trick?"

"There is no trick," Nolee said numbly. She felt like she was gazing at a woman who stood under a falling boulder, without warning her to dodge out of the way.

"Well, in any case, now all that remains is to see if the stories are true and I win anything." With that, the stylish young woman turned and strutted away, her high heels clacking on the old courtyard pavement.

Nolee faced her son. "What is it you're doing, my child? Tell me you don't understand any of it, the good or the bad. Tell me you are innocent, only a vessel for powers we can never understand."

But he told her nothing, only barked a single loud laugh as he watched a rooster in beautiful metallic colors chase a younger rooster away from the chickens that pecked in the courtyard.

***

Nolee arrived at the lottery office at three thirty...a full half hour late. Bolun Sep was standing outside, as if waiting for her specifically, smoking a cigarette. But when Nolee stopped her motorbike beside him, and swung herself off its saddle, instead of growling at her as usual he only nodded. It was as though they had agreed to meet when all the rest of his numerous ticket dealers were gone.

She gave him the money, and again no unsold tickets. And then she stared at him expectantly.

"Do you know," Sep told her, "that every single ticket you sold last time was a three-number winner?"

"So people have said. But I didn't print those tickets, Bolun."

"True enough. But I've been hearing that the winners all received a number from your son." Sep gestured past Nolee at Cee, seated in the bike's sidecar. "A prediction, or a blessing."

"He can't speak. They've all imagined it."

"And now these tickets you sold." He held up the thick wad of money. "Are these all winners, too?"

"I don't know," Nolee said. But in her gut she did. She knew they would contain, in part at least, winning numbers. The radio broadcast in only a half hour would simply confirm it.

"Nolee," Sep said uncomfortably, "I'm sorry, but whatever magic your son has—"

"Do you believe in such things?"

"Who is to say?" he snapped, defensive. "*You* must believe, if you allowed your customers to consult him! Whatever the case may be...I won't be giving you any more tickets to sell. I can't have workers who are influencing this process in an unnatural way. How can I explain that to the lottery department, if they should look into this strangeness?"

"I understand," Nolee said solemnly. And truly, she did. She had not wanted any more tickets to sell. If Sep hadn't just now cut her—as she had expected him to—she would have reassigned. But she was relieved that he hadn't mentioned Uhi's death. Relieved *that* was not the reason he was letting her go.

He paid Nolee her ten percent share of the sales. "I am sorry," he repeated, and he looked like he was sincere.

"Thank you for having allowed me to work for you," Nolee said, then returned to her bike and started it up.

She saw that Sep continued to stand there in front of the lottery office, clutching the wad of worn dirty bills as he watched her leave. Beside her, Cee lifted one of his stick-like arms and jerked it as if he might be waving goodbye.

***

They listened to the government radio broadcast. As always, Maik wrote down the mechanically recited numbers. And then they waited for the inevitable flood of people who would descend upon the house wanting to buy tickets. Nolee knew she would be sending away many disappointed people this evening.

While they anticipated the inevitable, Nolee, Maik, and Teng sat on the kitchen floor with the now silent radio in the middle of their circle, like a ouija board. In the living room, they heard the TV, and Maik's ten-year-old daughter Laiki speaking to Cee in a sing-song voice, encouraging him to eat the thick rice and pork soup she was feeding him with a spoon. Maik had told her two children they needed to start helping take care of their poor cousin.

Earlier that afternoon, before leaving for the lottery office to give Sep his money, Nolee had told Maik her beliefs about the death of the funeral man, Uhi. At first Maik had impatiently dismissed such a thought, but Nolee had kept on about it in an intense whisper, until Maik ultimately grew quiet and thoughtful. At last, Maik herself had said, "Poor Mr. Uhi. No wonder Cee wasn't able to give him any more numbers. A person only has one death day."

Now, as they sat on the kitchen floor, Nolee said quietly as if speaking to herself, "I haven't heard of any more deaths. I hope no one connects Uhi's death or any others that might occur with Cee and the numbers he gave them. If they make any such connection, mobs will come here to kill my son."

"None of us will ever speak of this matter outside these walls," Maik swore severely. "Right, husband?"

"Of course," he grumbled. "Do you think I'm stupid, woman?"

Nolee took Maik's hand and squeezed it, her eyes going wet. "Thank you, dear cousin. You are my greatest blessing."

"Your son is your greatest blessing," Maik said. "Hear me... Cee did not kill Uhi. He did not curse him. He only...he only *saw*. Saw Uhi's destiny."

"How do you know that?" Teng said.

"I know it in my heart."

"Since when do you believe in such things?"

"I believe what's in my heart," his wife stated. She reassured Nolee, "You will find other work. Until then, Teng and I will care for you and Cee. Don't be afraid of anything."

"Aren't you afraid for *us?*" Teng asked Maik. "And our children? Who knows if Cee is cursed or not? Who knows how dangerous he might be to our family?"

"Teng!" Maik cried.

"We can go," Nolee said, lowering her head. "We can go far from here...to some village where there are few people whom we might harm."

"No!" Maik said, shooting her husband an angry look. "We've been fine all this time. We will continue to be fine. You aren't going anywhere."

Teng rose to his feet and pulled out his pack of 777 cigarettes. "Whatever you crazy women want. I'm going outside for a smoke." Then, he jerked his head suddenly, his expression one of alarm.

"What?" Maik asked him.

But Nolee had heard it, too. Her son Cee's deep, gurgling voice in the next room.

Teng darted toward the living room. Jumping to their feet, Nolee and Maik rushed after him.

Ten-year-old Laiki was kneeling close to Cee, on his blankets spread upon the floor, the spoon of rice soup poised in her hand. Teng swept Laiki up in his arms and swung her away from Cee. The soup spilled from her spoon.

"What did he say to you?" Teng demanded of Laiki, spinning her around to face him. "Did he tell you numbers? Did he?"

Nolee stood behind Teng, her fingers pressed over her mouth. She looked at Cee with horror, and guilt, and crushing sorrow. She should kill him. And then kill herself. It would be the kindest thing for all of them.

But Laiki laughed with confusion and pushed herself out of her father's arms. "Dad," she said, "what do you mean? Cee can't talk. He was only making those sounds he makes."

Teng sighed, and dropped his face into his hands, wagging his head.

Maik put an arm around Nolee's shoulders and said, "It's all right, cousin. It's going to be all right now."

Teng stood up again, and wheeled back toward the kitchen. "I need that smoke!" he called back over his shoulder.

All through this, Cee had continued to watch the Western cartoon on the TV mounted on the wall. A cat chasing a mouse all around. He brayed laughter. He laughed and laughed.

***

People died in the town, as people die everywhere, on many different dates and in many different ways.

And two years after Nolee stopped selling lottery tickets, her husband Hiok—who had never come to visit his son Cee again—was hacked to death with a machete by his girlfriend's secret lover, when Hiok caught them in bed together and the confrontation escalated.

It was on the sixteenth day of the eighth month.

THE UNICORN FARM

The Nia-Fa Theme Park was by far the largest tourist attraction of its kind in the country, privately owned by a consortium of corporations but sanctioned by the government because of its touted cultural importance (not to mention the park's revenue, of which the government naturally partook). The park's loose theme was its country's religious foundation, focusing on both the harmonies of Heaven in the presence of the Ten Jeweled Gods, and the suffering of the damned under the Ten Demon Lords of Hell. At the front of the park was a gorgeous temple devoted to the former, resting amid resplendent gardens, but more popular of course were the multiple spooky ghost train attractions pertaining to the latter.

Also contained within the sprawling grounds—interconnected by innumerable trams, a miniature train, or rented bicycles if one liked—were a vast hotel with a series of karaoke rooms, a shopping mall and adjacent restaurant/banquet hall, an outdoors concert stage, a water park with man-made beach, a giant roller coaster, and a sizable zoo.

Nah was sixteen, just old enough now to work, though only on weekends since she hadn't yet finished school. She tended a juice stand called the Tiger Bar, near the long string of big cat enclosures. A green tent-like pavilion shaded the numerous outdoor tables. Today, however, all these tables stood empty, like the dense rows of unrented bicycles toward the front of the park. Bored, Nah did her homework atop her booth's counter, which she had first wiped down to remove its customary stickiness.

It was the off season. Not the customary time for family vacations, no holidays to draw tourists, and today no children on class trips, disgorged in uniformed waves from their buses. Occasionally one of the great cats let out a half-hearted grumbling roar, as if to test its ability to still do so. A lonely sound, but to Nah a measure of company.

She wore eyeglasses with narrow dark frames in a Western style, which she had pressured her mother to buy for her. She had a round, quiet, studious face, and she was very short and rather more curvy than most of her fellow students. Her mother, who had a stocky build, had proudly assured Nah that in their country, a meaty body was to be envied. It meant a woman was well-fed, no hungering peasant. Not that her mother was affluent; far from it. Nah was obliged to turn over her earnings to her struggling parents.

Despite her mother's reassurances, Nah envied her twenty-year-old cousin Ti, whose similarly challenged family shared the same house. Ti—whose lazy-lidded eyes and lazy movements came across as sensuous—was atypically tall for their people, thin as a reed, and that was the look Nah coveted. Ti was something of a neighborhood legend; every boy stumbled over his words when talking with her. Ti had recently won a job at an internet café, not so much because of her computer skills but because she drew in more boys to play their noisy first-person shooter games. The internet café was just at the corner of their street. Ti was so delicate she appeared frail, and so her father hadn't wanted her driving far on a motorbike to work at the

Nia-Fa Theme Park as Nah did. Apparently Nah's father held no such qualms. Either he deemed her to be more fit, or less precious, than Ti's father considered his daughter.

Things were so slow today that Nah manned her station alone. In busier times there were two of them behind the counter; one to tend the register and one to make the smoothies or iced coffees. It was so quiet, in fact, that Nah decided it was safe to abandon her post for a trip to the restroom.

She came out from behind her counter, and trudged down the paved path toward the nearest restrooms, which were recessed like the mouths of caves in a wall of painted plaster meant to pass for rock. This path took her away from the tigers, lions, and smaller tree cats into the direction of the unicorns.

Nah was about to enter the cavern designated for females when a commotion near the fence of the unicorn enclosure, which a sign called the Unicorn Farm, caught her attention and she paused to look that way.

Two Western tourists—both the man and the woman blond and, to Nah's eyes, almost frighteningly beautiful—appeared to be arguing with one of the uniformed zoo workers, gesticulating toward the unicorns on the other side of the high fence and their shallow, dirty moat. Nah studied one Western language at school but this appeared to be a different idiom, from another of the Western countries, so she could only speculate as to the cause for their agitation. The worker seemed just as confused, and looked quite stricken, as if the foreigners might be blaming him personally for whatever it was that had aroused their emotions. Nah was embarrassed for her countryman. But her admiration for the golden-haired couple made her sympathetic, also, to whatever it was that had stirred them to such extremes.

She followed, with her eyes, their jabbing gestures as they pointed toward the unicorns, which indifferently nibbled the bundles of leaves the worker had just hurled over the top of the fence for them.

Nah's people tended to shun open confrontation, loud and shameful displays of emotion (unless drunk or enraged by dramas over love or money). So instead of summoning guards or even the police to oust the tourists, the zoo worker finally just turned away and called to two of his coworkers. Together, the three zoo workers entered the unicorn farm through a padlocked gate and herded the dozen animals out of sight, into their barn at the back of the enclosure.

This only seemed to frustrate the tourists, and they cried out all the louder, unsatisfied. The white woman held her digital camera aloft, waggling it over her head like a weapon, suggesting to Nah's mind that the woman was threatening she had incriminating images captured within. Finally, though, with both the unicorns and the workers vanished, the blond couple turned away and reluctantly continued along.

The handsome young foreign man looked over at Nah and caught her eye. Nah looked down quickly, as if guilty, though she didn't know for what.

***

All day Nah had only sold one pineapple drink, one coconut drink, and two iced coffees—and one of the coffees was for the worker who had been confronted by the passionate tourists. The buoyant young man joked with Nah, though not in a flirtatious way. She didn't invite such giddy behaviors, as her cousin did. Nah was normally exceedingly reserved, but her curiosity had been aroused, and the man's open manner inspired her to ask him what had so upset the foreign couple earlier.

"Oh, I'm not sure exactly," the worker replied, "but I think

they were mad about the way we take bile from the unicorns."
He didn't say *unicorn*, of course—that was a Western word,
used for tourists, representing a conflation between a Western
mythical creature and a superficially similar mythical beast of
this country. What he had said was in fact *ni-liq*; this being the
actual animal named after that fabled beast. The worker went
on, "You know how Westerners are about animals…while they
stuff their fat bellies with hamburgers and chickens raised in
tiny cages." He laughed.

That had been the most Nah had interacted with another human being all day.

In regard to her poor sales, it didn't help that it had been
gray today, with spotty rain on and off from morning until now,
as Nah closed up the juice stand for the night. Well, her boss
Tendu would pay her the same either way.

She began the long walk to the area where zoo person-
nel parked their motorbikes. Sweeping trash from the
broad pathway, an old man she often exchanged greetings
with looked up at her, leaned on his push broom, and said,
"You shouldn't be walking alone in the dark, young girl."
Nah smiled at him. Did he harbor the archaic attitude that an
unmarried female should always be chaperoned? Where was she
to find her chaperone, then? "I'm all right—thanks," she said
softly.

"You never know if some guest to the park, with a sick mind,
has hidden on the grounds after hours. Or if a dangerous animal
might have escaped!"

"Thank you for your concern," Nah said, waving as she continued walking, her sandals slapping the pavement. "Good night!"

In one person's mind, she thought, the worst possible thing was
to be the object of someone's amorous attention. In another person's mind, the worst thing might be an absence of such attention.

She started past the fence to the so-called Unicorn Farm, and though she often passed right on by, tonight she paused there as if she might see the animals anew through the blue eyes of the beautiful foreign couple.

Seven of the dozen ni-liq had drifted out of their barn again, though three of those rested on the ground with their delicate legs folded under them, blinking their long-lashed eyes serenely, while four snuffled at the dirt for fragments of food they might have missed.

The ni-liq were a rare breed of antelope that lived in the mountainous central portion of the country, in deep valleys of coniferous trees. Their hide was reddish-brown, with black stripes along their sides, a black stripe down the nose, and white slashes upon the cheeks. In the middle of their head was a single thick horn: long and straight and black.

In the wild, ni-liq naturally possessed two long horns, but centuries ago men had perfected a way of transplanting the horn buds of a young ni-liq to the center of its head, touching each other, with the growing horns finally fusing together as one. This alteration was a tribute to their mythical namesake, a sacred creature that appeared in religious fables.

But the placard attached to the outside of the fence—which was tall to discourage thieves—would have tourists believe the unicorns were naturally one-horned. Tourists might believe it, not knowing better. Her countrymen pretended to believe it.

Nah wondered if that couple today had known better, though, and objected to the practice...in addition, as the young worker had suggested, to the siphoning of bile from their bodies.

Each of the ni-liq had a milky white plastic bottle hanging from its side like some pendulous tumor. The bottle's opening was attached to a catheter in the animal's body, allowing bile to drip from the gall bladder into the bottle. Each day the accumulated bile would be harvested. This process was openly described on the placard, without shame or apology, as was the purpose for collecting ni-liq bile. The highly prized bile was added to rice wine or various medicines, which when consumed were said to stimulate virility. For the same reason, when a ni-liq died its horn was smashed to powder to add to wine or other elixirs. And in general, it was simply considered lucky to consume what was nicknamed "unicorn blood."

Nah was startled when the old night cleaner with his broom stepped up beside her to gaze in at the placid beasts. "Saying a secret prayer to them?" he asked. "Hoping that the young man you love will marry you?"

Nah ignored his teasing; there was no such man. Instead she asked, "Do you think they feel pain?"

"Pain? All animals feel pain, my dear. Even this animal." He tapped his breastbone.

"From those things stuck in their sides, I mean."

The old man shrugged. "They know no other existence."

***

The next weekend was bright and dry, so Nah didn't have to wear her plastic poncho as she rode to Nia-Fa Theme Park. She got there an hour early. It was mostly just to get out of her crowded little house, have some time to herself before her long shift began.

This morning Ti, brittle creature that she was, had complained of suffering a back ache again. She and Nah shared a room together, sleeping on mattresses on the tiled floor. So Ti had stretched out on her front with her pajama top removed, while Nah kneeled beside her and rubbed hot, aromatic oil into Ti's long bony back. Ti's head lay pillowed on her folded stick-thin arms. She stared into space, maybe dreaming of her latest crush, and with her vacant blinking eyes reminded Nah of the resting ni-liq she had watched last weekend.

After rubbing the fiery oil onto her cousin's skin, Nah had then used the edge of a spoon to scrape the oil deeper into her flesh. Afterwards, as always, Ti was left with a symmetrical pattern of vivid red stripes down either side of her spine. It was a common practice, but Ti asked Nah to do this so often it was almost as if she welcomed it as a physical pleasure, as opposed to a remedy for pain. Nah half-recognized in herself a strange mix of feelings when she was working on her fragile cousin. It felt good to be scraping at her pretty skin—so uncommonly white for their people, and white skin was another symbol of affluence. It suggested this person didn't labor out in the sun. Nah's meatier flesh was brown. Nah would realize, as she applied the requested torture, that she had clenched her jaws together.

But at the same time, this intimacy between them—the baring of Ti's skin, the almost religious anointment of oil, and the rhythmic motions that elicited little moans from the older girl—made Nah feel something else, deep and restless and intense, that she was afraid to scrutinize closely. She found she *awaited* these pleasurable torture sessions...hoped for them.

Ah, but the homely realities of the human body, behind the pretty veneer. Did all the boys who hungered after flower-like Ti realize that her bare feet smelled like vinegar? Her plucked armpits emitted a sour tang? Her palms sweated so badly, that after she had been chatting with some boy on the family's computer she left little pools on the glass table upon which the glitchy old machine rested? These earthy material details did not disgust Nah, though, but rather endeared Ti to her. And they also consoled Nah...affirming that no human being was a radiant, perfumed god or goddess. Even the many statues of the Ten Jeweled

Gods throughout the Nia-Fa park, on close inspection, showed cracks and flaking in their brightly colored paint.

During their time alone behind their closed bedroom door this morning, Ti had said nothing about going to Nia-Fa herself that day, so when Nah was on her way to the zoo to start her shift—on foot and eating an ice cream she had bought from a stand that had just opened for business—and spotted Ti walking hand-in-hand with a young man with spiky hair, she stopped dead in her tracks and stared at them. Looking about, Ti finally noticed Nah, too, and flickered a big nervous grin. She pulled the boy over to her cousin.

"This is Ghip," she said, introducing the boy. "He comes into the café a lot."

"I thought you were working today," Nah said.

"I only told my father that."

"If he finds out you lied to go with a boy, he'll beat you."

"I'm twenty years old now! My school friends are already getting married…some already have babies!"

"Tell that to your father."

"Don't be jealous of my fun," Ti scolded, pouting.

"I don't care what you do!" Nah retorted, avoiding the boy's eyes as he listened to this embarrassing exchange. "I'm just trying to warn you."

"I'm not stupid, Nah."

"You didn't tell me you were coming."

"You didn't tell me you were going to work early. But I planned on bringing Ghip to see you in the zoo, to buy juice from you as a surprise." Ti smiled proudly, and wiped her sweaty palm on the outside of her long, blue-jeaned leg before taking Ghip's hand again.

"Then I guess I'd better go to my stand and start getting things ready."

"You can be late a few minutes…it's off season, right? Come on, why don't you go into the Tenth Hell with us? Ghip has never seen it before. He'll be so scared he'll need us both to hold his hands."

"Ha!" the boy said. "It's you who'll be scared, not me!"

The boy was handsome. Nah could see why Ti was smitten. Ti always went gaga over some cute boy…until the next one diverted her attention. Nah was surprised that Ti wanted her along now, instead of clinging to Ghip alone as they navigated the spooky darkness of the Tenth Hell. Was it love for her cousin, or was Ti simply not done showing off?

"If Tendu sees I'm late," Nah said, referring to the manager of the theme park's zoo, "he'll shout."

"Come on," Ti insisted. "We'll walk you to work right after."

"You don't have to worry, Ti, I won't tell your father."

"That's not why I'm asking! Let's go…it will be fun with the three of us!"

Nah didn't know how the boy felt about it, but finally murmured, "All right."

***

There were nine other Hell attractions—some of which you walked through, following a trail of phosphorescent footprints, while in others you rode in little rickety trains, or chains of boats pulled through water smelling of chlorine. The Tenth Hell was one you walked through…more open, more vulnerable. The outer structure was a gigantic, glossy black monster's head, with a single glowing red eye in its center, representing the Tenth Demon Lord of Hell. As the three of them purchased their tickets, from the demon's tusked jaws emanated a looping, crackling recording of sinister music and the howls of the damned:

those who had sinned in the mortal world. Those who gambled too much. Those who drank too much. Those who ate meat without first thanking the soul of the slain animal. Those who practiced infidelity. Those who were ungrateful to their religious leaders...to their country. In other words, Nah thought, the Ten Realms of Heaven must be entirely empty.

They mounted the steps and passed between the demon lord's jaws. Nah had no intention of reaching for Ghip's hand, but he took hold of hers and squeezed it tight, as if to prevent her from being dislodged by whatever supernatural forces might buffet them. Nah saw Ti wipe her hand on her leg again before taking Ghip's other hand. Then they slipped through black curtains and were enfolded in utter darkness.

At this early hour they were the only living souls braving the black maze. Its other occupants, springing from recesses in the walls or gliding down on wires from the ceiling, were mani-kins painted in fluorescent colors, with ghastly papier-mâché faces, though several of them wore rubber masks that Nah knew depicted characters from Western horror movies. The damned were shown suffering their appropriate tortures. One wretch sprang up screeching from a pit seething with dry ice, his head and torso covered all over with plastic spiders, scorpions, and centipedes. Another, chained atop an altar, was being eternally decapitated by two crudely animatronic demons working a giant saw. Meanwhile, jets of air or bursts of screaming erupted from out of nowhere...and the black-gloved hands of hidden workers (even as she flinched and shrieked, Nah wondered if they made the same money she did) groped at their passing ankles.

Ghip never once let go of Nah's hand. If anything, he held it tighter—to reassure her, or himself? Once, when an unseen hand stroked the back of Nah's head, she crushed her body up against Ghip's side, her breasts pressed to his arm. She heard him

laugh, and he leaned close to her ear to shout, "Don't worry...
I'll protect you."

In the darkness, it was easy to imagine that it was just the two
of them...that Ti wasn't holding his hand on the other side of
him.

Shyly, though, Nah put a little distance between them again.
Anyway, she reproached herself, she had been through this attraction a number of times before...why was she feeling so unsettled?

The final scene before they emerged into harsh sunlight again,
like souls purged and reborn, was the most ambitious. Here was
the Tenth Demon Lord of Hell, the obsidian-skinned hermaph-
rodite whom all the other nine demon lords had impregnated
together, so that he/she could give birth to an Eleventh Demon
Lord of Hell, thus upsetting the balance between Hell and the
Ten Realms of Heaven. The looming animatronic monster—its
single red eye a hypnotic spinning spiral, steam hissing out of its
snapping jaws, and a rubber human skeleton clutched in each
fist—presented an immense swollen belly, pregnant with the
imminent Eleventh Demon Lord.

But just then, as the three of them stood at the railing in front
of this frightful display, from out of the darkness came the Holy
Monkey—Cholukan—sitting astride a beautiful striped ni-liq
with a long golden horn. The mechanically propelled unicorn
charged the demon lord, and thrust its horn straight into the
hole of his/her navel.

More steam and horrible roars blasted from the demon lord's
mouth. The golden-furred monkey manikin let out cackling
laughter. The demon lord him/herself, of course, was not killed
by this attack, but the pregnancy was aborted. A great flood of
red-dyed water gushed from between the monster's legs into a
waiting pool.

Then a door slid open to their right, with daylight hinted beyond, and the three of them turned toward it, hands still linked, as the bellows of thwarted rage and the laughter of Heaven's triumph faded away. Illusions left behind them…back to the material plane.

***

Nah was surprised when she returned from work, that evening, to find the house in agitation. At first she feared Ti's excursion with Ghip had been discovered, but as her mother shooed Nah outside again she explained that they were all going out to karaoke tonight, as the guests of a man named Goh. Goh's father was one of the directors of the Oki-Me Electronics Plant, where Ti's father Zuy worked shipping boxes of circuit boards to Western countries.

They stood in the dirt courtyard in front of their house—Nah and her parents, and Ti and her younger brother and their parents—and in only minutes a candy-yellow car zipped around the corner, scattering neighborhood hens, and came to a stop in front of them. Somehow they all managed to pile in.

Grinning into the rearview mirror, the expensively-attired Goh exclaimed heartily, "Great to meet you all—Zuy has told me a lot about you. Especially *you*," he said, and Nah could tell he was looking at Ti now, in the mirror, crushed in the center of the back seat by the adults as if she were being prevented from fleeing.

They rode through teeming streets at jarring speed, Goh constantly heeling his car's horn to warn motorbikes, bicycles, and pedestrians out of his way. Meanwhile he played a tiny TV fixed to his dashboard, as if to impress his guests with its noisy chatter. Currently it was showing a program called *The World Slasher Cup*. It was a cockfight competition. Nah looked away, out the window, when two roosters with spurs on their ankles went at it in a mad flurry of wings.

The karaoke place was a tall, thin tower of concrete. Their party climbed up narrow staircases to the third level, where the host ushered them into their private room. The walls were covered with silhouetted figures of singers with microphones, guitar players, dancers, like the shadows of invisible ghosts. Goh ordered beers and plates of fruit, crunchy snacks, and dried squid.

Zuy navigated his daughter between himself and Goh on one of the room's long sofas, the two men starting on the beer and talking around the girl, who sat uncomfortably with her hands pressed between her knees. Nah was sure her palms were soaking. Goh took up one of the microphones while the young host readied the room's TV and karaoke machine. Goh offered the mike to Ti, but she declined, even after he pressed her. "Okay, I'll start, then!" he announced, and launched into boisterous song, leaning forward on the edge of the vinyl sofa.

Beer after beer, song after song; Goh dominated the proceedings, like a strutting rooster himself. Zuy didn't sing, but his wife did, and Nah's mother also. Ti's brother sang one song in his teenager's breaking voice. Nah declined when Goh offered her his mike, but he didn't press her. He simply leapt into another song, this one a Western number to demonstrate his dubious language skills.

At one point Ti and Nah escaped together to the restroom out in the hallway. Immediately Ti hissed, "Ten beers already. And he's going to drive us home?"

"He's trying to show off."

"He's ugly," Ti said. "And loud."

"He's not too old. And he has money."

"If he has so much money he should pay a surgeon to fix his monkey face."

Nah giggled, and the two cousins returned to the booming private room.

***

"A man in my position," said Nah's boss Tendu, while she made a smoothie for him in her blender, "has got to have a perceptive eye. It's easy to overlook a quiet girl like you...to mistake you as dim-witted or dull, to underestimate you. Another might tell you that you do yourself a disservice by keeping to the shadows. But I see just the opposite. I see a serious, hard-working girl of intelligence. Very unlike most of the silly young girls working here, who flirt with every foreign tourist no matter how old, hoping he'll whisk them away to the golden land."

Nah said nothing, listening to his words but concentrating on making the best smoothie she had ever concocted, fearing this was some kind of test masked as a casual visit. Had he noted that she'd arrived at her station thirty minutes late yesterday, when Ti had visited? She waited for a trap to be sprung, fanged jaws to snap shut.

Tendu had come around to enter the shadows of the booth with her, and he noticed her book lying on the counter. He pulled it to him, and began paging through its thin, cheaply photocopied pages. "Ah, you see? A studious girl. What is this, my dear?"

"Biology," Nah told him.

"Ah-ha," Tendu said, pausing at some of the pictures. "My children like animals, too." He set the book down and turned to watch her pour the blender's contents into a tall plastic cup.

Nah covered the cup, pushed a straw through the slit in its cover, handed the zoo's manager the drink and watched him suck upon the straw. Their eyes were linked as he did so. Finally

Tendu smacked his lips and said, like a character in a Western movie who had sampled a rare wine, "Perfection!" He placed the cup on the counter. "As I say, I've had my eye on you, my dear, and I believe you're ready for a new position."

Nah maintained her silence, reserving her gratitude until he explained.

Tendu continued, "Your maturity is evident to my appreciative eye. You are a girl on the cusp of womanhood. On the cusp of better things. It's a confusing time in one's life, I know, a time when many forces and many potential decisions pull at you, but I for one want to facilitate your evolution! You do understand evolution, don't you, being a student of biology?" He winked at her—maybe another movie mannerism. "We will be opening another concession stand soon, over there." He pointed across the way. Past the Unicorn Farm. "But this one will be more upscale, selling much more expensive wares. In the past, we have sold our unicorn blood only to dealers outside Nia-Fa Theme Park…but now, we'll be selling unicorn blood products ourselves, directly to our visitors. Bottles of unicorn blood wine, but we will also be serving it by the cup. And I want you, my dear, to man this new refreshment bar on the weekend shift."

Tendu moved closer to Nah, and reached behind her to run a hand down the back of her head. Nah shuddered. It felt exactly like the caress of the ghostly hand yesterday morning in the Tenth Hell.

Tendu said, "Because I am giving you a position of greater importance, I am offering you a higher wage as well." He told her what it was. Twice what she was making now. Her parents, she knew, would be ecstatic. After all, except for her meager allowance, the money would all go into their pockets. She didn't question it. It was an inevitability.

Tendu's stroking hand had continued down her long black

hair, and come to a stop on her back, resting heavily between her shoulder blades like some parasitic animal.

"What do you think?" he purred. He was so close she could smell the smoothie on his breath. The park all around them seemed utterly abandoned. Somewhere, a big cat roared out in loneliness.

"Thank you, sir," Nah said in a shaky whisper.

"Perfect," Tendu said, in his own shuddery whisper. With apparent reluctance, he stepped back from her, his hand trailing away from her back slowly, his fingertips brushing her ribs as they withdrew. As he retreated, though, his elbow struck his cup on the counter. It tipped over, the cover came dislodged, and a thick white pool spread across the surface, soaking the delicate open pages of her book.

***

Sometimes after it closed to regular guests the park would host special after-hours events: an informal business celebration, a birthday or graduation or bachelor party, perhaps even a late wedding or funeral feast. These events might take place at any one of the park's varied sites, though usually in its banquet hall, of course. Tonight's special event, however, was situated at the tables of the Tiger Bar. Nah wasn't sure of the reason, though the smartly-dressed men—and they were all men, discounting the young prostitutes on their arms—gathered outside the cages of the big cats and rowdily toasted the animals with their beers and glasses of Western liquor. Maybe it was for luck, or the men hoped to commune with the animals' potency. If a caged, bored, and dispirited tiger or leopard could be considered to have any potency.

Tendu himself was present to oversee the event, and tend to

these important guests whomever they might be. He directed Nah to bring trays of glasses from her new refreshment stand by the Unicorn Farm. Here, arrayed for sale were bottles filled with cloudy yellowish or amber solutions, most of which were variations of rice wine with ni-liq bile—unicorn blood—as an added but vital component. Some of these bottles boasted cobras, or giant black scorpions, stuffed inside and preserved by the alcohol like biological specimens. In addition, there were bottles of powdered unicorn horn, and even a number of entire horns for sale. These long black spikes were particularly expensive, and rested on shelves inside a glass showcase below the counter.

Sometimes Tendu instructed Nah to bring the party full bottles, and she poured out portions in the lifted glasses of the rowdy men. One of these men fumbled at her bottom as she started away, apparently in an attempt to squeeze a buttock, but she slipped from his grasp and didn't look back as she returned to her refreshment stand. She heard men whooping and laughing behind her, and her face radiated heat.

Tendu came to praise her, and ostensibly to assist her, as she switched dirty glasses for new ones at her work station. She could tell by his slurred voice and his breath that he had been joining in the interminable toasts with his guests. His breath stank of the cobra wine, which smelled like rice wine if it had fermented inside a reptile terrarium. She knew that the snakes were still alive when they were crammed into the bottles.

Leaning in close, Tendu said warmly, like a father, "I was not wrong in my appraisal of you, my dear. Such hard work. So uncomplaining. Such poise." He put a hand on the exact center of her back, as he had that other time. Strangely, it made Nah think of things Ti's brother had told her once about pressure points martial artists learned. His hand's weight seemed to inhibit the action of her lungs. In an intimately frank tone, he said, "You are not the most beautiful of girls, but it's your innocence and humility that give you charms beyond the all-too-common beauty of these little whores." He gestured with his head back in the direction of the distantly rambunctious men and the companions they rented to outdo each other.

"Thank you, sir," Nah said in a voice so low she wasn't sure she had even spoken, as she went about her work without looking at him.

"Mm," he grunted as he lost or discarded his affected eloquence. Tendu's hand slid down to the small of her back, and putting pressure there he subtly but heavily drew her nearer to him. As if unbalanced by the drink that sloshed in its skull, his head suddenly dipped low and his lips sought hers. But Nah, her nerves crackling and alert with fear and revulsion, pulled away in time to avoid them.

"Huh," Tendu chuckled. His wobbly head weaved back again like a snake that had missed its strike. She could tell he was both embarrassed and direly irritated. She felt his eyes on her back, like his hand, as she turned away to pour more wine into glasses. Then he said, "Hey…turn around here a moment."

She hesitated only a second, then did as commanded and faced him, though she kept her eyes averted. Once her mother had advised her that when a woman rode on a crowded bus and a man groped her bottom or breast, it was best—simply easier—to ignore it lest there was a scene, an ugly confrontation. It was just the way of men.

"Put out your hand," Tendu commanded softly.

Nah obeyed, extended her left hand. She was right-handed. For what little it was worth, a half-gesture of resistance.

Tendu made a fist but extended his index finger. This rigid finger he placed in Nah's palm. "Close your hand," he instructed in a whisper. She did so. Then, slowly, Tendu pushed his finger deeper into her fist, withdrew it almost all the way except for the tip, pushed it in again, back and forth, and he said in a quiver, "This is nothing so grave, huh? Easy enough. What's the difference, really? Innocent...easy...hm? I can do so much for you." He darted in to kiss her again. Their noses bumped. "I can do so much *to* you..."

But again Nah withdrew, extricating herself from his hold without actually shoving him away, though she wanted to.

Tendu wouldn't meet her eyes after that, as he turned to rejoin his guests without volunteering to carry a tray for her. "Ungrateful little bitch," he muttered, loudly enough for her to hear as he stumbled away. "Fat and ugly. Who else will take pity on you as I do?"

Tears started down Nah's cheeks. She was glad Tendu couldn't see them, to draw vengeful satisfaction. As she bent over her fresh tray to lift it, one drop fell from her jaw into one of the many tiny glasses. One of the men would drink her tear with the rest of his potion. She wondered what her pain might impart to him.

***

"Mom," Nah whispered to her mother that night, when they were alone in the kitchen preparing dinner together, "I want to quit my job."

"What?" her mother exclaimed, turning to her. "Are you losing your mind? After the raise in pay your boss gave you?"

"I promise you, I'll find another job. I'll even work after school every day."

"Don't be foolish...you're making good money there, they like you! They'll probably give you even more, later!"

A surge of muffled noise upstairs caused them both to look

toward the high ceiling. A man's raised voice. Zuy. And was that shrill weeping? The commotion was coming from the bedroom Nah shared with Ti.

"What is it?" Nah's father said then, coming into the kitchen after having heard his wife's excited tone.

Nah's mother faced her husband and repeated what Nah had said, though Nah had purposely kept her voice low to prevent him from joining in this discussion.

Her father scowled at her and said, "Don't be crazy…we need that money, and now more than ever, to help with wedding preparations. Of course Goh's family will pay most of it, but there are always things the bride's family are responsible for, and—"

"What wedding?" Since these were her parents, talking about helping fund a wedding, Nah experienced a delirious moment in which she imagined that after meeting her in the karaoke place that night, Goh had (drunkenly) asked Nah's parents to let him marry her.

"Ti's, of course," Nah's father said. "Don't you hear them discussing it up there?"

***

Nah cringed inside when she saw Tendu approaching her refreshment stand, but her face remained impassive. He was wearing dark glasses, which he wasn't wont to do, and this made him appear more ominous to her. But when he stood across from her with the counter between them, he smiled. Had he forgotten his drunken actions, and comments? Was everything back to normal between them?

"How are things going?" he asked cheerily.

"Slowly," Nah said.

"Of course...of course. It will continue this way for a time." Somewhere nearby a peacock cried out twice. "But I think I've found some extra work for you to do, a special project, to help keep you busy. And it will pay more money...a large bonus, in fact."

Nah was silent, watching him, waiting, glad he hadn't come around behind the counter, close to her, like before.

He was not content with her silence, though, and prompted her, "Are you interested?"

She shrugged.

Tendu was forced to go on. "If things prove successful, it might be an ongoing thing. Once every month, for the same client. But maybe others will want to acquire the same services later. All the better for us both. Right now, I'm talking about one of the gentlemen who attended our gathering the other night. Like me, he has a keenly appreciative eye for innocence. He approached me about you."

"What does he want?" Nah asked, hating to utter these words, as if even having to ask were a defilement.

"He wants to slow his aging. He wants to regain some virility. He wants a special elixir that we don't carry in a conventional container." Tendu swept his hand to indicate the rows of bottles beside the serving counter, filled with their cobras and scorpions and poisonous sea anemones. "The container is...you." Again, that bright smile under his dark lenses.

"What?" Nah said, numbly.

Tendu leaned closer and lowered his voice as if to spare her embarrassment, though no other person was even within sight of them. "When do you bleed again?"

"What?" Nah repeated. She heard a distant lapping surf inside her head, but peripherally caught sight of that old man who swept the walkways, and realized the sound was the slow

approach of his broom, shooing the dusty grit that always returned.

"When is your next period?"

"I…"

Tendu's grin was gone. Just those black lenses remained, her
face reflected in them doubly. "*When?*"

"Maybe," Nah answered, trembling, "maybe next week."

Tendu straightened up. "Perfect. Your innocent blood is what
this old man craves. Your body will discard it. You have no use
for it. But you can make a nice lump of money from that dead
blood. You would be foolish to say no."

Nah's face was burning. She wanted to shout a curse at him,
but she had never shouted a curse at anyone in her life. She
wanted to sweep her arm across the ranks of bottles and dash
them all to the pavement to shatter, their fanged snakes and
barbed bugs lying in pools for ants to nibble on. Expensive po-
tions for ants to lap up. But instead she asked in a tone that
sounded to herself like whimpering, "How would I…collect it
for him?"

"He would want to drink it from you directly," Tendu said
simply. "You would lie upon a table, and he would sit at the end
of the table. Like a doctor, examining you. And you could close
your eyes…maybe take a little nap…and he would quench his
thirst." The grin had returned, bigger, brighter, like a scimitar.
"Don't worry, I wouldn't be there. No one else would watch…
or ever know. Over in a flash, and you would have—and here it
is—a month's salary for only a few minutes of work. Not even
work."

Nah realized she had been wagging her head. "It's horrible,"
she said hoarsely. Her eyes were filling up.

"I understand it makes you shy discussing this. If you weren't
as innocent as you are, our client would never have requested

you. But think of your family…I know you help support them. Think of what you could bring home to them. Isn't that worth compromising your chasteness for a few moments, once a month?"

"Please," Nah sobbed, tears flowing openly now.

"Please what?" Tendu snarled. "Please don't give you a fat bonus? Please relieve you of your work and send you home to your parents today? Please, *that?*"

A strange thought came to Nah in the midst of her helpless sobbing, the sobbing that shook not only her body but her very soul, shook her soul on the frayed string that dangled it over a bottomless black well called Destiny. That thought was: this rich old man is the one who got my tear that night.

And he liked its taste.

***

On her thin mattress that night, with Ti having cried herself to sleep beside her after confiding that it was Ghip she loved, Nah dreamed of the unicorns.

She was in the theme park after closing hours…maybe after midnight…and there was no one, not even a security guard. Though distantly she heard—along with the faraway cry of a peacock—the shuffling rustle of a broom working ceaselessly and futilely to keep the labyrinthine pathways clean.

She walked past the mountainous bulk of the Tenth Demon Lord of Hell, a silhouette against the night sky, blotting out whole constellations. She was afraid to look in that direction but couldn't help herself, and saw a figure standing just inside the tusked jaws beckoning to her with slow scoops of his arm. She couldn't see his face in the darkness but somehow she knew it was Ghip. Ghip wanted her to go with him into the depths of the demon's guts, to hold her hand so they could search for Ti together, as when Cholukan searched the netherworld for his kidnapped love. But Nah couldn't go there with him, couldn't help him retrieve Ti, so she quickened her pace. She had another destination and purpose.

She arrived at the zoo, again with no security guards to be found at its entrance arch. She walked its paths feeling unnerved, imagining that the gate to every cage and enclosure had not only been left unlocked and open, but that every restraining barrier had dissolved entirely; that the animals all roamed freely in the darkness just beyond the irregularly-lighted pathways.

Yet she came to the pen of the twelve ni-liq unharmed, to find the delicate antelopes all outside their little barn structure, though resting on the ground with their legs folded beneath them. Hearing her approach, their single-horned heads all raised in unison alertly, their black eyes wary, nostrils snorting.

Somehow Nah had a single stolen key in the pocket of her pants, and she moved around to the side of the enclosure and unlocked the gate's large padlock. The gate squealed as she hauled it open. She left it standing wide open behind her as she stepped inside the Unicorn Farm.

The animals all rose to their hoofed feet, still wary but also hopeful for feeding. They watched Nah lower and cross the little wooden bridge over their dirty moat. They shifted back from her a little, but she put her hand out slowly, gently, and stroked one animal along its graceful neck with its coarse, bristle-like coat.

"Stop! Wait!" a voice boomed. It was a voice over a loudspeaker, crackling and distorted, like the recording that during open hours emanated from the mouth of the Tenth Demon Lord of Hell ghost train ride. Dazzling spotlights blasted into the Unicorn Farm from every direction.

The animals panicked, but somehow they knew enough to flee toward the wooden bridge...and the open gate in their high chain-link fence.

Nah panicked, too. Before it could bolt along with its fellows, she flung her arms around the neck of the ni-liq she had caressed and, slinging one leg over its side, vaulted up onto its back.

She clung to the antelope's neck and leaned her body low like a jockey, as it sprang after its fellows, the last of the twelve to clomp loudly over the wooden drawbridge and spring through the open gate onto a paved pathway.

"Stop! Halt!" that demonic, mechanical voice commanded as the animals scattered every which way, with springy loping/hopping bounds, the plastic bottles fixed to their sides bobbing and slapping. One bottle became dislodged and dropped behind, rolling, spilling its prized contents.

Now, at last, several men appeared...running out of the shadows, yet they were too indistinct for Nah to make out as security guards or zoo workers. But she could tell they carried rifles in their hands, apparently old army carbines, and their muzzle flashes burned her retinas briefly, their thunder cracking the inside of her skull. She saw one antelope that had been keeping pace alongside her own go down in a roll and a terrible splay of long fragile legs. More thunder claps. A horrible squeal from the throat of one unseen animal as it went down, also.

But her own mount galloped on, and on, darting down one off-branching pathway, then abruptly switching to another, leaving the lightning flashes and echoing booms far behind.

She knew her animal was the only one that had survived.

Nah didn't know where they were headed...didn't know if they would truly escape the theme park entirely...but at least they were running. Fleeing. Leaving their prison behind forever, or for only a few more precious moments.

***

Nah told her parents the first bonus was for helping harvest the bile from the ni-liq, though this was a lie, of course. Only several of the older, seasoned zoo workers handled that operation. But one day she did watch them perform the collection of unicorn blood, and seeing her observe from outside the chain-link fence, one of the men smirked and gave her a lewd wink. The wink told her this man knew the source of her bonus. She was certain he was not the only one.

Her parents had been delighted. And Tendu had been delighted. Knowing now to keep some distance from her, and refrain from touching her lest he spook her, Tendu nonetheless said, "Maybe one day I'll have a drink from the fountain of youth, myself."

Nah was tempted to reveal the truth to her cousin Ti, seeing as how Ti had been very open in expressing her misery at being betrothed to the wealthy Goh instead of her handsome young Ghip, but Nah couldn't bring herself to do so. She only continued to listen to Ti's sobs.

"I want to throw myself to my death," Ti wept, lying on her front as Nah rubbed hot oil into the flesh of her back. But this time Nah felt no strange, restless urges. All hunger had been burnt out of her. The thought of desiring another human being's flesh sickened her. Ti went on lamenting, mournful but also enraged, "I want to throw myself off the roof of that karaoke place he took us to that first night!"

"Don't say that," Nah said at last. "Yes, you don't love him, but he can take care of you. He'll be a husband. You will be respectable. Maybe you're lucky."

"Lucky?" Ti cried, propping herself up on one elbow to twist her head around. "Lucky to be sold like a piece of meat, so my parents can benefit? You think that's lucky? I call it Hell!"

"I know," Nah murmured, soothing her cousin with more gentle motions of her hands. "I'm sorry. I only mean…perhaps there are greater Hells."

***

His name was San-koy. She didn't know if he were in his fifties, or sixties, or even older; she couldn't judge the age of old people. She thought maybe she remembered him from the event, that night, but the men had all looked the same to her, give or take a decade or two: grinning, drunken, burying their faces in the necks of young whores with bright fake smiles.

Whores like me, Nah thought.

The first time he couldn't become aroused, though he had tried milking himself while he fed. Afterwards he had muttered with disappointment—Nah had feared, disappointment with her—but after wiping his chin with a handkerchief he had politely thanked her, as if concluding a business meeting in a boardroom instead of a transaction in one of the rooms of the theme park's immense (but at this time, barely occupied) hotel.

Tonight, upon entering the room where Nah had already been waiting for him, sitting in a chair instead of on the bed, San-koy again paid her in advance as if to allay her obvious discomfort. He had come in carrying a long, silk-wrapped parcel under his arm. He set this parcel down on the edge of the entertainment center where a large flat-screen TV rested, and unfolded the satiny wrapping that had bound it to reveal a full ni-liq horn, slender and black. San-koy smiled at her and said, "A purchase I made at your very own concession stand, just now. Your friend Tendu aided me in your absence."

He turned from her to switch on the TV, and flicked through various channels. "Why are you sitting here in boredom, my child?" At last he came to a rerun of the soap opera *B-2*. "Ah… here's a good one. Watch this…take your mind away." In a grand-fatherly sympathetic tone, removing his jacket and folding it over a chair, and next working at the knot of his tie, he cooed, "I know…I know. You will be on your way home soon, sweet thing." Maybe he had seen the moisture brimming in her eyes.

Did you drink my tear? Nah wanted to ask him. Did it make you hunger for the taste of my blood? The taste of my soul?

Down to only his underpants now, his body cadaverous, he said, "Please disrobe, my dear." As if he were embarrassed to go further, strip fully, unless she did so first.

As she had last month, Nah left her glasses on. She would feel too vulnerable without them. She had to hold onto something… some partial mask or last vestige of a barrier between them.

Surveying her as she lay back atop the bed's quilt, San-koy grunted to himself, as if admiring this living chalice, or acknowl-edging a grim challenge to his manhood. He turned, reached out and ran a hand along the length of the fused ni-liq antlers. Self-consciously, he told her, "For luck."

Nah lay solid and splayed as if dead upon a coroner's metal table. She turned her face away, toward the TV, grateful now he had put it on. She avoided seeing San-koy at the foot of the bed, depressing the mattress now, ignored the wetness of her own dribbling tears as they fled her eyes.

On the TV, a character named Moop had followed her hus-band Din out of their apartment, up to the roof of the building, and discovered Din kissing *B-2*'s primary protagonist, Laiki. Moop shrieked like a madwoman and ran to the edge of the roof to throw herself off, but Din and Laiki rushed over and grabbed her, and pulled her back to safety. Nah was reminded

of Ti—like Moop, the bride in an arranged marriage—and her
threat to throw herself off the roof of the karaoke establishment.

Right now, Nah wanted to throw herself off the edge of the
world. She felt herself teetering there, her bare toes projecting
over the edge, and a strong wind lapped at her body in rhythmic waves. But it wasn't the wind prodding her body, and her
feet projected over the edge of a bed. She didn't want to look,
knowing the view would dizzy her, nauseate her with vertigo,
but when San-koy lifted his face she couldn't stop herself from
turning her head to look at him.

His lower face was smeared red, like a lion that had been feasting on the opened belly of a gazelle. His eyes were glassy with
desperate ravenousness. He started scrabbling further up the
bed...climbing atop her. She saw that this time, either actually
or psychosomatically charged by the ni-liq horn, he was fully
engorged. And that he meant to enter her.

Nah started to roll to one side, before he could pin her down.
This hadn't been part of the agreement. Tendu had told her San-
koy only wanted her red life fluid.

"Hold still...hold still," San-koy rasped, in a voice meant to be
calming but which quavered with loss of control.

"*No!*" Nah cried. She pushed a hand away from her chest and
kicked at his legs. He closed a fist in her hair to stop her from
slipping away. As a result, they both toppled off the bed and
thumped to the floor in a tangle.

"Ow!" San-koy had banged an elbow sharply against the edge
of a bedside table. He released Nah and they both scrambled to
their feet. Nah made a dive for her clothing, folded in a chair
beside the TV's entertainment center. She was sobbing with jolt-
ing shocks to her whole frame.

"Where do you think you're going?" San-koy blurted, reaching out to grab onto her hair again. He jerked her back toward

him. "I already paid you, you dirty little thief!"

Nah slapped at his arms, but he only tugged her head lower to throw her off balance. His horn bobbed close to her face. She reached to either side of it and raked her nails down his abdomen.

"Aaaiiieee!" the old man wailed, and he released her long hair but struck her in the ear with his fist. The blow made Nah stumble backwards and strike her bottom against the edge of the entertainment center. Remotely, she heard the familiar, mournful theme music of the drama *B-2* as it cut to a commercial break.

"Ugly little cunt!" San-koy raged, eyes blazing in a face still half-masked with her blood. He lunged toward her, cocking back his arm to punch her again.

Nah found her left hand rested on a long, hard pole. She closed her fingers around it, jerked it out in front of her and gripped it in both fists. She thrust it forward and San-koy plunged straight into it, rather than it into him.

The ni-liq horn entered his mouth, splitting his lower lip in half on the way in. Its point broke through the roof of his mouth. The weight of his forward momentum drove the shaft up further, behind his eyes into his brain.

Nah let go of the horn and clamped both hands over her mouth to seal off a scream. She quick-stepped backwards, to avoid the fallen San-koy's thrashing limbs, and the blood spluttering out onto the carpet.

She watched as his writhing became less frantic...more like the unconscious restlessness of a person suffering a nightmare. The gurgling/bubbling at the back of his throat, as he swallowed his own blood, slowed and lessened. At last, as she continued staring in a state of unreality, the old man went still and silent.

***

Nah regretted three things as she rode away from the hotel on her motorbike. Rode through the tall front arch of the Nia-Fa Theme Park.

She regretted that she might never see Ti again…and hoped without her moral support, her cousin didn't literally throw away her young life.

She regretted that she had left the hotel room with only the money San-koy had already given her, without thinking to empty his wallet as well.

And she regretted that she hadn't phoned her boss Tendu to summon him to the hotel room, telling him there had been a terrible accident, and stabbing him with the ni-liq horn, too, as he stepped through the door.

Why not steal more? Why not kill more? The damned could only descend so far. There were only ten levels to Hell.

Nah didn't know where she was headed…didn't know if she could truly escape retribution, and damnation…but at least she was running. Fleeing. Leaving her prison behind forever, or for only a few more precious moments.

ULTIMATE NAILS

When the salon on the other side of the traffic rotary changed its name from *Resplendent Nails* to *Superior Nails*, Juyen changed the name of her salon from *Glorious Nails* to *Ultimate Nails*.

"Let that tapir-assed bitch with her plastic nose and silicone tits and diseased hole top *that*," Juyen spat.

Her husband Zam laughed and wagged his head. He had heard of men's penises likened to a tapir snout, as an insult, but now he found himself trying to visualize a tapir's rear end. "I actually think the name of our salon—both salons, really—sounded more important before."

His wife swiveled slowly to train her eyes on him like black death rays. "Her title before was a boast about her salon. Now, it's a statement against *my* salon. Are you too much of a grinning idiot to realize that?"

"And so now we have to pay for a new shop sign, and everything else that might bear our name?"

Juyen took a step closer to him and hissed, with a mixture of menacing and seductive fierceness, "Yes, we will—if you ever hope to visit *my* hole again."

Juyen, with her huge smoldering eyes, and modernly styled short hair beveled in back to show off her long neck, was the most exciting woman Zam had ever taken to bed. She had honed her sexuality like a warrior would sharpen his sword edge. And Zam, uncommonly tall and rugged for their generally diminutive people, his head shaved down to a black stubble in the current tough guy style, had taken plenty of women to bed—including almost every nails technician in Juyen's stable, at one time or other. He was sure Juyen knew about this, and that rather than being afraid it would undermine her stature in her workers' eyes, allowed such frivolous affairs as a means of keeping her husband close to home, contented, and grateful. He was certain she reasoned that if he had to cheat, it should be in a way she felt she controlled.

They both turned to look out the open front of their salon again, across the bustling rotary with the bronze statue of the Ruby Empress stranded on the island at its center, arms outstretched, as she was orbited by motorbikes and occasional cars and trucks, all of them beeping their horns at each other incessantly. Through this vortex of chaos the husband and wife could see *Superior Nails*, and a delivery man climbing off a scooter out front. He was carrying plastic bags through which bulged stacks of white styrofoam food containers.

"Nice of Fai to buy lunch for her workers every Friday, isn't it?" Zam said teasingly.

Juyen whipped her head around to glare up at her husband again, the muscles twitching in her hardened jaw. She whispered, "Speak a little louder so all my workers can hear, why don't you? You, who are so concerned about us spending money." But then she smiled. He was afraid to look at her smile, and gazed outside again. Juyen said, "Go out right now and buy lunch for all my workers. You're going to do that every Friday from now on. But first, go over there and find out where he works." She gestured at the parked scooter. "But don't let those bitches in Fai's salon see you. Buy our lunches from the same place. And pay that boy a nice tip to spit in their food every Friday, before he brings it by."

"You're going to pay that boy every week to spit in their food? But they won't even know it!"

"*I'll* know it!" Juyen said, widening her eyes.

Zam bit off whatever else he might have said. He only nodded quietly and began to cross the threshold.

"Hey, wait up!" Zam's brother Frang came out from a room at the rear of the salon, adjusting his jacket. He wore a white suit, his hair greased back like a movie gangster. He said loudly, "Don't you hate when you get finished wiping your ass, then another spurt of shit comes out and you have to start wiping all over again? You know what I hate worse than that? When the fucking toilet paper runs out when you're still wiping! Who is it that looks after the water closet these days?"

Juyen jerked a thumb at her newest worker, who looked like she was trying to hide behind her white face mask and bent lower over the feet of a middle-aged woman whom she was giving a pedicure. Lavatory duties and pedicures were for newcomers.

Frang leaned down close to this girl and said sweetly, "Next time you don't leave enough toilet paper in back, I'll use your hair to wipe my ass. Got it, doll?" And he stroked his hand down her long hair.

"That's enough crudity out of you," Juyen snapped. "You're going to upset my poor customers." But the middle-aged woman was only tsk-tsking Frang and chuckling. "Go help your idiot brother run an errand, you shit-mouthed brain-damaged boil on my ass!"

"I would love to be anything on your ass," Frang said, as he strutted past Juyen on his way to join Zam at the threshold. He was still adjusting his jacket, and in so doing exposed a revolver with a four-inch barrel, tucked in his waistband.

Juyen took him by the elbow. "Moron," she said. "If the police ever catch you with that they'll back you up against a wall for execution."

Frang kissed his fingers and rubbed them together, signifying that he'd offer a bribe if such a situation ever arose. "You pay me for protection, don't you, gorgeous? This is a harsh world, you know." Then he slipped out of Juyen's grasp, and he and Zam stepped out onto the sidewalk. There, Frang said to his older brother, "What, she doesn't know you have a gun, too?"

"I don't flaunt it the way you do," Zam muttered, glancing back to be sure they were out of his wife's earshot. Seeing they were in the clear, he confided, "She has my balls in her hand, Frang."

"I'd kill to have my balls in her hand," the younger brother joked, lighting a cigarette. "Actually, it's more like she wears your balls between her legs. But don't start complaining. Before you met her, you were just a punk on the street. Now you've got money in your pockets, a roomful of young beauties smitten with the boss's husband, and a wife beautiful as a model. Or beautiful as a demon...either way. But you want a demon in bed, you have to make a deal with it. You have to pay the price."

Lighting his own cigarette before they started across the street, Zam looked up behind him at the sign *Glorious Nails*. He sighed fatalistically, slapped his kid brother across the back of the head, and said, "Let's go buy the girls some lunch, you tapir-dicked boil on my ass."

***

That evening, when the salon had closed for business and the girls were all heading out to return home after an interminable work day, one of the workers, named Jha, knocked on the doorframe of Juyen's little back office. Frang had already left, but Zam was slumped in an ornately carved and glassily lacquered wooden chair, a long leg slung over one of its arms, watching TV while waiting for his wife to finish scribbling columns of figures in a child's school workbook. She kept stacks of these brightly-covered books, not trusting computers to store her records. Juyen looked up and called for Jha to enter. Zam sat up a little in his hard chair, only mildly curious, but then sat up even more when he saw the girl who accompanied Jha into the office.

Jha had worked for the salon for several years, and was pretty enough; he had slept with her a few times, but didn't care for her unfortunate halitosis. The young woman beside her, though, was another matter. She was a little shorter than Jha, a little younger, and infinitely more lovely. Her teardrop-shaped eyes were poignant in their shyness, her small pouty mouth like a rosebud on the verge of blooming, the neat line of her bangs imparting a schoolgirl's innocence. Despite her short stature, she was perfectly proportioned, her skirt showing off long slender legs. The mix of girlishness and sexiness made for a heady brew.

"Madam," Jha said with her usual meek and respectful tone, "this is the sister I told you of—Ghoo."

"Ah!" Juyen exclaimed, "and just as lovely as you claimed." She smiled and motioned for Jha's kid sister to approach. "Come here, child."

Ghoo did as requested, shuffling closer to Juyen's desk with awkward steps. She flicked a sideways glance at Zam. He had hoped the girl would notice his handsomeness, and he had been prepared for her, grinning at her broadly. What a sweet little pastry she was!

Even Juyen, he thought, looked like she wanted a taste, reaching to the girl's smooth cheek and cupping it. "My oh my," she said, "a flower, indeed."

"Indeed," Zam echoed aloud, unconsciously. His wife glanced his way, and his guts tightened their coils, but no jealousy flashed in her eye. Rather, her smile grew brighter.

"I had a thought recently," Juyen said, "and your face has made that thought crystallize in my mind. Yes, yes...I think you're exactly the girl I was waiting for."

Jha smiled. "You'll take my sister in, madam?" she asked.

"No," Juyen said.

Jha's smile fell like a bird that had struck an invisible wall. Even Zam was stunned. His wife prided herself on having amassed, she felt, the prettiest batch of nails technicians in the city. Ghoo was lovelier, in her delicate way, than all of them. Juyen had just called Jha's sister a flower! Did she see Ghoo as *too* innocent-looking, then?

"I have another idea for you entirely, my flower," Juyen cooed.

"What idea is this?" Zam spoke up.

"Well, my dear slow-witted husband, Ghoo is so striking and fresh a beauty I'm sure any salon would want to snap her up to grace their premises. Especially, our good friend Fai across the street."

"Fai?" Zam said. "You mean—"

Juyen addressed Jha. "Don't bring Ghoo in our salon again. I don't want our hateful neighbors to see her here. Take her back home, Jha, and I'll tell you more about my plan in the morning."

"But," Jha stammered, looking back and forth between her sister and her employer, "you are giving her a job, madam?"

"Yes, yes, don't be so dense." Juyen made a shooing motion. "I told you, I'll tell you more when you return in the morning." She smiled at Ghoo in goodbye, uncharacteristically gentle. "And you, my pet, I'll be speaking with you on the phone."

"Thank you, madam," Ghoo said sweetly, as her older sister hustled her through the doorway.

Juyen turned to her husband. "The prettiest bullet I have ever seen."

"You mean spy, don't you?"

"I mean bullet. And I expect you, husband, to take her under your wing. Safely away from our shop, of course. Charm her, beguile her, make her yearn to do anything to please you."

Zam grinned. What an agreeable assignment! "If you say so," he replied.

"I say so. Now, this is what I'm thinking…"

Zam listened, until his grin withered and his face grew solemn with the effort of masking his horror.

***

At forty-four, Fai was a dozen years older than Frang's sister-in-law Juyen. Frang had heard Juyen make much of Fai's age, and Fai's rhinoplasty to affect a more Western nose with tiny triangular nostrils, and Fai bleaching her face five shades lighter than her neck and body, and wearing such heavy dark eye makeup. Frang had to agree that Fai's face looked a bit unnatural—too tight to stretch properly in a smile—but he highly approved of the breast augmentation that Juyen particularly liked to mock. He had gripped those huge, steely spheres only minutes ago while riding the woman. She had panted up into his face, exhaling an odd odor he didn't care for, and he wondered if Juyen was right in claiming Fai had had all her teeth pulled out for being discolored and decayed, and wore dentures instead. Whatever the case, he held his breath whenever they kissed.

Yet Fai's inky hair was still lustrous, her body still firm. Her curvy hips, widened by bearing children, supplemented the voluptuousness of her bosom. Frang actually found it extremely exciting that she was fourteen years older than himself…like a naughty auntie. He would never dare call her that teasingly, though, or bring up the subject of her age at all.

Despite their having just finished a loud, frenzied bout of lovemaking, Fai quickly pulled on a silk robe to hide her body demurely, or self consciously, as she left the bed to go shower. Frang stayed where he was, feeling lazy, and lit up a cigarette. Listening to the water run, he glanced at his expensive Western wristwatch to make sure he wasn't too late returning to *Ultimate Nails*, where he would again lounge about lazily and smoke cigarettes in his role of security muscle.

He'd told his brother Zam he had bought the wristwatch himself, but in truth it had been a gift from Fai. Since they had begun seeing each—always secretly, always at her home—she had never let his cock or his wallet go hungry.

She had approached him, initially, with a phone call. He had been curious about her proposal to meet, and agreed. At that first meeting she had gone down on him, and sent him home with a wad of bills, which she tucked deep down into his trouser pocket while holding his gaze meaningfully. Their locked eyes had been like a handshake.

She returned from the bathroom, toweling her hair, and stood over the bed looking down at him with a taut smile, her beauty severe and weirdly wrong. Then, she reached for his pistol, which he had set down on a bedside table when he'd undressed, and turned it toward him at arm's length.

"Hey!" Frang cried, covering his face with his arms. For one flaring moment he believed this had all been an elaborate trap, a trick to get him to lower his guard and trust her.

Fai laughed and returned the old, tarnished revolver to the table. It was difficult, and dangerous, to acquire modern firearms in their country. She said, "Oh, my poor boy...you don't think I'd really mar your prettiness, do you?"

Frang clamped down on his anger, forcing himself not to explode. If he displeased her, he knew, there'd be no more bulging breasts or bulging wallet. So he grinned and chuckled. "Every gangster needs a gun moll."

Fai ran seductive fingers down his shin. "My cute little gangster." Her nails lightly raked him, leaving white trails of ploughed skin cells. "So what do you think about the globes?"

For a second he thought she was referring to her chest, but then he remembered the plot she had suggested before they went to bed. He sighed. "It's so elaborate, Fai. Look, if you don't want to worry about Juyen anymore, just let me kill her."

"*Men*…always wanting to do things the men way. So brutish, no finesse. But I suppose you dream of a hefty prize for doing away with her, eh? Well, help me with these spirit globes and I'll make you very happy, my hungry little pet."

"You know I'll do anything for you, gorgeous."

"You amuse me with your offer, though. You could kill your own sister-in-law? And put your widower brother out of a job?"

"Maybe he could come work for you." Frang shrugged his naked shoulders. "But if not, there are other jobs."

"I sense some sibling rivalry between you two."

"I love my brother," Frang protested.

"You love money, and your prick." Fai caressed his leg again. "But that's all right…so do I."

***

Zam had sat watching attentively during the first phase of Ghoo's makeover. Normally when he came to this beauty salon—alone or with his brother—he'd have the works: haircut, eyebrows trimmed, wax cleaned from his ears, a massage and fuck in the back room. But he wanted Ghoo to feel she had his full, rapt attention. And actually, she did. If the girl had been striking before, in her fresh state, she was even more dazzling now...a gemstone polished to a luster.

"Look at you!" he crowed, standing up from his chair and clapping his hands together. "That color is amazing!"

Ghoo grinned shyly, like a child.

The stylist had colored Ghoo's hair a dark coppery red. Beaming proudly at her work, the hair stylist said, "Next we give her a more sophisticated cut."

"Not too short," Zam advised sternly. He loved his wife's short hair, but he wanted to demonstrate to Ghoo that he had an intense interest in preserving the beauty she already possessed.

"No, no," the stylist reassured them both. "Then after the cut, we shape your eyebrows."

"Not too thin!" Zam insisted, even more sternly. "Too-thin eyebrows make a woman look old and mean."

"Not too thin," the stylist promised. "We will make her sophisticated while still celebrating her youth. After shaping her brows, we do her makeup...and teach her how to reproduce that look herself."

"You are so kind, sister," Ghoo said softly, with a little half bow.

"And after *that*," Zam said, reaching to Ghoo and taking hold of her small hand, "I bring you shopping for a new wardrobe. My own personal gift to you, my dear." Though Juyen was really the one footing the bill today. "You must look your very best to be an *Ultimate Nails* girl, eh?"

Ghoo grinned bashfully again and averted her head somewhat as if to hide her smile behind her shoulder, but Zam saw how her eyes turned to the side to stay fixed on his own, glistening with a dark hunger that belied her innocence.

But then hunger always glistens darkly.

***

Every morning, before she unlocked the retractable shutter over the front of *Ultimate Nails*, Juyen brought her motorbike—as brightly red as varnished nails—to a stop at the edge of the traffic island at the center of the rotary. Here loomed the majestic and lovely bronze statue of the Ruby Empress, her arms spread wide, and cupped in each palm a red glass orb…symbolizing her gifts to her beloved pet, Cholukan.

To bring good luck for a prosperous work day, Juyen would leave a bright new coin in the grass at the base of the statue's platform. Late at night, when traffic was sporadic (though it never entirely ceased in this busy city), beggars and the like stole out to the island and took the money, no doubt muttering prayers throughout, begging for forgiveness and pointing out the desperation of their situation. Juyen didn't care what became of the money later; she knew the Ruby Empress, most gentle of the gods and goddesses, was charitable.

There were other offerings at the foot of the platform. Not just coins, but bills, prayers written on scraps of paper, a rotting melon, a bottle of rice wine with a sea anemone preserved inside, a pack of 777 cigarettes, a submarine sandwich swarming with ants, joss sticks stuck in the ground, several still smoldering, and a child's tattered old teddy bear. Juyen figured the toy's owner had died in an accident at this busy roundabout, and the parents or other surviving relatives were petitioning for the tiny soul's straight journey to the Ten Heavens.

Juyen knelt in the grass, raised her hands to her forehead pressed palm-to-palm, and intoned, "Oh great Empress, as I love you, bring me good fortune and deliver absolute ruin to my enemies, for surely they do not love you as I do. I will devote my life to you, immaculate goddess, if you turn your benevolent face from the spiteful and unfaithful Fai and allow her just fate to smote her like a bolt of lightning."

As Juyen opened her eyes, lifted her head, and prepared to rise she spotted something resting in the yellowed, overgrown grass that she hadn't consciously noted before. It was another offering: an egg-like red glass globe the size of a melon, much like the spheres held aloft in the idol's hands. But she shuddered when she saw it, for she knew that this glass orb contained a ghost.

She couldn't actually *see* a ghost inside this ruby ball, but she knew it was there. When someone died in a violent manner, such as a murder or a traffic accident, a monk might be paid to place one of these spirit globes at the site of the tragedy. After the ball had rested at the site for ninety days, the tormented spirit would have been coaxed from the place of its body's demise. Thus lured inside the consecrated sphere, like an animal into a trap, the spirit would be reunited with its fleshly vehicle, when the ball was interred at the body's grave plot.

Juyen guessed this ball contained the soul of the child whom had owned that weathered teddy bear.

She raised her joined palms to her forehead again and whispered another quick prayer, urging the tiny spirit on to the Ten Heavens. She didn't want to attract bad luck to herself by not acknowledging the soul in its transition. Like mortals, ghosts were touchy creatures.

***

"Did you go to nails school, darling?" Fai asked the angelic eighteen-year-old who had come into *Superior Nails* meekly inquiring about employment. "You can't work here or anyplace respectable without certification."

"Yes, aunt," replied the young woman—who had introduced herself as Ghoo—addressing Fai in the respectful way of a small town girl. Ghoo came from the green rural outskirts of this city, Haikan. So did her sister, Jha, of course, but Ghoo made no mention of her sister. She rummaged in her handbag clumsily, spilling a few brand new articles of makeup to the floor. After apologetically stooping to retrieve them, she produced a folded paper and handed it over.

Fai gave it a glance. "Ah...a vocational program in high school." She passed it back to Ghoo. "I'm not impressed with your certificate...but I am more than impressed with your loveliness." She reached up to cup Ghoo's face in her hand, much as Juyen had done a few days ago. But Ghoo was all the more stunning now, with her coppery hair and model-perfect makeup, her outfit smart and chic: a navy blue skirt and matching blazer, and a white silk blouse open just enough to show rounded cleavage produced by a new pushup bra. Despite her sophisticated veneer, Ghoo grinned like a nervous child, and Fai remarked, "You have the cutest, most adorable smile I have ever seen."

A customer who was having her nails painted with dragonfly designs, listening in on the conversation, piped up enthusiastically, "If she wasn't so young I'd swear she was Pe Dhu!" Pe Dhu was the sweet-faced actress who had played the character Laiki in the television drama *B-2*.

"Yes!" exclaimed the technician who was painting the miniature dragonflies, twisting around to see Ghoo for herself. "Exactly Pe Dhu!"

Fai took hold of Ghoo's hand and squeezed it. "We can add to your nails skills...I have no concern there...but no one could possibly add to your beauty. At *Superior Nails*, we pride ourselves on having the loveliest nails technicians in all of Haikan. Yes, absolutely, you must join our family."

Ghoo bowed deeply, and said, "Thank you, thank you, dear aunt." She heard one or two of the other workers snicker at her peasant-like formality, and when she straightened, she could see a few of the technicians sneering at her with their eyes, though white masks covered their lower faces. It made Ghoo feel self conscious, even a little afraid that somehow they could see through her guise, could detect the plot of which she guiltily was a part. And yet, rationally she understood these few hostile women were merely jealous because Fai was making so much of her beauty. A simple matter of rivalry.

Still holding Ghoo's hand, Fai raised it for close inspection, having noticed her nails: painted with delicate flowers boasting metallic silver petals. "Your nails are exquisite," Fai said. "Your own work?"

"Y-yes," Ghoo squeaked. It was a lie, and she hated lying, but it was all for Zam. She would do anything to make Zam hold her hand as Fai was doing now.

In reality, it was Juyen herself who had painted the ten silver flowers. It was like Juyen putting her signature on a piece of artwork.

***

Two walls of the apothecary featured floor-to-ceiling rows of little wooden drawers, labeled with yellowed index cards, while the other two walls were lined with shelves. These shelves were filled with glass jars containing powders fine or grainy, whole leaves and flower petals, strips of tree bark, dried insects and lizards, bird feet and mummified animal embryos. One large jar was stuffed full with monkey heads pickled in alcohol, their faces squashed and unhappy. The air smelled of all these things combined.

Yet this was only the main room, for the general public. There was another floor, above, that most customers would assume merely provided the owner's living space. But Zam had made advance arrangements, and the elderly proprietor led his two guests through a curtained doorway and up a steep flight of steps to the second level, which was a special extension of his shop below. The old man was no taller than Ghoo, and his spectacles with their round black lenses suggested blindness, but from the way he navigated this place Zam couldn't be sure. Maybe full blindness hadn't yet descended, or perhaps it had long ago but he was just intimately familiar with his surroundings and their contents.

"There are two powders," the proprietor began explaining, moving around behind a wooden counter like the one downstairs. He bent down, and they heard him open a cabinet on the counter's far side. Then, a crash as a large bottle fell out of the cabinet to the floor. "Ah! Damn her! How many times have I told that stupid daughter of mine not to shift the items around down here!"

"Are you cut?" Zam asked, trying not to smile with amusement in case the old man wasn't entirely blind.

They heard their host push glass shards out of his way with the side of his foot, muttering swears. "I'm instructing my daughter in my art, for lack of a son. But her mind is only on boys, boys, boys."

"That's the way of women," Zam said, turning to wink at Ghoo.

His wink made her cheeks go hot with blood.

"As I was saying," the proprietor went on, producing two vials from behind the counter, one in each hand. "This fungus," and he raised his right hand, holding a vial containing a brown powder, "is a dangerous pathogen, which can cause rapid infection in a human host. In this dehydrated state, it is quickly activated when introduced to water."

"What are the symptoms of the infection?" Zam asked.

"Swift necrotizing of flesh…even bone."

Ghoo shuddered, hugging her arms tight across her chest.

"Obviously," the old man said, "the person handling this fungus should wear a face mask so as not to inhale it, and rubber gloves."

"Easy enough for you to do that, in a nails boutique," Zam whispered, having leaned down close to Ghoo, so close his lips brushed her ear through her burnished hair. She shivered, but this time out of excitement rather than horror.

"Moreover," the old man continued, "it is wise to swallow the contents of this other vial before handling the pathogen." He held up the vial in his left hand, this one filled with a white powder. "It is an antifungal agent derived from bacteria. Should the pathogen be introduced into one's body, this powerful agent will destroy the fungi cells, so that an infection will not take hold. I would recommend swallowing the entire contents of this vial, mixed in a glass of water, one day before handling the pathogen, so that the agent is fully dispersed through one's system."

"An antidote in advance," Zam said.

"Yes. It may of course be used after an infection has begun, but by then much damage to the body's tissues may already have taken place. So I stress again," and once more he held aloft the vial in his left hand, "take this a day in advance."

"Understood," Zam said. "Thank you. We'll take them."

"Very good." The proprietor reached under his counter again for a small cardboard box, filled with a nest of shredded newspaper, in which to safely package the glass vials.

Zam glanced at Ghoo, saw her unhappy expression, and steered her aside with a hand gently pressed to the small of her back. "What is it, my beauty?" he asked in a hushed tone.

"Fai is…she's good to me," she said hesitantly, in a tiny creaky voice, dreading his disapproval.

"Am I not good to you, dear?"

Ghoo's cheeks flushed red. "Of course!" She looked directly into his eyes, her own wide and moist. "Oh, of course!"

He cupped her cheek in his palm, as Juyen had done, as Fai had done, but it was Zam's hand she had been waiting for.

"Do you know," he said, "how lonely my soul has been? My wife…you see how driven she is, how consumed with her business. Yes, I understand, one must be dedicated to one's business to make it succeed. But she has neglected me more and more, Ghoo, until she no longer sees me. I have faded into the background, faded from her heart. I accept this sad fact, as I say, but I have been empty for some time. Until…until the day I saw *you*."

His words were so earnest, he began wondering if he were speaking the truth…about the spiritual desolation at his core. About the excitement this girl had awakened, his jaded heart turned to a sack full of dragonflies when she first walked into the office with her sister.

He saw Ghoo's plump lower lip trembling with emotion. "Me?" she said.

"Yes, Ghoo. You have filled that empty place inside me."

Tears formed in her eyes, twin quivering menisci. "Oh, Zam. But your wife… Juyen has been good to me."

"Yes. Juyen has been good to you. And Fai has been good to you. But it is I, Ghoo, who loves you."

The tension of the menisci broke, and tears rolled down both Ghoo's cheeks. But at the same time, she smiled that bright adorable smile of hers.

"Will you do this for me, Ghoo?" Zam said. "Let Juyen succeed with her plan. Let her business become even more successful, and fill her even more. Fill her so much that she won't see us anymore. Won't see us, won't care, when we go off together to start a new life of our own."

Did he mean *that*, he wondered? No, now he knew he was going too far...he had it too good with Juyen. And could even this angel excite him more than his demon did? But he would hold her like a stolen diamond in his hand, as long as he could, until it fell through his fingers.

She took his hand from her cheek, moved it to her lips, and kissed the center of his palm, while emitting a little sob.

The kiss and the sob made him start to go hard in his trousers. He wagered she'd be in bed with him by week's end. How long had it been since he'd had a virgin? The dragonflies fluttered madly in his heart again, like the dried insects in one of the apothecary's jars all come miraculously back to life.

The proprietor pushed the closed box across his counter, clearing his voice to regain their attention. "Young love," he joked. "If only there were an antidote for *that* infection."

***

What a house of horrors, Frang thought, looking around him. It was like a museum in hell; a collection of exhibits geared to frighten even the demons.

The black marketeer's name was Whep. His head was entirely shaved bald, and his neck was blue with prison tattoos. It was from Whep that Frang had purchased his handgun and bullets. In one room of his house, Whep had dozens of pistols and rifles to offer, generally old military items. Also, swords, machetes, or knives for those who couldn't afford a gun. But Frang had never been in *this* room of Whep's home before.

Shelves on the walls and tables arranged around the room displayed Whep's most unusual wares. Several prayer books bound in the leathery skin of monks. The toothless skulls of stillborn infants, which when buried at the corner of a field inspired fecundity. A leering stone demon head, broken from a statue guarding some ancient temple lost to the deep forest, which might be buried on the property of one's enemy. A jar containing a number of human penises, bleached by the alcohol they were preserved in. A hinged glass box containing a dagger with its blade caked in old brown blood. Intricately carved ni-liq horns. And a row of red glass orbs, varying slightly in size but all of them seemingly empty. Except that each ruby ball had a label taped to its side.

Whep waved his arm at the spirit globes, smiling to show his few remaining teeth. "What would you like? Angry male ghost? Female? A child wailing for its mom for eternity?"

"Where do you get these?" Surely they weren't exhumed from grave plots; by then, the spirit inside would have moved on to the afterlife. "Do you steal them from accident and murder sites, before the families can come back for them?"

"Friend Frang, you know better than to ask me that. I steal nothing." Whep spread his arms innocently. "I only buy what my contacts bring to me, no questions asked. That's the way I like to do things…please take note. No questions asked."

Frang took a wary step nearer to the red glass spheres, arranged like a strange crop of fruit, afraid to look at them too long lest ghastly faces surface within them, but he saw only his own reflected visage. "Are you *sure* there's a ghost inside each?"

"I will guarantee it."

"And…it will be angry? If released from the globe, it will haunt its location?"

"It will be *furious* to be denied its proper resting place, trust me. It will take a whole monastery of monks to exorcize it."

Frang brought out his wallet, brimming with Fai's money. "Well, why not make it a female ghost, then? That seems appropriate."

***

Zam rejoined his wife late in the evening, at their two-level house, after having been away from the salon for so many hours that she had gone home without him. She was chopping scallions for soup when he sauntered in. Looking up at him, she asked, "So?"

"Everything's ready for tomorrow. She drank the protective potion. Almost vomited at the taste." He chuckled at the memory.

"And?"

"And what?" Zam nonchalantly opened the refrigerator for a 777 beer.

"Where was it you took her to drink this potion?"

"A café."

"Ah." Juyen smiled. "You took her to a hotel. If it was really a café you'd have told me its name."

"Juyen...you hurt me with your accusations." He took a swig from his can.

His wife stepped close to him, reached up and took hold of his ear with one hand, and—stretching it out—placed the edge of her knife's blade behind it. "Don't lie to me or I'll add this to my soup."

"Hey, hey, hey," Zam said, but not with too much alarm. It wasn't the first time she'd put a knife's edge to him, at one part of his body or another. "You know I'm devoted to you, Juyen!"

"You're devoted to that tapir snout you call a cock. So, how was it when you kicked down her door for the first time? Did she cry out that she loved you?" Juyen lowered the knife, released his ear. "Did she whimper and moan as if you were torturing her?"

"Such talk, wife," Zam sighed, raising his beer again.

Her face stretched in a blade-like grin. "I see it in your satisfied eyes...I saw it in your swagger when you came in. She moaned and sobbed when you lapped her young pussy." She set down the knife, with bits of scallion clinging to the blade, and cupped his crotch through his trousers, still grinning up at him. Zam looked down at her then and realized she was excited about visualizing him in bed with Ghoo. Was this part of the reason she let him frolic with her staff?

"What is it that you want?" he asked casually, as if he had no clue.

"Show me what you did to her," she whispered.

So they went up to their bedroom, and though he didn't admit that these were the same acts he had performed with Ghoo at the hotel, it was understood between them.

He buried his face between his wife's legs, gradually worked his tongue down lower, teasing her perineum. "Yes," she hissed through her teeth, lifting her head from the pillows to watch him, "that's your world, right there. That's where you live...on that little strip of real estate between my pussy and my asshole."

"Mmm," he grunted, in what might pass for agreement.

"And you never want to leave that little island, do you?"

"Mm-mm," he grunted.

"Lick my asshole," she commanded, resting her head back on the pillows again. Staring at the ceiling, she asked, "Did you tell your brother about our plot with Ghoo?"

"Mm-mm," he grunted in the negative again.

"You don't trust him?"

Zam lifted his head, gazing at her along the length of her

body. "It's just, the fewer people who know about this, the better. What we're doing tomorrow…it might lead to death. We might become murderers."

"Stroke me with your fingers while we talk." He obeyed, and closing her eyes, in a shuddery voice she went on, "All I care about is that no one will ever dare have their nails done in *Superior Nails* again. No one will risk working in *Superior Nails* again. There will *be* no more *Superior Nails!*"

"Whatever you want," Zam muttered, as if this put it all on her, and exonerated him.

"Can our country girl really do this? Is she nervous?"

"Of course she's nervous. She's afraid they'll realize she's the one who's responsible. I told her of course they'll make that connection, but before that happens we'll pull her out of there. As far as Fai is concerned, Ghoo will have vanished without a trace."

"But can she be trusted later, or will it be too much for her poor conscience? What should we *really* do with her when she's completed her mission?" When Zam stopped working a finger in and out of her, Juyen opened her eyes to study him. He was looking at her with an expression like the one he'd worn when she'd first told him the plan about launching a biological attack on her rival. "Ah…you're worried about her, huh?"

"She'll do whatever I say, Juyen. You don't have to be concerned about her loyalty."

"If she were loyal to me, she wouldn't be fucking my husband." Juyen smirked. "But don't worry…I won't hurt your little pet. And you're *my* little pet, aren't you? Get up here and fuck me now."

Zam climbed up her body as instructed, and tucked his cock into her. Propped above her on stiff arms, he began churning her insides dutifully. Staring with fierce eyes at where they were joined, Juyen said huskily, "I'm like the Ruby Empress, and you're like my good little monkey, Cholukan. Oh…yes…fuck me, monkey! Fuck me, Cholukan!"

***

Where *Ultimate Nails* had five whirlpool spa chairs, *Superior Nails* had six. Fai had ordered the sixth chair only a month earlier, after sending a friend pretending to be a customer over to *Ultimate Nails* to report back on what she reconnoitered. The friend informed Fai that Juyen had just bought a fifth chair. Fai ordered her sixth the same day.

Despite being gushed over for her beauty, as Ghoo was the new girl it was her responsibility to clean the foot spas at the start of the day before the boutique opened for business. She got down on her knees to do so. No one asked her why she wore her face mask in addition to gloves as she wiped out the spa basins, but she half-heard a few giggling comments behind her back.

Bent low over the first empty foot tub, Ghoo sprayed a solution of water and bleach (though she had cut back on the amount of bleach Fai had instructed her to use), then wiped down the inside of the basin with a sponge. When she had finished, with her hunched back hiding her actions, she shifted a hand to her front jeans pocket and surreptitiously palmed a small glass vial containing a brown powder. After uncapping the vial, she sprinkled a dash of the powder into the tub, as if lightly seasoning a soup…not so much that it would draw attention to itself. She then tucked the vial into her jeans again before rising and moving on to the second foot spa chair.

Water, the old man had told her and Zam, would activate the potion.

Ghoo trembled throughout all this. Her fear at being discovered in this act of sabotage made her nauseous. She was sure

guilt added to the stew burbling in her guts. Poor, trusting Fai!
But just when Ghoo considered spraying and wiping clean,
again, the foot tubs she had contaminated, Zam's handsome face
manifested before her mind's eye like the image of a god in a
rapturous vision.

He had mused aloud that if the women who used the whirlpool spas had shaved their legs recently, the fungus would have
a better chance to enter their bodies through tiny abrasions in
their skin. But when he had seen that Ghoo's eyes had gone wide
with dismay in reaction to his musings, he had taken her head
soothingly in both hands and pressed his lips to her forehead.
Then her eyelids. The tip of her nose. Her lips...

From there, they had ended up in the hotel room's bed. But
even as inexperienced as she was, Ghoo had never believed they
had only gone to a hotel so that Zam might coach her and help
her prepare the protective elixir.

When she reached the sixth and last chair, Ghoo had to hold
onto one armrest as a wave of sizzling blackness passed over her
vision. Her gorge rose, but sank away again, like a roiling ocean
wave. She moaned aloud.

Was this something more than just fear and guilt? Was this
sickness a consequence of love—not just emotional, but physical? When a man first entered a woman, was some fundamen-
tal change triggered in her system? And though he had quickly
withdrawn from her at the moment of climax, spurting onto
her belly, she wondered if one of his microscopic snakes had still
managed to find its way inside. Her mother had once sternly
cautioned her that these snakes might reside in the tear that
first wept from a man's tool before he even penetrated his lover.
Might Zam's child, infinitely small, already be clinging to the
inside of her womb?

"Dear? Ghoo? Are you all right?" The familiar voice, so near, caused Ghoo to gasp and snap her eyelids open. She hadn't even noticed she'd squeezed them shut—having gone from blackness to blackness.

It was of course Fai's familiar, oddly *wrong* face hovering there…seemingly too close, as if to eclipse all else. Ghoo blinked up at her speechlessly for a moment, thinking Fai had said something entirely different, such as, *"What do you think you're doing there? What is that dust you've sprinkled in my foot spas?"*

Instead, Fai took Ghoo's arm and helped her to her feet, helped support her. She said, "Poor baby, are you sick?" She gently pulled the mask from Ghoo's face to see her better.

"Maybe," Ghoo managed to get out, "maybe it's the smell. The nail polish. The acetone."

At the hotel, Zam had joked to her that he believed the fumes in nail salons drove all the workers crazy over time. Ghoo had wondered if that explained a few things about Juyen and Fai both, and probably that was what Zam had been implying. His words about the toxic fumes had come to her aid just now.

"It can take some getting used to, dear, but—" and here Fai paused to sniff the air through her pinched little nostrils "—we haven't even begun working yet. Do you want to step outside and get a breath of air?"

"I feel like…like I need to lie down."

"Of course. Maybe it's waking up so early for work; it's new to you." Fai wagged a finger in the young woman's face. "Don't you be staying up late at night. Come, now." Still supporting Ghoo, Fai led her toward the back of the salon, where a staircase led to a second level. "I have a cot in my office, remember? You can rest up there till you feel a bit better."

"You are too kind, auntie," Ghoo whimpered.

Fai looked down at Ghoo and saw that her eyes had filled with tears. "Oh!" Fai exclaimed, obviously touched.

Stifling a sob, Ghoo said, "I'm sorry. I'm sorry for the problem I'm causing!"

Fai put her hand to the girl's cheek, which was filmed in perspiration. "Oh stop it. You're such a sweet, dear child!"

***

Frang donned a full-head motorcycle helmet, with a dark-tinted face shield. He had never cared to use a helmet with a face shield before, and most people didn't, but it would conceal his identity...as would the nondescript motorbike he sat astride. He had borrowed it, for a fee, from the black marketeer Whep.

Frang had told his brother he wouldn't be coming into *Ultimate Nails* today because he was suffering a debilitating hangover. A plausible enough story, since he had frequently taken days off for this reason. So frequently that an angry Juyen had often questioned to his face whether she really needed him for security at all, when she already had her husband to dissuade street gangs and gangster types from trying to wring protection money from the salon. She would then go on to say she had only really given him a job for Zam's sake. Though she always relented later, her threats to cut him from the payroll had much to do with Frang having gotten into bed with Fai both literally and figuratively.

Several blocks away from the rotary in whose orbit both *Ultimate Nails* and *Superior Nails* faced each other, like the constantly tipping plates of a scale, Frang started the rented bike and set forth. Adrenaline flushed through his system.

Hanging between his legs in a double layer of plastic shopping bags, like the fresh produce families brought home from the market each day, was the red glass spirit globe.

He grew increasingly nervous as he approached *Ultimate Nails*.

He didn't want to stop his bike in order to perform his task, lest he be recognized somehow despite his disguise and in case anyone should attempt to detain him, and yet he knew he couldn't fulfill his mission while maintaining a high rate of speed. So his best bet, he calculated, was to slow down but not stop, deliver his package, then gun the motor and disappear back into the anonymous throng of bikes.

Frang entered the wide roundabout, and it swung him in its gravitational pull, like the hand of a clock turning toward a predestined hour, finally slinging him out toward *Ultimate Nails* directly ahead. Even from here, within the salon he could make out a few of the familiar girls who sat nearest to the building's open front, and moreover, Juyen herself working the front desk.

Frang removed his right hand from the handlebars, reached forward into the doubled plastic sacks and drew out the crimson sphere, like a giant crystal apple. He cradled it against his thigh. Closer to the boutique...closer.

Was it just his imagination, or did Juyen look up and meet his eyes for a moment through his dark face shield as he came parallel with the front of the salon? But she dropped her gaze again to the foreign fashion magazine spread before her atop her counter, and in that moment Frang hurled the globe like a grenade through the open front of *Ultimate Nails*.

He didn't linger to see whether the globe shattered or was merely chipped, or simply thudded to the floor unbroken. Even if the ghost at its core were not released, he knew the reaction of workers and patrons alike would still be one of great aversion. He faced forward again, satisfied, and had just squeezed the throttle when a little girl maybe two years old skipped from the curb into the swarming street ahead of her older brother, before he could take her hand.

Frang twisted his handlebars abruptly to the left. He veered around the child and just avoided striking her, but in so doing bumped hard against a young woman riding her own motorbike alongside him. She went right down, and snapping his head around Frang saw a bicycle that an elderly monk had been vigorously pedaling close behind the woman ram into her downed machine. The flimsy bicycle came up short, throwing off the blue-robed monk, who came to land directly in the path of a truck bearing a load of melons. Frang jerked his head forward again, but heard some terrible sounds behind him.

Frang was fighting with his own wobbling bike, almost kept it upright, but ultimately overbalanced and he too went down... skidding along the street with the vehicle atop his left leg.

Frang heard people crying out all around him, including the woman whom he had knocked down...and including himself, as the momentum of his bike dragged him across the pavement like a potato across a grater.

***

The red glass orb *did* break—on the floor right beside the front counter, behind which stood Juyen. At that moment a regular customer named Whi, the owner of a jewelry store who always tipped generously, was coming toward the counter to pay. The globe shattered directly in front of Whi, and she jumped back with a yelp as small chunks like a scattered handful of rubies clattered all around her and ticked against her shins. Half of the sphere remained intact and rocking, like the bloody top of an exploded skull.

Juyen and Whi looked down at this wobbling bowl, and both instantly recognized it for what it was. Whi reeled away from the counter and fled for the street, screaming shrilly, payment for her ten glossy nails forgotten. Juyen cried out, as well. She was torn between her fear of touching the thing, and her impulse to snatch up the bowl before any more of her customers, or her workers, saw it. Only a second or two of hesitation, and at last she convinced herself that at this point the orb itself was harmless, a vessel emptied of its poison, but already it was too late. More exclamations of horror shot up all throughout the salon, as workers lifted their heads to see what the commotion was, and customers stood up craning their necks, even those soaking their feet in the spa chairs.

In synchronization, workers and customers alike went from gazing aghast at the rocking bowl, to whipping their heads this way and that as if following the darting of an invisible fly. In terror, they were all looking for a ghost.

And then, still in synchronization, workers and customers alike burst up to scramble madly for the street. In the screaming stampede, tables were overturned...nail polish spilled in thick pools like congealing blood...bare feet slapped wetly out of whirlpool basins. These barefoot customers shrieked even more sharply as they trod on glass shrapnel, but that didn't stop them from fleeing *Ultimate Nails*.

Juyen dropped to her knees to sweep all the fragments toward her. She seized the bowl, unmindful of its jagged rim, and thrust it behind the counter. Looking up at her crew as they abandoned ship, she shouted, "Stop it! I'll fire all of you! You're panicking my customers, you stupid bitches!"

Ghoo's older sister Jha raced past, and Juyen made a grab for her leg but only managed to furrow the girl's skin with her claws.

Juyen looked up as a final figure stood over her. Her husband Zam, the last person remaining in the salon besides herself. In his fist he held a nickel-plated snub-nosed revolver, which he had fetched from a locked drawer in their rear office. His strong jaw was thrust forward with rumbling fury. "Did you see who threw it?" he asked.

"Someone on a bike, I think," Juyen said. "Go! Go kill them!" Then, like a shattered thing herself, she broke down into sobs of hopeless rage. "We're haunted now! Word will spread throughout Haikan! We're *ruined!*"

"Fuck my mother," Zam hissed, and he charged out onto the sidewalk where all the workers and their customers had already dispersed to every direction like startled pigeons. He kept his gun close to his leg, to minimize the chance of it being seen, but he squeezed its ivory grip as if to crush it.

Alone in *Ultimate Nails*, Juyen sprang to her feet when she heard something rattle to the floor behind her. She scanned the back of the room, and saw a small glass bottle of nail polish rotating on the floor. Perhaps it had been upset in the crazed dash of women, and had finally dropped off a table edge, but Juyen knew better. Especially when the bottle wouldn't stop spinning slowly around and around and around.

"Forgive me, spirit," she whispered to her empty salon, pressing her hands together in front of her bowed forehead. She squeezed her eyes shut to unsee the spinning nail polish bottle, but this didn't stop the flow of her tears. Tears of dread. Tears of defeat. "Forgive me."

***

Fai had been so busy with familiar routines in her salon—tending the front counter, overseeing her workers, chitchatting with several of her customers, buying fruit for her girls from a bicycle vendor selling door-to-door, and purchasing lottery tickets for herself from a child hawker who wandered in from the sidewalk—that it wasn't until she decided she needed to catch up on some work in her office that she remembered the new girl

Ghoo was still in there, resting. With a start, Fai checked her wristwatch. Ghoo had gone upstairs to lie down on the cot in her office before they'd even opened for the day's business… almost three hours ago, now.

"Oh!" Fai said, upset at herself for being so distracted and forgetting her newest employee entirely. She hurried to the staircase at the back of the room, determined to send the poor delicate child home to rest properly until she was strong enough to return to work.

Fai reached the closed door of her office, cheap aluminum with a frosted plastic panel in lieu of a window, and when she pushed it open it was as though she had set off a booby-trap— a blast of stench striking her in the face like a solid concussive wave. She gagged, and quickly covered her lower face with one hand. Had the sick girl vomited? Or shat herself in her clothes? Or both?

Fai's office was so small that it only took two steps inside to stand over the cot that was pushed against one wall. The cot upon which Ghoo lay. But…could that disjointed shape be Ghoo? The room had no window, and the overhead fluorescents were off, the only light entering through the doorway. Fai had just started leaning forward to shake Ghoo's shoulder with her free hand, when she made a strangled sound of horror behind her hand and backed up two steps into the threshold again. Her eyes adjusting to the murk, Fai better made out the thing on her cot. That is to say, her eyes made out what her mind could not.

For a heartbeat or two Fai thought someone had piled bleached white branches on top of Ghoo's sleeping body. Or…deer antlers perhaps? But then Fai came to the realization that these white, coral-like forms had grown out of Ghoo's body. Grown from her bare arms and legs, pushing past her clothing to thrust out from her collar and from under the hem of her shirt. Grown from her neck, from her scalp, from her jaw. At the same time, these sprouting appendages had left Ghoo's own flesh withered, caved in on itself, as if all the muscle beneath and all the fluid in her young body had been leeched away. Even her pigment seemed leeched away, leaving her flesh as bloodlessly white as the branch-like growths themselves. This new, fast-growing matter was replacing Ghoo's own. Life for life.

"Oh no...oh no," Fai chanted in horror behind her hand. "No, no, no..."

Hearing Fai's voice, Ghoo turned her head on her pillow. Even in the dimness of the room, Fai saw that one of Ghoo's eyes was gone, leaving a socket scoured to the bare bone. On that same side, her lips were missing, bare teeth jagging up her cheek.

Ghoo croaked, "Zam?" It was the last word she said. On her dying exhalation, a puff of white spores rose up to float in the air before Fai.

Fai had no idea what she was witnessing, but some intuition told her that those hovering motes could be harmful if she ingested them. Fai did not know, as Ghoo had not known, that the daughter of a blind apothecary owner had carelessly rearranged the order of his wares beneath his work counter. Just as the blind man himself had not known, when handing over the two substances to his customer Zam, that the vial of white powder he had held in his left hand had been the pathogen, not the antifungal agent. And the vial of brown powder in his right hand the antifungal agent, not the pathogen.

Fai went shrieking down the stairs, panic having taken hold, and in her hurry one of her plastic sandals slipped loose and threw off her step. She pitched forward as if diving into a pool, and as if to further this image, thrusting out her hands to break her fall. Her stiffened arms could not withstand the weight of her plunging body, however, and both wrists snapped. She rolled onto her back, wailing like a madwoman, holding out her shattered arms.

Her girls ran to her from all around the room. Crouching beside her, one of the concerned nails artists asked, "What happened, Fai?"

Even as she asked, several other of the young women started upstairs to see for themselves. On their heels, a few curious customers followed...despite Fai's hysterical protests.

Immediately, from upstairs came more screams. Screams upon screams.

***

When Zam lunged out onto the sidewalk he was dazzled by the sun, and by the chaos that confronted him. Traffic still churned thickly around the whirlpool of the roundabout, but in front of the salon stood a cluster of bikes as if they had washed to shore, bearing those who had witnessed the triple accident or had stopped to avoid crashing, themselves. Zam strode toward the nearest two of the three fallen victims. One, a young woman, was jabbering and sobbing wildly, pointing her arm accusingly in the direction of the third victim. She wailed more loudly when two passersby lifted her by the arms to lead her toward the sidewalk. She hopped on one foot. Some of those who had stopped to watch held out their cell phones to make videos of her.

The truck had come to a halt abruptly, so that some of its load of melons had cascaded down its sides, lying smashed in the street like organic spirit globes. The old monk lay smashed in the street, himself, torn into two halves with his blood and guts smeared in a long swath by the truck's wheels. For a moment Zam was transfixed by this image, but people quickly crowded around the monk, blocking him from view, and Zam turned his attention to the third victim, who had fallen and been dragged further along the street. The hopping woman was still pointing toward him.

This man was gathering himself to his feet painfully, at the same time taking his bike by the handlebars to pull it out of the street, even as riders nonchalantly glided around him. The man wore a helmet with an uncommon full-face shield, tinted almost black. As Zam stared at him, the dusty and frayed rider glanced up and froze, as if he had picked out Zam in particular from the crowd. This wary reaction told Zam all he needed to know; that this was the man who had ruined his wife's, and thus his own, livelihood. He broke into a run, still squeezing the ivory grip of his revolver. With Zam's arms pumping, the flashing nickel-plated gun was more openly visible to anyone who might look toward him. It was visible to the man in the identity-concealing helmet.

***

Frang had his bike upright again and on the sidewalk, out of the current of traffic, and was about to sling one leg over the saddle when he saw Zam in the distance, staring directly at him. He doubted Zam recognized him as his brother, but he had little doubt Zam realized this was the person who had lobbed a su-pernatural weapon into *Ultimate Nails*—especially when he saw Zam start sprinting in his direction.

Frang jumped onto his seat, wincing at the pain so thorough-ly dispersed throughout his banged and scraped body that it seemed to have no particular source. He prayed his bike hadn't been too damaged to function properly, but before he could even start it he heard a loud report from further down the street, like a firecracker going off at a street festival. He looked up again and saw that Zam had stopped running to assume a firing stance like an action hero from some Western movie, holding his gun in both hands to take aim. At this distance, with a snub-nosed revolver Zam would be lucky to hit the side of a building if that were his target...but maybe luck *was* with him right now, because this second bullet clanged against the bike's body near Frang's right leg.

With a yelp, Frang tried to start his bike. It didn't turn over.

Zam was charging forward again, to close more of the distance between them. People who had seen him fire the first two shots had leapt aside, out of his path.

Frang was surprised that his brother had given himself over to his anger so completely. He had always been the more cautious of the two of them, the one more concerned about trouble with the law. Frang supposed Zam felt that now with Juyen's salon essentially destroyed, he had nothing left to lose. But Frang still had a lot to lose, including his life, and he wasn't willing to sacrifice that even for a brother. When he tried starting his bike once again, and was again unsuccessful, he swung himself off it, let it drop to its side, and darted straight out into the swirling traffic of the roundabout. Bikes swerved sharply around him, their riders cursing him. One woman had to stop outright to avoid striking him, and the person behind her slammed against her rear wheel, jarring her.

Any citizen of the hectic city of Haikan knew that the best way to cross a street was to simply walk forward into the midst of traffic and let it work itself around you, rather than trying to pick and dodge one's way through the streaming bikes and other vehicles. Frang had decided to gamble on trusting these riders to avoid him as he cut across the rotary, hoping that in the dense mix his body would present a more elusive target, and trusting that Zam would be afraid to fire a third time lest he hit some innocent bystander.

He was wrong to trust the traffic…and as wrong to trust his brother as his brother had been to trust him.

***

When he saw his enemy recklessly plunge right into traffic, Zam skidded to a stop and assumed a firing stance again, keeping a bead on his enemy as best he could. Still bracing his pistol in both hands, he fired a third time, aware that this left the five-shot revolver only two more cartridges in its cylinder.

The bullet didn't get anywhere near Frang this time, instead plowing between the ribs of a young girl who was riding on the back of her boyfriend's bike. Zam snarled an oath when he saw her slump backwards limply and fall away, to be bounced over by the bike that had been riding behind them—in his current state of mind, more furious that he'd missed his opponent than that he had hit an innocent.

The helmeted man had almost reached the traffic island that formed the nucleus of the rotary, when one of the countless motorbikes looping around it collided with his hip. The man went down, rolled back immediately to his feet, but now as he continued toward the traffic island Zam could see he was loping along as if injured and, hopefully, in agony. The man fell to hands and knees as he reached the island, scrambled up onto it on all fours like a desperate animal. Zam leveled his gun at the man's back again.

With the revolver's two-inch barrel too short to give the projectile the spin it needed to fly straight, this fourth bullet again went wide, and struck one of the twin red glass orbs held in the palms of the bronze statue of the Ruby Empress, representing her gifts of sight to Cholukan. The glass ball shattered, its chunks raining down at the statue's base, and now Zam was horrified where he hadn't been horrified by accidentally shooting that girl. It was as if he could feel the statue's metal eyes shift in their sockets to blaze at him spitefully. Finally, the red haze of blind hate lifted and he realized what he was doing. He realized how many people were watching him from the sidewalk, from windows and tiers of balconies, even videoing his actions with their cell phones. The police would surely be on the way…and surely now, on top of everything else he had lost, his very soul was damned.

And then a bullet smashed into his upper left chest, just below his collarbone.

Zam staggered backwards a few steps but managed to stay on his feet, momentarily too shocked and stunned to feel pain, or to understand just what had happened to him. But when he heard a second shot fired at him from the rotary, and felt something whiz past his left ear as it bored through the air, his eyes latched onto the figure standing atop the base of the Ruby Empress's statue, leaning back against her body for support, so as to give himself a clear line of sight above the heads of all the bike riders. Zam saw that his helmeted foe had a handgun of his own, and also held it outstretched in both hands, but his gun had a longer barrel and was more accurate.

Zam felt blood flowing down his chest and knew at last he'd been hit, but he thrust his pistol forward again in just his right fist this time—barely even aiming—and fired his fifth and last shot. His bellow of frustration and self-pity almost drowned out the gun blast itself.

Two more bullets were fired back at him in rapid succession. One passed harmlessly above his left shoulder. Though in fact his opponent had been aiming toward Zam's chest, the broadest target from a distance, the other slug passed straight through the front of his throat and crashed into one of his cervical vertebrae.

Zam was dead before he fell onto his back.

***

"Forgive me, goddess," Frang muttered, looking straight up at the Ruby Empress's face from below. He almost hoped that with the helmet's dark visor covering his face, she wouldn't be able to recognize him to slate his soul for later damnation. "It was my brother who defiled you," he added, glancing toward her outstretched left hand, which now only held the jagged bottom hemisphere of a red glass sphere.

He had seen his brother drop to the sidewalk. He had felt a mix of satisfaction and regret, and relief that Zam had probably not guessed his identity even up to the end.

Succumbing to the pain from his smashed pelvis and his scoured flesh, he slid down the front of the Ruby Empress's legs to sit between her feet on her pedestal. His right arm dropped heavily to his side, the pistol still gripped in his fist. He heard police sirens approaching. How could he flee from them now, in this condition? They would put him in jail. Ultimately they would back him up against a wall for execution by firing squad.

His head sagged, and his despairing eyes finally noticed where his brother's final bullet had ended up.

In the yellowed grass at the foot of the statue's platform, some bereaved family member had placed a red glass spirit globe like the one he had thrown into *Ultimate Nails* only a matter of minutes earlier. Zam's wild, stray shot had exploded the spirit globe into shards.

In his mind's eye, then, Frang saw a ghost loom up right in front of him, its face only inches from his own: the angry face of a very young child, its eyes as enraged as those of a demon, its mouth stretched impossibly wide in a wail he couldn't hear but which rattled the cells of his brain. The sirens of police vehicles, though, as they pulled up at the edge of the traffic island, substituted for the ghost's unheard cry very nicely.

Frang lifted his revolver again, slipped its barrel past the lower edge of his helmet, pressed its muzzle to the underside of his jaw, and fired a bullet up into his jangling, beleaguered brain.

***

Not even a month after the nail salons *Superior Nails* and *Ultimate Nails* had folded, a brand new nail salon named *Heavenly Nails* opened for business at the roundabout.

MOTHERBOARD

Leep was playing a computer game when his two-year-old sister Fhu Fhu was killed.

The game was based on the adventures of Cholukan, the Holy Monkey, specifically focusing on his adventures in Hell rescuing the beautiful virgin who had become his obsession. But Cholukan could return to the mortal plane at various points in the gameplay, transported with the magical help of the Gold-Scaled Dragon, and visit the pretty little hamlet where the virgin Bhi Tu lived and from whence she had been kidnapped by demons.

In this village, Leep (in the form of Cholukan) could save his game progress at a temple, buy supplies or upgrade weapons at various shops, and restore his health at an apothecary. He welcomed these stays in the village, and often prolonged them, strolling the flower-bordered lanes between simple cottages with tiled or thatched roofs, playfully chasing and scattering the ducks by the edge of the pond, talking with everyone he met on his meanderings. Leep felt more comfortable interacting with these people than he did those who lived in his own neighborhood.

Leep associated many things in his life with specific colors. He found colors sometimes held mysterious significance other people were apparently not conscious of. For instance, he strongly associated *green* with this little fantasy village inside the Cholukan game. Green was the color of transcendent peace.

As exciting as the game was, in Hell where it primarily took place, Leep would have been quite content if all it offered were these excursions into Bhi Tu's hamlet.

Leep's mother had asked him to watch Fhu Fhu while she cooked, so he hadn't put on his headphones as he normally would to properly immerse himself in the game. So it was that he heard a single odd squawk come from just outside. After which he heard his mother shout from the kitchen, before she began screaming outside in the little courtyard of their home.

That was when he remembered Fhu Fhu.

He jumped up from the computer desk and rushed outside in time to see his stepfather's car rolling forward, to move its rear wheel off Fhu Fhu's body. Leep's mother was pushing the back of the car, as well. When the wheel was off Fhu Fhu, Leep's mother swept the child's limp body up against her chest and turned to run back inside the house. Leep's bare-chested stepfather scrambled out of the car and raced after his wife.

Later, Leep would learn the sequence of events, for an old neighbor woman who had been sitting in front of her home had seen everything while husking ears of corn. Overhearing that her father was going to the market, Fhu Fhu had gone out to the car unbeknownst to her parents, patting at its tail end and waiting for her father to come and load her inside. But when he had slipped into the car and begun reversing it out of the courtyard, he hadn't seen his daughter behind the vehicle.

Once the whole story was filled in for him, Leep screened it like a film in his head, countless times over the months to come. Especially in the days immediately following Fhu Fhu's death it became a nearly ceaseless loop, seemingly running even when he was asleep. The film loop raised endless questions for him, such as: why hadn't his stepfather put on a shirt before going to the market? Why hadn't his stepfather thought to bring Fhu Fhu with him? Why had Leep's panicking mother carried Fhu Fhu inside the house instead of into the car, so they could bring her straight to the hospital? Not that it would have mattered, ultimately, but her actions seemed illogical to Leep. Did she see the car as untrustworthy, at that point, a thing of menace?

And mainly, for whatever reason, Leep thought about the dress Fhu Fhu had been wearing. It was a thin little dress of a bright reddish-orange color. Sunset orange. *Orange*. Why had his mother selected this dress specifically that morning? Was there some significance to it, some cosmic symbolism that was lost on him? When she dressed her daughter that day, his mother hadn't suspected it would be the last time (because others changed Fhu Fhu into her white funeral dress, after they had bathed her; Leep's mother was in no condition to perform these duties herself). It could have been another dress, another color, but it wasn't. So many things could have been different. But they weren't.

In an alternate system of events, Fhu Fhu could have still been alive.

When his mother rushed past Leep into their house, carrying his crushed sister, she met his eyes and shrieked, "You were supposed to be watching her! Stupid! *Stupid!*" She might have hit him if she weren't so preoccupied. Leep just stood there helplessly, saying nothing, feeling dream-like and disconnected. His shirtless stepfather chased after his wife, looking stricken and guilty...but as far as Leep knew, his mother never ended up accusing her husband. He had supported them ever since the death of Leep's father, who had been accidentally electrocuted working on power lines.

In the days and months that followed, Leep's mother would point at him and sob, "It should have been *you* killed, instead of your precious sister!"

"Now now," his stepfather would soothe his wife, now that he was assured she didn't blame him for their daughter's death, "you know the boy is crazy."

In the past, before his stepfather had come along to care for them, Leep's mother would sometimes weep in despair, "It should have been you killed, stupid child, instead of your father."

And though Leep could understand this sentiment, he himself didn't wish he had been electrocuted *instead* of his father—a good-humored, patient man, who had taught Leep how to use the family computer. Rather, Leep wished he and his father had been electrocuted *together*.

There was one man in Bhi Tu's green village who tended a vegetable garden in front of his cottage. His dialogue was minimal—just things like, "Have you talked to the monk yet? He can help you remember where you have journeyed thus far." Or simply, "Good day to you, Mr. Monkey!" Leep liked to stop and talk with this villager in particular, though, because he bore a superficial resemblance to his father.

But within hours of Fhu Fhu's death, Leep's mother tore their computer system apart, and carried the components out into the courtyard one by one, dashing them to the ground, littering the dusty pavement with broken pieces of plastic, metal, and bare electronics. The villager tending his garden still trapped inside, unseen, like a miniature genie.

***

Leep never joined his coworkers in the large cafeteria of the Oki-Me Electronics Plant at break time. Instead, he would sit at one of the computer stations adjacent to his work area, munching a snack he'd brought with him, and making use of some private time to go online…since his family still didn't have a home computer, even six months after Fhu Fhu's death.

One of his favorite computer activities of late was to access a virtual globe program, which allowed one a full geographical perspective of the world via composited satellite information…viewing the planet from afar as an alien explorer might, or zooming in so close that it was as if one stood as a tourist in the street of a given city, no matter how far away it might actually lie.

In his own country, he could view the grounds of the Nia-Fa Theme Park. The gigantic monster heads one entered to experience the ten Hell attractions were made humble and small seen from far above. Sometimes he typed in his own house's address, and could hover above it like a bird, making out the courtyard and even his stepfather's parked blue car, but to zoom in more closely everything became blurred. There was no street level view available for his humble neighborhood.

"Trying to peek in pretty women's windows?" one of his coworkers, Ran, teased him upon returning from the cafeteria. She was a few years older than Leep, who had just turned twenty.

"He's trying to peek in yours," joked another worker, an older man named Ketpo, settling in at his work station—one of many in a long double-sided row. Mostly it was young women who worked the assembly, soldering, testing, and inspection areas, but Ketpo had injured his back in an accident in the warehouse.

On Leep's first day it was given to Ran to train him in soldering the PCBs (printed circuit boards), and at that time Ketpo had joked, "Hey Ran, who's your new boyfriend?"

"Jealous, old man?" Ran had replied.

Leep had said nothing, but his face had burned.

Now he quickly closed down the virtual world program and returned to his own work area beside Ran's. Before resuming her work, Ran covered her lower face with a surgical mask, like workers in nail salons used to protect themselves from fumes, or like many women used when riding motorbikes to keep from inhaling exhaust and dust.

On his first day—a month ago now—Leep had worn the spare mask that Ran offered him, but when he realized Ran was the only worker who wore these protective masks he became self-conscious and never donned one again. At the time Ran had explained to him in a cynical tone, "Besides the fact that we're cheap labor, we make these circuit boards in our country for the same reason why you only see our people doing nails in Western countries. That is, it's okay for us to breathe in poisons so long as white people don't have to. People who work on these boards are exposed to lead, acid, formaldehyde, carcinogens. I'm not trying to scare you off, because I know you need the money just as much as I do, but I only want to make you aware. You see Phoop down there? With the short hair?" Ran had lowered her voice and nodded at a woman toward the far end of the assembly line. Leep had had to shift in his chair to see past all the blue telephone-style cords that hung down from overhead like jungle vines, their ends attached to the wristbands they all wore, grounding them. "She's been here for five years now, and she recently gave birth to a son with no arms...just little stubby fingers growing out of his shoulders."

Overhearing this, Ketpo had folded his arms up close to his chest, wiggling his fingers at his shoulders and crossing his eyes.

"Stop it!" Ran had hissed. "Do you want her to see you? How cruel!" She had then said to Leep, "Ketpo just proves my point. If he wore a mask like me, these fumes wouldn't have made him crazy."

Though his face had remained impassive—as it almost invariably was—Leep had flinched inside at the word "crazy." He had heard it all his life. Terms like autism and Asperger syndrome, or schizophrenia, bipolar disorder, Down syndrome, were all but unknown in his country. At best, someone might be thought of sympathetically as "slow." A person suffering major depressive disorder was simply "sad." There wasn't even really "quirky" or "eccentric." There was only crazy. One was either crazy or not crazy.

While the others got settled back in from lunch, reaffixing the blue grounding wristbands that tethered them like prisoners, Leep snuck away to the men's room. Seated on the toilet, he saw an ant sniffing through the channels of discolored grout between the floor tiles. This was the third day he had seen a single ant exploring these avenues. He now believed it was the same creature, unable to find its way out of this grid-like maze. He was careful, standing up, not to accidentally crush it. He considered catching the ant somehow and bringing it outside to set it safely free, but he knew he was late enough back to work as it was.

Sure enough, his team leader Moop was waiting for him upon his return. Scowling as always, arms folded across her chest, severe in her white smock. Ran had whispered that Moop had marital problems of some kind. Moop said to him sharply in front of the others, "Why don't you ever go to the restroom during your break? Why do you wait for break to be over to go?"

"Sorry," Leep muttered, taking his seat and fixing the shackle of his wristband.

Moop moved closer to him, and watched him as he resumed working. Her presence close behind him made Leep nervous, and he was afraid to make an error, but after a few minutes Moop said, "You're doing very well at this."

"Thank you," he said without looking up from his section of the long table.

"I understand this is the first job you've held?"

"Yes," Leep said. "My mother said it was time I helped my family."

"Very good. I'm sure she's proud."

***

When he had handed her his first week's pay from Oki-Me Electronics, his mother had said, "It's the least you can do. Do you know what a good worker your sister would have grown up to be? Do you remember how she would pretend to paint my nails? Only two years old! She could have had her own salon one day. So smart! She would stand behind me and pretend to brush my hair. She might have been a hair stylist!"

Leep himself remembered how on several occasions Fhu Fhu had stood up behind him on his computer chair while he played, and rubbed his shoulders as if to give him a massage...but he didn't bring this up. He didn't remind his mother how Fhu Fhu would cry when he went to the market to buy some things for their dinner, if she couldn't go along with him. "Brother!" she would be calling after him as he left her behind.

"Now now," Leep's stepfather comforted his wife, eyeing the money in her hands wistfully but not daring to ask for it, "our precious baby waits for us to rejoin her one day in the Jeweled Heavens."

Leep himself did not believe in the Jeweled Heavens as described in holy texts. They were an outdated product of an ancient faith. It was illogical that there would be no progress in the spirit realm, while things here on the humble mortal plane were ever surging ahead. To him, beliefs should change with the times…become updated for a modern age.

Yet he said nothing about his sister or his opinions on obsolete religions, after having given his mother the money. He only turned away to go upstairs to his small bedroom.

There, he sat cross-legged on his mattress on the floor, and watched a cartoon on his little TV with its poor reception. His sister had always enjoyed this program. He watched it for her… hoped that somehow she could see it through his eyes.

He was silent as he watched the cartoon, his face mask-like, but tears flowed down both his cheeks.

***

"I've got another headache," Ran moaned through her mask, soldering green PCBs beside Leep. "I tell you, this place will be the death of me."

"Poor dear," Ketpo teased. "Kiss her, Leep—make her feel better."

Leep kept his head down to hide his flushed cheeks.

Ran said, "Shut your rice hole, old man."

"Oh, it's just a little smoke from the solder you're smelling!"

"You'll believe me on your death bed. Do you see how poor people who live near this plant and other electronics plants in our country bake old circuit boards to melt them down, just to collect tiny amounts of precious metal? Have you heard how sick these people get?"

"Yes!" cut in another of the assembly workers, a woman named Lhut who wore her fashionably auburn-dyed hair clipped up in a rooster tail behind her head. "Have you ever seen that family that sits begging on a bench in the park by the river?" She pointed in what she felt was the park's direction. "Mother and two children! They were poisoned from the mother melting down circuit boards, and because they sleep in one bed, one night all three of them fused together into one wretched creature!"

"Oh, I know who you mean," Ran said. "Yes, it's terrible, but that's a gigantic tumor, Lhut…people can't blend together like that."

"I'm telling you, they did! I've seen her…it's more than a giant tumor." Lhut shuddered.

"Anyway, yes," Ran said, "I also heard she was one of those who melt down circuit boards for metal."

Their talk made Leep want to go to the park at the earliest opportunity, to look for this monstrous beggar woman. He hoped it truly was that she and her two children had merged together into a single being. He liked that idea.

***

The various assembly teams at Oki-Me focused on different types of computer components—these utilized by foreign corporations, banks, and even government agencies in their data storage systems. An assembly line might be dedicated specifically to 3.5" disk drives, or 2.5" disk drives, and so on. The line that Leep worked on assembled input/output modules containing expansion cards, these cards being the circuit boards he and Ran soldered.

Even when he wasn't soldering the printed circuit boards—only placing the finished i/o modules atop rubber mats on the shelves of wheeled racks, to be brought for testing and inspection—the complex mosaics of their surfaces fascinated him. Standing apart from his assembly line, with no one nearby and piles of cardboard boxes on wooden pallets forming a screening wall, he would often pick up one of the modules to study it up close, turning it this way and that, flipping it over to view its underside. Ran had told him just one of these light, seemingly flimsy little modules averaged six hundred dollars in value overseas, but that wasn't what fascinated him.

What intrigued him was how similar their surfaces looked to cities and towns as seen from a great height, on the virtual globe program he visited during his breaks. He imagined this was how cities looked from an airplane. How they looked from space. Eventually, he had come to imagine that these circuit boards *were* cities...not miniature cities, and not terrestrial cities, but full-sized cities afloat in outer space.

There had been some cataclysm, a catastrophe that had destroyed their home world, but these people had seen it coming, had had enough time to prepare. They had launched a fleet of cities into space, and the city-craft had scattered like dandelion seeds to the depths of infinity.

Each craft was its own unit, self-sufficient, the star colonies varying in size and configuration but sharing common features. Designed purely for interstellar—not atmospheric—flight, they did not need to be aerodynamically streamlined in design. Take this craft, for instance...this rectangular i/o module he held in his hands. Its raised edge, by which it was slotted home like a bureau drawer, was a vast metal wall to help shield the city from particulate radiation in the event the electromagnetic shields faltered.

The city itself was primarily *green*. That is, the foundation upon which it had all been laid out was green, though of course it was not grass or any other vegetative matter but a glossy synthetic surface, its color chosen to soothe the colonists with memories of their dead home world. The conductive pathways of the circuit board's copper "traces" became streets and roads. These streets connected numerous silvery dwellings for the individual colonist families, arrayed in dense rows like suburban neighborhoods, with occasional open areas that served as parks. Trans-formers, transistors, resistors, capacitors, potentiometers, induc-tors, fuses, diodes, oscillators, the battery: all were structures of varying size and function. The general uniformity of the little silver houses was broken up by the larger components, and these became water towers, factories, food production facilities. Huge complexes that helped generate the breathable atmosphere, or the artificial gravity, or helped power the city's platform on its course through the cosmos. A microprocessor or a gray RAM square might be a gigantic shopping mall where the colonists could purchase new clothing and other necessary articles, dine in restaurants, and divert themselves with any number of en-tertainments, including cinemas. (Leep had seen Western shop-ping malls on television, though nothing quite like them existed in his country, not even the so-called Ruby Mall downtown: a glorified department store. Malls were as exciting a concept, in themselves, as an alien world.)

Because there is no "up" or "down" in space, the so-called un-derside of the city platform was inhabited, as well. There were no large components here, this being the "solder side" of the PCB, but "through-hole paths" from the more complex surface of the board to this flatter side enabled the colonists to travel freely from one surface to the other, perhaps when they com-muted to and from work. The underside of the city was devoted primarily to more housing.

Staring down from on high, Leep came up with a name for this particular city adrift in the void. He dubbed it Motherboard.

"Leep?" he heard a voice call for him, somewhere on the other side of the wall of stacked boxes. The voice caused him to jump, and he almost dropped the module with its expensive expansion card.

He quickly set the module back down on its rack. He wasn't

tempted to stash Motherboard away so that he might view it again later (and he certainly wasn't tempted to smuggle it out of the building when he left for home tonight). After all, there were so many identical i/o modules on this same rack, and there would be more of them on the racks tomorrow. Any one of them could be Motherboard.

He would be patient. Just as he waited for his breaks to open the virtual globe program, when the time was right he would visit Motherboard again.

***

Later that afternoon, Leep listened with his head lowered over his work as Ran—in one of her extra-animated, extra-vocal moods—prattled on to him, "Everything can be broken down into the data it's composed of…everything. Even a rock is composed of data, do you know that?"

"Maybe you're right about these fumes being poisonous," Ketpo remarked.

"See what I mean, Leep?" Ran said. "Even Ketpo's rock of a brain is made of data. Though very little."

"Har har," Ketpo said. "Everything is data, huh? I think that's a video game you're thinking of. In a video game, rocks, trees, houses, and silly young girls are made from data."

Keeping his voice low in the hope that Ketpo wouldn't hear him, and without looking up at Ran, Leep asked, "Are people's souls composed of data, too? Do you think our souls could be stored and transferred like computer data?"

Ran swiveled in her chair to stare at Leep for a few speechless moments, as if she couldn't believe these words—so many, and of such a nature—had come out of him. At last she replied, "I don't know about our souls. But our minds, yes, one day I think so."

Leep couldn't understand how she differentiated between the mind and the soul, but he didn't ask her. He was embarrassed he had asked her as much as he had, especially when Ketpo snickered derisively, having overheard his questions.

***

Leep teleported onto Motherboard.

It was how an individual was able to travel between one colony ship and another—within certain limitations of distance, of course. The scattered fleet's scientists were ever trying to perfect the technology, so that one day all of them might teleport to a brand new planet and leave the space craft behind.

In his case, though, he wasn't teleporting to Motherboard from another ship, but from a blighted world that had not proven satisfactory for the colonists to settle. He had been sent there as a scout, and was grateful for leaving it behind, if only for a time. He still had business to conduct on that unhappy world, and wasn't looking forward to going back there.

But right now he was deeply pleased to be walking these placid, ordered streets again. Up close, the pervasive *green* foundation for the multitude of little silver houses and assorted larger structures no longer appeared like grass, but its hue put his heart at ease all the same. A sunny-faced colonist walking along the spotless, plastic-perfect street in the opposite direction beamed at him as they passed each other and chirped, "Good day to you, Mr. Leep!"

In his unhurried meandering Leep came to a park where little robotic ducks waddled ridiculously, cutely, by the edge of a pond of languid liquid mercury. Here he found a woman sitting with her two children on a bench, watching the ducks. Leep stopped before them, for a moment a tad confused; from a distance, seated as close together as they were, he had thought the three of them were a single being.

The mother looked up, grinned and exclaimed, "Hello, Mr. Leep! Welcome back!"

"It's good to be back," he replied.

"Good news, perhaps," the mother said, as her children giggled at the ducks, some of which bumbled into each other comically, while others bobbed on the mercury's reflective surface. "I hear our scientists have scanned a distant planet, which seems capable of supporting life. They are calling it Oasis. It could prove our future home!"

Leep asked, "When do they think we might reach it?"

"Oh, it could still takes years for that, I'm afraid. It's so far off."

This pleased Leep. Though he didn't want to admit it to the woman, he was quite content on Motherboard, and rather preferred that the ship never ceased carrying all of them through the peaceful, silent expanse of space.

His wrist comp beeped, and he lifted his arm to gaze down at the device's tiny viewscreen. A familiar, angry face was framed on the screen. "Oh," Leep said, with a new sense of urgency, and much regret. "I have matters to attend to. I have to go back."

The mother frowned sympathetically. "Already? Poor boy! It must be so hard. Good luck."

"Thank you," Leep said. And he vowed as much to himself as to the woman, "I'll be back soon."

He touched a key on his wrist comp, sending a signal to the city's teleportation facility. Immediately his location was established, and in an unseen flash he was disassembled and whisked back to the blighted world like an attachment to an email. His molecules and his mind transferred like data...and his soul along with them.

***

"Where were you?" Moop fumed. "You've been gone from your station over an hour! Look at the work backed up! Were you in the restroom again? Do you have some problem I should know about? Chronic diarrhea?"

With his face pulsing hot inside, Leep sat at his section of the long table and bent low over his work. He heard Ketpo snort, suppressing laughter.

Moop went on, "You can stay home if you like. I'm sure you have a toilet at home, right? You don't need to come here if you'd rather shit than work." Then she turned on her heel and stomped off.

Leep poised his soldering gun above a circuit board but didn't dare lower its hot tip. His hands were subtly trembling, a disharmonious vibration only he would have noticed. He could feel Ran's eyes on him, and he said very softly without looking over at her directly, "I wasn't gone for over an hour."

"Leep," Ran said in a sympathetic tone, "please be careful. Maybe Moop is exaggerating a little, but it was about an hour."

"I was only loading parts on the rack," Leep protested. Already he had said more than he usually uttered in an entire day at work. At work *and* at home. "Maybe fifteen minutes."

"It was an hour, Leep," Ran insisted gently. "Just watch out, all right? You don't want to get on that little tyrant's bad side."

"Daydreaming too much," Ketpo remarked.

***

This time Leep was careful to use the restroom during his lunch break, closing the virtual globe program earlier than he usually did, to assure that he would be back to his station on time. He had angered Moop enough for one day.

As he sat there, he spotted a tiny ant wandering between the tiles. It had to be the same one he'd been seeing in here lately. Would it never find its way back to its nest, poor thing?

But he noticed another ant, not far from the first. And then, a third. Three of them. So, the creature wasn't all alone after all. Leep smiled.

***

His father had used to bring him down to the park by the river, to see water puppet shows or simply to sit and have a cold drink as they watched lazy rafts of leaves glide by on the current. Aside from walking along the park's periphery on some errand for his mother, Leep hadn't actually visited it for several years now, until this bright weekend afternoon.

The park was mostly green, but not *green*. It was littered with trash and with humans. As he walked its paths, he passed young lovers, and laughing children who reminded him of Fhu Fhu. He tried not to remember her right now, not out here in the open like this. He preferred to conjure her in the solitude of his room when he watched her cartoons on TV. But even as he pushed thoughts of Fhu Fhu away, perversely memories of his father blossomed like flowers growing from a grave.

Just as he hadn't actually witnessed Fhu Fhu's death but had replayed it in his head innumerable times, so had he done with his father's death—actually, before Fhu Fhu's accident and on to this day. His mind had made a movie of the incident based on the script he had learned from those who had witnessed the event. He saw his father, a field worker for an electric power supplier, brace a ladder against a wooden street pole: a former telephone pole made obsolete by cell phones. From the top of the pole branched a mad tangle of power lines, so abundant it seemed they upheld the pole rather than the other way around. But the top of the metal ladder accidentally touched one of the drooping black cables. His father stood there still gripping the base of the ladder in both fists, staring ahead and seeming to tremble, for a terribly long few seconds before he finally slumped down to the ground, where he lay with waves of black smoke coming off him.

Leep liked to think that his father felt no pain in those long seconds. Instead, that he experienced his spirit being transferred out of him…maybe into the power lines themselves, to be spread throughout the web of the entire city. To go on living as a vibrant current, this electric ghost lighting homes and illuminating TV and computer screens. Leep's *own* computer screen.

Feeling saddened by this mental movie, which had begun to loop around and around, Leep considered returning home, but he was uneager to do so. When he'd left on his walk, his stepfather had been out in their little courtyard—shirtless—washing his blue car with a sudsy sponge. Did he still think there might be bloodstains on its surface, a year later? Leep had avoided riding in the blue car since the accident. The rear of the car to him resembled the red-eyed hateful face of a locust.

Just as he was considering whether or not to return home, however reluctantly, at last he spotted the woman he had hoped to find. As he had overheard his coworkers say, she was seated on a park bench. He quickened his pace as he approached her.

Surely someone else, a family member or friend, helped transport her here every day to do her begging. Her tumor was too enormous for her to be able to walk easily on her own. Leep thought it must weigh as much as the woman herself, pinning her down, splayed across her lap and spilling to either side of her onto the bench's seat. Much of the tumor was exposed, her clothing—though apparently adapted to accommodate her deformity—not sufficient to cover it all. These two overflowing mounds of flesh flanked her tightly but in no way resembled children, Leep was disappointed to find. They put him more in mind of shapeless masses of raw protoplasm, undifferentiated matter from which something had yet to take proper form.

The woman noticed that Leep was standing over her, staring, and she mutely lifted a hand to him.

Leep found a few coins in his pocket, and stepped forward to place them in her upturned palm. She nodded at him and withdrew her hand.

"Don't worry," Leep said to her in a lowered, confidential voice, "we're still on course. We'll reach Oasis someday."

***

Leep was soldering a PCB at the shared work table when he became aware of a barely discernible moving dot upon its green surface. The moving dot was *orange*, a shade close to red.

He felt an urgent impulse to dive down into the circuit board, as if plunging from a high cliff into the sea. To project his imagination into it…to teleport to Motherboard right there and then. But no, not in front of the others. So rather than give chase to the orange something, he swung a mounted magnifying lens toward him, one of those that other workers with less keen eyesight than himself used to do their soldering. But when he looked through the lens, the orange dot was already gone.

He had thought it had legs. A tiny mite, then? And if so, had it crawled inside some crevice of the circuit board, perhaps sensing his scrutiny?

When Ketpo and some of the others became engaged in a

noisy conversation, Leep used the opportunity to angle a little closer to Ran and murmur, "Can insects live inside circuit boards?"

"Insects?" Ran repeated. "Well, yes, I've heard of bed bugs in computers. And cockroaches, too—they like being inside anyplace warm. I've even heard people say they saw bugs crawling right inside their LCD screens."

"And mites?"

"Yes, I think I've heard of mites in computers, too. Why, Leep? Did you see a bug on your circuit board?"

"Maybe it wasn't a bug," he muttered, but more to himself than to the pretty young woman.

***

Leep had been careful to set aside the circuit board on which he had thought he'd seen a crawling orange speck. At lunch break, when the others had all gone to the cafeteria, he sat at the computer as he did customarily, but instead of exploring the virtual globe program he held the circuit board in both hands and stared down at it intently.

***

Returning to Motherboard, Leep encountered an alarming scene, disrupting the colony's usual placidity and distracting him from his search for the mysterious orange something-or-other.

Two members of the colony's security force, in their neat white uniforms and helmets, and carrying bulky white rifles, stood to either side of a large blue robot. Their guns were trained on it, ready to fire. The robot had the red-eyed hateful face of a locust.

"Mr. Leep!" one of the security officers exclaimed, when he saw Leep nearing. "Please advise! We caught this robot invading our city."

"I wasn't invading," the robot protested in a deep-chested, metallic voice. "I was drifting through space without a home, abandoned by my makers. I hoped to settle here with you humans."

"It could be lying, sir," the other security man warned. "Perhaps we should take no risks, and destroy it."

"Please!" the hulking machine rasped.

Leep held up a palm. "Wait. This is a city of peace. We don't want violence here."

"Please trust me," the robot begged. "I will work hard to earn my keep."

"We should give it a chance," Leep said.

The guards looked at each other, and slowly lowered their weapons. One of them said, "If you say so, sir. If you trust this robot, we have to trust you."

"Harmony *is* our way," the other guard admitted.

"Thank you, kind people," the robot said, and maybe its red-eyed face wasn't actually hateful-looking, after all.

"But just be careful where you walk," Leep advised the automaton. "You're so big, and we have many children playing about. I don't want you to accidentally crush any of them."

"I promise to be very careful," said the robot.

"Then welcome to Motherboard," Leep said.

"We'll help it get settled in, sir," one security guard said. "And we'll give it a tour."

"Wonderful," said the robot. It started tramping away with heavy, clunking footfalls, the guards escorting it on either side, and swiveled its head around to wave back at Leep as it departed.

Satisfied with how he had handled the situation, Leep tilted back his head and smiled at the heavens. The artificial atmosphere tinted the sky a faint blue, but beyond its translucency was the blackness of space and its myriad pale stars, just barely visible. As he gazed upward, Leep became aware of something else looming behind the thin blue haze of atmosphere. Gradually he realized it was a great face, vast as a god's. Its features were ghostly, rather vague, but the longer Leep stared the more it became evident the god-like face behind the sky was smiling benevolently. And then, holding the face's gaze, Leep realized something else.

The face was his own.

***

A woman's shriek startled Leep, and he was jarred so badly that he felt as though he had been dropped from on high into his chair in front of the computer. He gripped the circuit board in his hands more tightly, so as not to drop it, its hard edges pressing into his palms like knife edges. For a moment, he thought it was his mother's voice, crying out in the driveway while he sat in front of his computer game.

He looked up to see his coworker Lhut standing nearby, staring at him with ballooned eyes. Lhut, with her auburn-dyed rooster tail, who believed the woman in the park was a conjoined family.

"What is it?" Ketpo asked, startled by the woman's scream as well, swiveling around in his chair to look.

Lhut pointed a quivering arm at Leep, her eyes still wide. "He wasn't there a moment ago! I blinked and then he was there! "

Ran jumped up from her chair and rushed to Lhut's side, gently holding her arms. "Lhut, what are you saying? Leep must have just come back from the men's room."

"No," Leep spoke up. "I was here. I've been here through lunch."

"Lunch was finished a half-hour ago," Ketpo told Leep. "Don't lie and say you've been here all along. We all know better. Where do you think Moop is right now? She's looking around for you."

"I was here," Leep insisted softly.

"You can't lie, boy. You haven't been here until just now."

"He's a ghost!" Lhut sobbed, as Ran put her arms around her. "A ghost!"

Ketpo tapped the side of his head behind Lhut's back. "You win, Ran," he said. "These fumes *are* poisonous."

"Come on," Ran said to Lhut, walking her away, "let's get you a drink of water." She glanced back at Leep oddly over her shoulder.

Leep looked down at the circuit board in his hands. In the past, any of the i/o modules could have been Motherboard, but this unfinished PCB was the one with the *orange* mite. He had been jolted out of Motherboard before he could search it out. So he surreptitiously turned his back to the others and slid the board into the front pocket of his loose-fitting trousers. He started to walk away from his work area.

"Hey," Ketpo called, noticing him, "where are you going now?"

Pausing for a moment without looking around, Leep said quietly, "To the restroom."

"*Again?* With all this work backing up, and Ran and Lhut already gone off who knows where?" The man wagged his head. "Boy, when Moop catches up with you you'll be out of here."

"Yes," Leep said in a slow and thoughtful tone, thinking about what Lhut had seen. "I think I'll be out of here." Then he walked away.

***

On his way to the men's room, Leep changed his mind and turned instead toward the cafeteria. He wanted to see Ran first, and she had pulled Lhut away saying their coworker needed a drink of water.

"Leep," he heard Moop call out from an aisle that adjoined the one he was walking down. The aisles in this section of the plant were bordered by racks containing plastic bins filled with cables and other parts, and so far the racks had shielded him from Moop's view.

Swiftly, unnoticed by anyone in this fairly empty area, Leep moved to a nearby corner of the sprawling work floor and backed himself into it until his shoulder blades touched the meeting of the walls. There, he dug the oblong circuit board out of his pocket. Gripping it in both hands, he stared down at it fixedly…even as he heard Moop's voice calling his name again, nearer and louder.

He stood in this same pose on a street of Motherboard, but now instead of the circuit board he was staring down at his wrist comp. On the mini computer's little screen, sandy with static, he saw Moop walking toward him. Was she looking straight out of the screen in his direction? He doubled his concentration. The static cleared, the image sharpened, and Moop kept on walking right past him. Over the device's tiny speaker he heard Moop cry out once more, "Leep, you better have gone home! You better have quit! If I find you, you'll be sorry your mother brought you into this world!"

But her words grew fainter as she stomped farther away, and then Leep transmitted himself back to the unsuitable planet.

***

Lhut screamed again, and dropped the bottle of water she'd been drinking from to seize hold of Ran. Ran whipped around to see that Leep had entered the cafeteria. He hesitated just beyond the threshold, afraid to proceed further and frighten Lhut more.

Surely her cry would attract Moop and others.

"Keep him away!" Lhut pleaded, frantic. Then she let go of Ran to point at Leep accusingly, and commanded, "I banish you, ghost! Be gone!" But when Leep only stood there blankly, Lhut abandoned her exorcism to bolt for another doorway at the opposite end of the cafeteria, leading out to the shipping department and loading docks.

Without even understanding the situation, the teenage girl who worked behind the cafeteria's counter took in Leep's admittedly ghost-like, immobile face and dove into the kitchen.

With Lhut gone, Leep started toward Ran again, walking between the empty tables. She stood waiting for him to reach her, unblinking.

"Leep," she began uncertainly. Then she seemed to falter. Lhut's terror had apparently infected her. She managed to get out, "What are you doing?"

Standing before her shyly, he said, "I just wanted to say goodbye. Thank you for teaching me. You were nice to me."

"You're…leaving?" Ran stammered.

"Maybe you can come with me, if you want. I think I could teleport you, too, if I tried."

Leep wasn't always good at reading the expressions of other people, but if he were to guess, he would have thought that Ran's face conveyed both fear and awe. Still unblinking, she stared at him for a long second and politely shook her head. "I have to stay here, Leep. I'm sorry."

"It's all right," he said. He lifted a hand. "Bye."

Ran mirrored his gesture. "Bye, Leep."

Then he turned back toward the doorway, hoping to make it to the men's restroom before Moop or anyone else spotted and intercepted him. He didn't look back as he left the cafeteria, but he sensed Ran still standing there, watching him depart.

***

"I know you're in there, you crazy boy—I saw you go in!" Again Moop pounded her fist on the restroom door. It wasn't locked, but she was clearly afraid to come in. Still, it could only be a matter of minutes, at best, before a man came into the restroom looking for him. "I'll see that you're fired—do you hear me?"

Leep understood that in being incomprehensible to Moop, he had made *her* into the crazy one. Poor earthbound Moop, so violently unsettled. So representative of her blighted realm. She made him grateful he wasn't one of its indigenous race.

Seated on the closed toilet lid, Leep stared with full focus at the narrow circuit board gripped in both hands. Its green surface so dense with miniature detail. But now that detail started rushing up toward his eye, as if he were piloting an airplane that was plummeting from the sky toward a glittering city below.

The last sounds he heard from the unsuitable world were the restroom door slamming open, followed closely by a fading voice that said, "He's not in here."

***

Motherboard was generous in size, considering it was a city that floated like a dandelion seed through space, and so the giant blue robot had scooped Leep up into its hand and carried him along as it clomped heavily through the neatly laid-out streets. Leep was always happy to reacquaint himself with the city, and he would have been content to be carried along in this manner for a much longer time, but suddenly he noticed a certain silvery cottage up ahead and commanded the automaton to stop and set him down.

A man was tending a little vegetable garden in the front yard of this cottage, and when he saw Leep walking toward him he stopped working, and grinned warmly with recognition.

"Welcome home," the man said.

Leep saw a figure move into the shadowed threshold of the cottage. A very small figure in an *orange* dress. She waved to him, inviting him inside.

He went to her.

DISTINGUISHED MOLE

"**D**octor," Oo said, having cracked open his frosted glass door and poked her head into his office, "I think you need to see this."

"What is 'this'?" he asked the nurse, trying to strike the right balance between authoritative (because he was the new doctor at the clinic, and wanted to establish a sense of respect) and friendliness (because Oo was extremely attractive, in her tight white uniform, glossy hair streaming from under her little cap).

"Our patient, Mr. Ep, who came in with pain in his left ear, and hearing loss."

"What seems to be the trouble?"

"Ear wax."

"More than you can dig out?"

"I'm...afraid to, sir. Perhaps we need to soften the wax with solution and flush it with water."

"And you can't do that?"

"I've never seen such impacted wax before, Doctor," she said sheepishly.

Dr. Bendo Tin sighed with just the right balance of irritation and indulgence, rising from behind his desk, and said, "Take me to him."

***

The middle-aged farmer, Rinpo Ep, sat where Oo had left him, a tray of probes resting on a wheeled table beside his chair. He was squinting in pain, though whether that was from his ear or the bright lamp positioned close to his face, turning his skin red, Bendo didn't know. He said to the man, "Good morning, Mr. Ep. I'm Dr. Tin. Let me have a look at your ear."

Ep looked up at him, scrunching his face more than ever. "*Huh?*"

"Your ear," Bendo repeated, more loudly, as he sat down where Oo had been sitting. She had followed him into the room and stood awaiting his orders just behind him. Bendo indicated his own ear and said, "I'm going to have a look."

"I don't want you to clean my ears," Ep protested, pulling away from Bendo where he hadn't bothered to pull away from the hot lamp before. "I want *her* to do it." He pointed at Oo.

Bendo sighed. He wanted to say that this was a medical matter, not a visit to the local barber, where a pretty young thing would lovingly excavate the wax from your ear while you lounged back like a dog having its belly itched. But he restrained himself and replied, "We are concerned your ears are impacted. This woman is only a nurse; I'm a physician."

"*You?* You're too young," Ep groused.

Bendo ground his lower teeth across his upper for one second, before responding, "Surely you can see I'm older than my nurse."

"Yes, but she's a woman. She's probably been digging wax out of her father's ears since she was ten."

"Eight," Oo said behind Bendo.

Bendo pivoted in his chair to frown at her. She looked regretful.

Ep said, "My daughter Kwen started cleaning my ears when she was just eight, now that I think of it." (He didn't add, though, that his daughter had been his son at that time. Stepson, actually. It was all too much to get into.)

Turning back to his patient, Bendo said, "But nobody has cleaned your ears in a while, I take it?"

"No," Ep admitted. "My Kwen is a grown woman now, with a life of her own."

Bendo took up a pair of forceps—not the simple hook-tipped probe Oo had been using, like those that barber shop cuties employed. He edged his chair closer to Ep and repositioned a magnifying glass that branched off from the lamp's base. "Face the nurse," Bendo commanded. "You can look at her, at least— how's that?"

Ep grunted unhappily, and then winced as Bendo leaned close and inserted the tip of his instrument as if it were an explorative extension of his eyes.

"Gods," Bendo muttered.

"*What?*" Ep asked.

"I said," Bendo told him, "this wax is badly impacted indeed. Hold still, please."

First Bendo worked the closed tip of the forceps past a hard black nugget of wax that completely plugged the entrance to the ear canal. Once he had rolled that boulder out, depositing it on a wad of gauze Oo extended, he found the wax behind it somewhat less fossilized. He dug out another large mass, only to find more wax still filling the canal beyond that. It wasn't until he had coaxed out four big chunks of wax that the canal became unobstructed, a little blood smeared on its pink floor. He imagined Ep's hearing had just improved vastly. But the canal was still not entirely clear. There was an odd object remaining, tucked up to one side as if hiding from Bendo. He took hold of its edge with the forceps, and carefully drew it into view, then out of the man's ear altogether. When he placed this object on Oo's gauze, she let out a cry and dropped the wad to the floor, scattering the black nuggets of wax. But the foreign object was still snared in the weave of the gauze pad: an inch-long winged cockroach, that had probably crawled into the man's ear while he was sleeping, when it had been much smaller, and become trapped there. It was dead—who could say for how long?

Ep looked down at the piece of gauze to which the dead insect clung, and muttered, "Fuck my mother." Then he looked up at the startled nurse and smiled soothingly. "It's all right, my dear. There-there."

"Sorry, Doctor," Oo said, crouching down at last to clean up the mess.

Bendo glared from one to the other of them. Things had to change soon at this clinic. He was tired of the distrust of his patients, and the incompetence of his underlings. He needed to command more respect around here, there was no doubt of that. He needed to prove himself to them.

And to himself.

***

"Come on, come on, everyone," called Dr. Vip, sweeping his arm, gathering in his staff like a teacher wrangling unruly children. The head physician at U Zi U Hospital directed his doctors and nurses to assemble on a few marble steps within the clinic's central courtyard, where a photographer from the city's newspaper waited to take a group shot.

Vip positioned himself at the center of the composition, on the top step so as to appear a head taller than those on the bottom step. Bendo chose to stand on the bottom step on the far left of the group. All the doctors and nurses wore white uniforms, but colorful plastic sandals. Vip turned and picked a gecko off the wall behind him, flicking it away, though geckos were not uncommon in the examination and patient rooms. Cats too frequented the clinic grounds, meandering through the open-air waiting areas, as did women in straw hats hawking lottery tickets to the ill and injured. No feline or human pest threatened to wander into the group shot, however, or Vip would have chased it on its way.

As the photographer lined up his shot, the older nurses glowered sternly at the camera, while the young ones like Oo grinned brightly. Bendo wouldn't have been surprised to see Oo hold up the V sign with her fingers.

Also at the center of the group, but on the lower step so as to appear shorter than Vip, stood a red-headed foreign tourist who had been coming to the clinic every afternoon for several days now. He had suffered a spider bite on his leg which became infected, his limb going swollen and fiery red. The clinic staff had been draining out pus and cleaning the wound, changing his bandages, and giving him shots of antibiotics in the hips. Of course, the pretty young nurses were always beaming at him, as did mothers waiting for their ill children to be seen, forgetting their wailing infants while they smiled hungrily at the white-skinned Westerner, dreaming of giving up everything here for a life in his country.

Vip had insisted on examining the man's leg himself whenever the tourist arrived from the nearby 777 Hotel, frowning with intense scrutiny at the wound and then writing a prescription for oral antibiotics to be taken throughout the day. And then a few minutes ago, Vip had had a brainstorm. With a journalist and accompanying photographer here to do a newspaper story on the clinic, he had pulled his Western patient over to the marble steps, and ordered a lab smock be brought for him, so that the tourist might appear to be a prominent foreign surgeon visiting a renowned clinic. Or he might even pass for a member of the clinic's permanent staff of international medical experts!

Bendo sneered. Here he was modestly standing on the fringe, the latest addition to the clinic's *actual* staff, with a fake positioned at center stage by that pompous liar Vip. Disgusting! Unprofessional! But everyone else seemed to find it quite amusing, all in good fun, including of course the overweight and sun-burned tourist. Vip kept a straight face, though, when the picture was finally taken. The venerable head physician of U Zi U Hospital!

When the group broke up, Bendo started toward his office so as to see his next patient, but Vip came up beside him, taking his elbow and turning him toward the young female journalist. As if anxious to detain the attractive woman longer, Vip told her, "This is Dr. Bendo Tin—the latest addition to our fine staff! He is a graduate of Haikan Medical College, where he won notice for his striking research projects and his imaginative thesis on cellular manipulation, so we are very fortunate to have him."

"Ah!" said the pretty journalist appreciatively, understanding only the "fortunate" part.

Another of the little clinic's seasoned physicians—Dr. Wak—stepped nearer to add, "And Dr. Tin is very fortunate to have *us*, aren't you, Bendo? So that we might give this lofty-minded young man a grounding in the practical experience and knowledge he *really* needs to embark on an illustrious career!"

Wak's choice of phrasing was not lost on Bendo. "*Lofty*-minded." "*Practical* experience." Yes, he had "won notice," as Vip had related, at school—but not necessarily favorable notice. His research and thesis had been much derided. If not, right now he might be working at one of Haikan's major hospitals, instead of at this tiny clinic on the city's outer orbit.

But ignoring Wak's patronizing tone, Bendo smiled politely to the left and right of him at the two older men. Both were still dark-haired, with Wak somewhat younger and more good-looking than Vip, but the two physicians had something more in common. They both had a prominent facial mole, raised and black like a beetle. Wak's rested on his left cheek, with a single long hair growing out of it. Vip's mole was on his chin, and *three* long hairs grew out of it. Such hairy moles were considered a sign of wisdom, so it was undreamed of to have them removed or the hairs trimmed. Several of Bendo's instructors at Haikan Medical College had possessed similar moles (including one frightening old female professor). What he wanted to know, though, was how it was that so many doctors and teachers were fortunate enough to be born with a mole that would put forth such luxuriant growths as they aged. Was it some mysterious genetic trait, that naturally accompanied whatever predisposed an individual for a medical career, or was it quite simply a gift from the gods?

All Bendo knew was he didn't have a single mole on his entire body, except for a flat brown mole near the crease of his bottom. Hardly a mole that he might flaunt to his patients and fellow physicians, though one could always hope a cute nurse might encounter it.

The journalist scribbled some more notes, but the photographer failed to take a picture of Bendo standing between Vip and Wak, as if he found the newcomer at U Zi U of insufficient importance.

***

For a research project in support of his dissertation on tissue engineering at Haikan Medical College, Bendo had used methods of his own design to reproduce cells from the muscles of a pig's heart, forming them into a simple, jellyfish-like structure. (He had seeded the cells in a fine "scaffold" of collagen, which he had cut into a flower-like shape.) This mock jellyfish, when introduced to an electrically charged medium, would respond with a heart's pumping action and thus "swim" like a real jellyfish.

Now, as he sat in front of his computer in his grimy little office at U Zi U clinic, a gecko stuck to the wall above his head making kissy sounds as if to mock him, he read a news story about bioengineers at a Western university who had done the same thing, but using heart cells from a rat supported by a silicone film. There was much excitement about the possibilities. An organic pacemaker! An artificial, organic heart! Swarms of bioengineered jellyfish that might eat oil spills! Oh, these revolutionary, visionary Westerners might make *millions* from their research.

And yet Bendo had been ridiculed by some at Haikan Medical College, his jellyfish either sneered at as a grotesque abomination or laughed at as a mere parlor trick, a sock puppet of living cells. One professor had scoffed, "We've been making dead frogs dance with electrical current for over a hundred years!"

Bendo swore under his breath as he read through the article again, his blood turning to magma in his veins as he considered the possibility that somehow these men had read his thesis. But on a third read, he had to admit that it was next to impossible for the Westerners to have learned of his research. It was like the airplane, developed at various spots in the world at the same time, with one lucky individual (or two brothers, actually) just getting there a little bit quicker.

If only it were not so difficult to obtain a visa to leave this country, he might go to another country where his ideas and skills would be appreciated. Be properly rewarded. Where he would be *respected*. Instead of being stuck here, where the best he could expect was—

"Doctor?" Oo had stuck her pretty head in through his open door, beyond which came the squalling of feverish infants, the crying of children taking a syringe in the hip, the ceaseless rumble of motorbikes in the street outside the clinic's high walls with their murals of the Gold-Scaled Dragon and that trickster, the Holy Monkey, with his red glass orbs for eyes.

"What?" Bendo snapped at her without taking his eyes from the computer screen. He felt like his own eyes were crystallizing into red glass.

"We have an emergency patient you should see. Dr. Vip and Dr. Wak have not returned from lunch."

He swiveled in his chair to face her, angrier still for the suggestion that he should only be considered if those doctors were not available. "What is this emergency? You can't slap a patch of topical analgesic on the forehead of another fevered baby?"

"It's a monk from Va Tung Va temple, Doctor," the nurse said meekly. "He was riding his bicycle near here and was run over by a truck."

Bendo sighed heavily. Very well, then. What else was he to do, now, but ensure that a monk's heart muscles didn't stop their mindless contractions?

He swiveled back to close the news story, bitterly hoping that the foreign researchers' discovery would go awry. That a horde of bioengineered jellyfish released in the ocean to cleanse an oil spill, for instance, bonded together into a single gigantic organism that would rise up to flatten one of those bright, shiny Western cities he would never get to visit.

***

Bendo could tell the moment he laid eyes on the monk (who had been carried on a canvas stretcher from the street to an examination room, right past all the waiting mothers, leaving a spoor of blood drops in his wake) that there was no hope for the old man. Bendo might just as well have ordered Oo to paste a topical analgesic patch on his forehead, for all the good they could do him. Nevertheless, he looked at the nurse—who had a hand clamped over her lower face against the smell of blood and squashed bowels—and barked at her to prepare morphine.

Was it the tenacity of human will, the power of the gods suffusing him, or just a mechanical quirk of anatomy that the monk was still alive, though he had been bisected below the navel? What miracle accounted for the fact that he hadn't yet bled to death or succumbed to trauma and shock? And yet another man might die from a mosquito's bite, attacked by invisible microorganisms. (Bendo supposed compression accounted for the not bleeding to death part.) He almost wanted to laugh that they had piled the monk's lower half onto the stretcher, too, perhaps in the hope that the venerable doctors Vip and Wak, working toward each other from either end, might stitch the man together again.

The monk reached out and seized Bendo's hand with a surprisingly strong grip. The grip did not seem urgent or desperate, however; it was more like the holy man was reassuring *him*. His eyes were locked on Bendo's (though whether he actually *saw* the doctor was another matter), his much-creased face composed, even serene. Bendo was reminded of monks who self-immolated in one protest or another, and admired that inner strength—though he himself had never been a believer in gods and magic, all those dragon lords and mischievous monkeys credited for life's vagaries of fortune. He bent over the monk and said, "We will do all we can for you." Which of course meant nothing but the syringe of morphine that Oo put in his hand, too frightened to stick the holy man herself.

"I should give you enough to put you out of your misery, old man," Bendo muttered as he withdrew his hand from the monk's grip and administered the injection. As he did so, he continued to watch the man's face. He was elderly, shaved bald of course, and on his chin perched a glossy black mole twice the size of Vip's. Furthermore, it sprouted a veritable waterfall of long silvery hairs. Had there ever been a finer mole? No wonder this man was so full of death-defying force.

Bendo himself did not believe in any literal, innate power or good fortune residing in a random melanocytic nevus. But he did understand the cultural importance of such a growth, so he admired and coveted the monk's impressive mole. In fact, it set his imagination whirring.

This man would perish soon, no matter how tenacious. Even a saint could not survive being split in half. Soon he would have no use for that mole of his. Bendo thought that when no one was looking, he might easily excise the mole with a scalpel, hide it away, and later on graft the growth to his own chin (though he might need to manipulate the cells with his special skills to make the transplant take).

Ahh...but that wouldn't work, would it? Firstly, despite his rather distracting wounds, the absence of the monk's mole was bound to be noticed by his fellows when it came time to have the temple's corpse-eating beetles strip away his fleshly vestments and reduce his body to bones. And then, of course, there was the matter of his own fellow clinicians wondering how Bendo Tin had suddenly sprouted such a magnificent mole. True, there were "congenital moles" and there were "acquired moles," yet one didn't acquire them overnight. No, it just wouldn't work.

But Bendo's imagination did not easily take no for an answer, and continued to buzz as the doctor set his empty syringe aside. Another idea replaced the first, like some organic thing springing to life in his head. A flower opening, a pig heart/jellyfish throbbing.

"Close that door!" he commanded Oo, motioning toward the threshold to the examination room, which was packed solid with gawking patients, nurses, and the blood-stained citizens who had transported the monk here. Just as at any traffic accident or crime scene—such as an all too common drunken machete attack—a number of cell phones had been extended, recording videos to be shared on the internet. "Give the man some privacy, all of you! Show some respect!"

To her credit, Oo pushed them all back, and managed to close the door, though their blurred shapes lingered beyond the frosted glass. She turned to face Bendo, but he was bent over the monk again, his back blocking his actions.

He had unwrapped another syringe, pushed its tip into the monk's mole, and drawn back on the plunger. As he did this he watched the old man's face for a reaction, but his quivering lids half veiled his eyes, which had rolled up white in their sockets. It wouldn't be much longer. Perhaps the last dregs of his life force, still charging his body, would permeate these stolen particles of him. Bring luck to this physician who had no faith in luck, only in tangible science.

"Doctor?" Oo inquired nervously, afraid to peek past him at the holy man, martyred to the material world, his blue silken robes smeared with blood and pulped green melons that the truck had been carrying. "Is he...?"

Straightening, slipping the syringe into his lab coat's pocket, Bendo looked again to the monk's face. "Yes," he announced plainly, "he is."

***

Bendo knew he couldn't pursue his project at the clinic in un-
disturbed privacy. He could certainly scare the nurses off, but
sooner or later Vip or Wak would stick their nose in his business. That was okay, though, since he had almost everything he
needed at home, and what he couldn't easily buy he could easily
steal from work.

Not that his apartment-cum-laboratory was spacious. It was
the only good thing about not having a wife: their elbows would
have been poking each other in the ribs at every movement. It
galled him that he had to live this way. A man of his brilliance—
there, he said it outright in his mind, *brilliance*—living like a
peasant in this closet of an apartment! No money, and hence
no space and no woman. Well, he would change all that. One
step—one cell, if he must—at a time.

The former tenant of this apartment, B-2, had used it as a hair
salon and to give massages; which, Bendo figured, meant she
had also been a prostitute. The little front room, its face open to
the bustling street, had served as the salon but also as the young
woman's living room, with a TV suspended from a bracket near
the ceiling. Crammed into one corner, a sink, fridge, rice cook-
er, and hotplate stood in for a kitchen. Behind a curtain at the
back of the room were a tiny bathroom and a bedroom nearly as
tiny, dank with the imagined dregs of sex.

Bendo kept the metal shutter that served as a front wall closed
and bolted at all times. He had set up a work table and shelves
of books and supplies in the former salon room, and his computer of course, but he had left the ceiling as it was. Dark, bare
wooden boards, from which numerous folded paper birds hung
on strings, along with dozens of stars cut from colored paper...a
crumpled and worn universe that the girl had probably formed

with her own hands, in the hours of boredom between customers. A project to give her something more artistic to focus on, apart from her usual drudgery. How he could relate.

Tonight, as had become his custom, Bendo rolled up towels and pressed them against the bottom of the metal shutter to keep out dirt and noise, to shut out the limitations of his culture and his country, before he returned to his own artistic project. It was the best he could do to establish a sanitary environment under these regrettable conditions.

Though he had been rusty at the start of the project, when he'd hit his pace he'd entered into a happy delirium that sustained him in the days that followed. It was like making love again after too long of an abstinence. This had become more than a bid for greater respect. It was a challenge of his *craft*.

One formula that helped fuel his efforts, one which he had never employed while in school, was the strong fermented rice wine he had taken to drinking in the evenings since starting at the clinic…in increasing quantities, as if in some ongoing experiment into his own personal tolerances. This evening upon arriving home he filled his little cup before he even began fretting over his petri dishes, having made some excuses for anxiously leaving work two hours early. As if his *real* work awaited him at home.

Bendo always listened to sad songs by female singers, too, while he worked. But then, weren't all songs in his country, by female or male performers, depressingly sad? Magically, the more he would drink, the sadder these warbling laments would become. They were like a future soundtrack for the hearts he would break when his fortunes finally turned.

At the beginning of this endeavor he had been careful in formulating a variety of growth media in which to propagate the explant cells from the old monk. He had had to take into consideration that the ability of cells to reproduce depended on the donor's age, and compensate for that accordingly. The base medium, which he tweaked differently for each petri dish, was his own unique recipe—and his skills in this area had gone unappreciated at school. Ha! Most of the professors there wouldn't know a growth medium from the fermented fish sauce they dipped their spring rolls in.

Yes, so many factors to balance as he established and nurtured the *in vitro* culture that he portioned out into his dishes. Cellular proliferation rate...the cycle of mitosis during the expansion of the melanocyte population...duration of the cells' productive period. He utilized "controlled death" (and how he loved that term; so god-like) conditions, optimal for cellular replication. Furthermore, when it came time to transplant the cells to his own body, he had to be sure they would be accepted. This would be accomplished through "chimerism," such as when a host received a bone marrow transplant from a donor, tricking the body into not rejecting foreign cells so that they would exist compatibly.

He refilled his cup with 777 brand rice wine as he divided his attention between inspecting the culture's progress, and steaming some prawns in a big metal pot on the hotplate he'd inherited from that unnamed girl. She haunted this apartment like a ghost, an invisible companion whom he felt an odd attachment to, for lack of anything more substantial. The more he drank, the more real her presence became, and he fantasized he was cooking for the two of them.

And the more he drank and the sadder the songs became, the more he spoke aloud to the cells as he hovered over them, studying their growth and nodding in approval. "Beautiful," he purred, "beautiful." As if he were appreciating a naked woman's entire body instead of mere scraps of human architecture. But when he came to examine his last petri dish tonight, his brow furrowed. Though he hadn't overfilled the dish with medium, it looked as if he had. A silvery-gray film had grown up over the edge of the dish, all around, and had even started overflowing onto the table itself in a thin, rubbery membrane. It looked like a gigantic amoeba, extending pseudopods as if to hoist itself free from its confines and escape. The growth had been so rapid since he'd checked this petri dish before work, that he felt if he stared at the membrane long enough he would actually see it inch forward.

"Too strong a medium in this one," Bendo muttered to himself, shaking his head but intrigued. He prodded the film with a gloved finger. "Overcompensated…definitely overcompensated for the age of the donor."

Meanwhile the feelers of the giant prawns hung out from under the pot's lid like a circle of fine tentacles. They had been alive when he'd brought them home in a plastic bag from a market just down the street, and had tried nipping him with the tiny pincers at the ends of their long, vividly blue forelimbs as he introduced them into the pot of water. When they were cooked he'd crack their shells, now turned orange, and dip the thick meat into a mixture of salt, pepper, and lime…another of tonight's formulations.

As soon as his cup was empty he filled it again, for the fourth time. He spoke more loudly to the room…to his cells and his invisible lover. "I will grow a fine mole, with long hairs like corn silk, and I will return to that backward medical school and strut before my professors and they will *envy* me my distinguished mole!" He was grinning wildly, yet also felt tears dribbling down his cheeks. Damn sad songs. But he only turned toward his computer, in which he played the CD, and cranked the volume louder. He then waltzed about his cramped little laboratory with the ghostly hairdresser/masseuse, bumping the central work table with his hips and spilling his rice wine. "Envy me!" he cried again, over the loudness of the music.

***

In his dream, it was his hairdresser/masseuse/prostitute girlfriend who sang the morose songs to him while he worked, yet she still remained unseen...somehow hidden from him even in apartment B-2's tight confines.

Bendo stood at his hotplate, tending a dented tin pot so large it rested on both burners. The pot was full of a bubbling concoction, a translucent gray sludge, which Bendo stirred and poked with a long pair of tongs. Rising into view and submerging again, at his prodding, were a number of hard white masks with empty holes for eyes, nostrils, and mouth. In the dream he knew the composition of the masks was organic.

As the masks boiled in the big pot, they gradually melted down and became more of that sludge, a sugary thick protoplasm. All that was left of the masks when they dissolved were support struts, or something of that sort, which resembled the long blanched forelimbs of a crustacean.

When the last mask had joined the broth, satisfied, Bendo took up a ladle in place of the tongs, scooped up a bit of the primordial ooze, blew the steam from it, and delicately drew in a sip.

He smacked his lips, and announced, "It's ready."

While his phantom lover went on lamenting.

***

Bendo awoke on his back on the floor, gazing up at the firmament of wooden boards and lazily twirling paper stars.

His head was aching at the front from the rice wine, at the back from perhaps falling and striking his skull against the floor. But the pain in his jaw was inexplicable. It wasn't until he sat up, with a drawn-out groan, that he noticed the syringe dangling against his neck, its needle still plunged deeply beneath his skin to the right of his chin.

He reached up and pulled the needle free, wincing as he did so, and examined the syringe's barrel. Whatever it might have contained, it was now completely empty.

"Gods," he hissed aloud, pulling himself to his feet. "Which culture? Which medium?"

He found several of his petri dishes swept to the floor, probably when he'd passed out, making it harder to determine which one he had filled the syringe from. Possibly from more than one dish, even, gods forbid? And then, even more frustrating, was one of the petri dishes that still rested on the table. Like the syringe, it was absolutely empty. And yet the label taped to it indicated this dish was the one in which he had observed that rampant cell growth last night.

Bendo whirled around, looking at the floor. It was possible he had destroyed the over-stimulated cells last night and then cleaned the dish out, but he didn't think so.

He got down on hands and knees, peeking under his shelving units. He took his search to the bedroom and bathroom. Finally, when he returned to the front room, he realized that a strong burnt reek he had been smelling came from the pot on his hotplate, which he had never shut off. All the water had burned out of the pot, which had blackened, the prawns inside charred and withered. He shut the burner off to resume his search.

It was then that he noticed one of the rolled up towels against the shutter's bottom looked somewhat disturbed. He unbolted the shutter and rolled it to one side. The metallic clamor, the stabbing brightness of sunlight, and the stench of gasoline from the chaotic street spiked into his skull.

Two boys stood on the sidewalk, looking down at something the older of the pair cupped in his hands. Bendo took a few steps closer to them, and got a look at the object. A flattened thing like a patty of grayish gelatin, ringed with long silvery hairs like cilia. It somewhat resembled some unknown type of jellyfish.

"Mutation," Bendo mumbled, in awe. "Spontaneous cellular differentiation."

His slurred voice alerted the two boys, who looked over at him.

"Hey!" Bendo barked, starting toward them again. "Give that here!"

Startled, the children spun and bolted, the larger boy still holding his newfound pet.

"Damn them," Bendo grumbled, standing helplessly as he watched the boys disappear around the street corner.

**

That day at work Bendo only experienced soreness in his jaw from having jammed the syringe in there so far (and he felt lucky he hadn't fallen on his face when he passed out, driving the needle in even further), but on the second day when he was shaving he noticed a small raised bump to the right of his chin. It looked like a pimple, with the red dot where he had injected himself forming its center.

On the third day, though, the bump had grown more distinct and taken on a bluish hue, like the fake tattooed beauty marks women often acquired.

Bendo experienced an exhilarating gratification, tasting of vindication, that he had succeeded in his challenge…but also a wariness mixed with that. The growth rate of his mole was more rapid than he had anticipated. Perhaps he had succeeded too well.

By the fourth day, with the mole going from blue to black, he caught Oo whispering to another nurse and motioning toward him. When the nurses saw he'd noticed them, they grinned shyly, nodding and waving. He smiled, once again exhilarated but wary. When Oo was alone in his office with him toward the end of the day, he casually said, "Nurse...that is, Miss Oo...I'm going to stop for dinner at a wonderful seafood restaurant near my apartment on my way home tonight. I'd like to thank you for the loyal service you have shown me since I began at our clinic. Would you care to join me?"

Oo blinked her eyes rapidly, hovering beside him awkwardly, and finally stammered, "I would love to, Doctor, but my mother...my mother has been ill, so I must cook dinner tonight for her and my father. Another time, please?"

"Oh...um, very well," Bendo said, quickly returning his gaze to his computer. "Of course, you must tend to your family."

He wasn't sure whether to believe her or not. Could it be he had misinterpreted the whispers of the two nurses earlier? Perhaps his mole wasn't sufficiently big, black, or hairy enough yet to impress them.

He was preparing to leave for the day—alone—when Dr. Vip called to him through the open door of his office. He ventured inside, and the smiling chief physician, seated behind his desk, invited Bendo to sit across from him.

"Dr. Tin," Vip said without preamble, "I can't help but notice there is an unusual discolored growth on your chin."

"What, sir?" Bendo asked, as if he had no idea what the man was referring to. But finally he touched his chin and said, "Oh... this?" He chuckled. "It's nothing, sir, just a mole manifesting late in life. I had an uncle with one just like it, and my mother has a mole on her chin, though hers is flesh-colored." This latter example was actually true.

Vip knitted his brows and cocked his head quizzically. "But the onset and development are so rapid, Dr. Tin, I fear it may be something other than a mole...such as a melanoma."

"Dr. Vip, with all due respect, would it be any more common for a melanoma to develop this rapidly?"

"There may be abnormalities in the genes that control cell growth," Vip replied. Bendo was surprised he even knew the concept of genes. "We should really do a biopsy on that."

Bendo sat up rigid in his chair and said, "Oh no...no, sir, there is no need for that."

"I really think there is, Doctor—I'm concerned about you. A biopsy will be easy enough, as you well know...I'll do it myself right now."

Bendo bolted up from his chair, more abruptly than he had intended. "Really, sir, that isn't necessary."

Vip stood up from his own chair. "Please, Dr. Tin, I *insist*."

Bastard liar, Bendo thought. The chief physician was intimidated by his ascendant mole—that was it. He wanted to nip it in the bud...put this upstart in his place...hold him back... castrate him, in effect.

"I can't, sir, not now...really, I must get home," Bendo stuttered. "My girlfriend has been ill and...and I need to cook dinner for her. She'll be expecting me."

"Doctor..." Vip started moving toward him. Bendo expected him to pull a scalpel out of his lab coat's pocket at any moment.

"I'm fine, sir, fine!" Bendo blurted, and he turned and darted out through the doorway. He called back, "Thank you for your concern, sir, but it isn't necessary! Isn't necessary!"

Vip was still calling after him as Bendo fled toward the row of motorbikes leaning in the shadow of the high wall surrounding the little clinic.

***

Bendo dreamed of owning a car, and not some laughable dwarf-ish toy like the city's garishly colored taxis, but a handsome West-ern vehicle. For now, however, like most of the city's inhabitants he got around on a motorbike. So he rolled his bike backwards out of the row, mounted and started it and sped out through the gate as if fleeing the scene of a crime. He almost smashed into a man staggering drunk and in shock onto the clinic grounds with deep machete wounds gaping shockingly in his body. Good—that would refocus the chief physician's attention.

Up until only a few years ago helmets for motorbike riders hadn't been required, but now it was strict law. Vip had told him the clinic had seen a marked decrease in head injuries, except with small children riding as passengers, for some reason (no small helmets?) overlooked by both parents and police in regard to that law. Helmet styles varied widely, most covering only the top and back of the head, though Bendo himself had chosen a full-head style with a darkly tinted face shield. He thought it made him look like a character from some exciting movie.

He didn't bother removing the helmet when he stopped at a seafood market on his way home and picked up a bag of live crabs for dinner. They rustled in the membrane of their plastic bag as he carried them back to his bike.

Bendo didn't remove his helmet until he let himself into his apartment, leaned his bike just inside where it cramped his space even further but wouldn't be stolen, then closed and locked the corrugated shutter again. As he lifted the helmet off his head, the lower part of the visor met some resistance on its inner surface and he felt a slight tugging at the flesh of his chin. Setting the helmet on his work table, now cleared of all his petri dishes with the success of his experiments, he reached up to touch his chin where the helmet's visor had met resistance. There, his fingers encountered a protuberance. It was rubbery but firm. It felt like the finger of a small child, protruding from his jaw.

Bendo darted to his tiny bathroom, slapped at the switch to turn on the fluorescent over his mirror. When he saw his reflected face, even though he believed in no gods he evoked them once again.

The rubbery protuberance *was* as long as the finger of a small child. Black at its base, it gradually shaded toward gray until its rounded tip was almost translucent. Again he touched it, fingered it, but more gingerly and with revulsion, as if it were some unpredictable parasitic insect affixed to his jaw.

"What, what, what?" he chanted, circling around and around his work table, since that was the only area with enough room in which to pace. "What, what, what?" As if to ask what was happening, and what to do about it, at the same time.

Until he could settle on a better course of action, he stopped his pacing long enough to fill his favorite cup with some 777 rice wine.

"Accelerated growth rate *increasing*," he blubbered after he had gulped the wine in one swallow, a few drops spraying from his wet lips. "I've got to cut it off, that's all. Got to cut it off…"

He pawed through his collection of medical instruments until he found a scalpel and some other articles he would need, and returned with them to the bathroom mirror, meanwhile ranting loudly, "Bastard monk! What kind of magic is this, huh? The same magic that kept you alive while split in two pieces, damn you?"

He might just become a believer in spiritual matters, after all.

Bendo filled a syringe with Lidocaine, then injected himself at the base of the growth. He grunted at the pain, the area no doubt tender from when he had injected the monk's cells in the first place. He withdrew the needle and injected more of the anesthetic on the other side of the anomaly, praying that the numbing effect would spread quickly. But the pain in this spot was even greater—so great that Bendo gasped and dropped the syringe. Its glass cartridge shattered. Lights flared in his vision like the flashbulbs of all the photographers he had dreamed, in school, would one day gather when the world caught word of his discoveries.

He grabbed at the edge of the sink in an effort to stay on his feet, but only knocked an open bottle of povidone-iodine into the basin, spilling its dark yellow contents. His fingers slipped off the stained porcelain, and he toppled backwards.

He seemed to fall down a deep dark well for a long, long time, until he lost sight of the circle of light where he'd entered it.

***

He dreamed that giant prawns filled his tiny apartment. Prawns with bodies as long as people. Like the cockroach he had removed from that patient's ear, they must have sneaked into his flat while still quite small. Since then, though, they had grown with unnatural swiftness, to unnatural proportions.

As if to avenge their charred comrades, the prawns he had recently steamed to death and then overcooked, the mammoth crustaceans had all reached out to Bendo with their long, beautiful blue forearms, and seized onto his flesh with their toothy pincers. They had all latched onto him at the same spot: his jaw.

They pulled at him, as if to rip away chunks of his flesh to feed upon. The pain was intense, beyond any pain even he as a physician would have believed possible. Maybe they wanted to dig into him for a morsel they coveted more than mere flesh. Maybe they sought to consume his very soul.

Yes, that was it, for he felt his essence being dragged out of his fleshly vehicle, just as he had meant to extract the succulent meat from the shells of their brethren. He looked down at his body as they wrenched him out of it, saw himself splayed senselessly on the floor of his apartment in a little puddle of Lidocaine and rice wine, like the discarded husk of a cicada.

***

Bendo's own groaning awakened him. The agony made him want to flee from wakefulness again.

As he had seen in his dream, he lay on his back on the floor of his apartment. His soul had not been torn out of this suffering shell. If only it had! He wanted nothing more than to be free of himself. Especially when his mind fully registered what his eyes were seeing.

Above him: the bare boards of the wooden ceiling, from which dangled the familiar folded paper birds and colored stars the nameless hairdresser had hung there. But there was now an additional, unfamiliar element. Perhaps a dozen long vines, as thick around as his wrist, had grown upward and fixed their ends to the dark wooden boards. These tubular, flexible growths were a silvery-grayish color, translucent, resembling the tentacles of a giant mollusk but without any suction cups. They were spread above Bendo like the cords of a parachute, anchored evenly across the whole span of the ceiling. And he knew the point from which they had sprouted, because he could feel a strange combination of pressure and tugging where they were rooted against the bone of his lower jaw.

The tentacles were his own flesh, commingled with the monk's. His own traitorous cells, run rampant…reaching out hungrily or spitefully, to embrace or throttle the very world should they continue to grow and grow.

Bendo gurgled a sob. It was the most articulate sound he could wring out of himself.

He tried to prop himself up on one elbow, as the first step toward sitting up, which would be the first step to standing, but he collapsed onto his back again. His weakness was not only from the pain, but from terror. While he waited for both to subside somewhat, he forced his eyes to their limits, to the right and left of him, in the hope that he would spot his scalpel on the floor and within arm's reach. But if it had fallen to the floor, and not in the sink, it was out of his range of vision. At this point he dare not even turn his head.

He wanted to sob to the monk that he was sorry for defiling his body…for the theft of his flesh. And he also wanted to curse the monk again, and voice the hope that his tainted old flesh poisoned and killed every one of his temple's sacred horde of corpse-eating beetles. But he could do neither.

Bendo lay there a long time, afraid to try moving again, listening to traffic passing in the street outside his locked metal shutter. Waited as the night deepened. He heard sad music playing loudly from a neighbor's apartment, recognized it as the melancholy theme song of the soap opera *B-2*, which they must be watching on television. The music made tears stream from the corners of his eyes.

But gradually the pain diminished and finally went away altogether, as if the Lidocaine had finally taken effect, though he knew intuitively that it had more to do with changes that were underway. He reached both hands up to his lower face tentatively, hesitated, then felt at his jaw with trembling fingers.

Yes, his flesh there was numb, but that gave him little comfort, because his flesh also felt different to the touch. It had the cool, fragile feel of gelatin, as if its surface might break if he probed it too forcefully. The numbness, and the gelatinous quality of his flesh, extended up both sides of his face to just under his eyes. He realized his face was liquefying. If he waited much longer to act, how far would this effect spread? Until his very brain liquefied?

Panic came over him anew, and he closed both hands around the single thick trunk that had emerged from his jaw, from which all its hydra necks had branched out. He pulled at the growth as if to uproot it. To his surprise, this desperate act bore results. He felt the thick root coming away from him in his hands. But unfortunately, though there was no pain involved, he realized the flesh of his lower face was sloughing away along with the root. So be it, then! He would get skin grafts, even if he had to beg Vip and Wak to do the work!

He continued to pull the root away, but not only did the gray, translucent flesh of his cheeks come away with it. When he finally tore the growth entirely from his face, and released the trunk to let his arms drop limply to his sides, he saw an odd object dangling at the swinging end of the octopoid form clinging to the ceiling. That swaying pendulum was his entire lower jawbone, bearing all its teeth.

Bendo moaned, and shut his eyes to escape from this nightmare. The theme of *B-2* played on, and fresh tears ran down the sides of his face, across his exposed cheekbones. His consciousness bled out of him, as if it were borne along in his teardrops. His body, spread-eagled upon the floor in a star shape, lay still for a long time. Then it gave one final, violent shudder, and went still forever.

***

The tentacled thing survived being struck by a surprised motorbike rider (a teenaged girl with glasses who'd been speeding, though she scrambled back onto her bike with only a skinned elbow and sped away in panic again). It even survived several machete whacks from a drunken man whom it also startled, consequently dragging one nearly severed limb for several hours until its wound healed. It quickly learned to stay out of sight as best it could, hiding in a coiled mass in some confined dark place during the day and moving about only at night...darting through streets, clambering up walls and across rooftops.

It was still glimpsed occasionally, though only briefly. Those who witnessed it in its furtive, slithering-scurrying movements described it to family or friends and a few times to skeptical police officers as a "huge spider"...a "land octopus"...the "hand of a giant ghost"...a "demon." One man who saw it up close noticed the partial face that grew from the neck from which all the sinuous limbs radiated. He told police it had only a lower jaw, and a rubbery mask-like face with wide, wild eyes. He couldn't quite express that the eyes stared like those of some tourist to a country he wasn't prepared to encounter...or a newborn thing in an alien world.

For the tentacled visitor's cells had not entirely stopped growing, and from the scrap of its host's face it had grown a little more of his face, including fresh new eyes with which to take in this disorienting, exotic but nightmarish world it had been cast into.

It collected observations in an attempt to understand its place in all this. It peeked into open-air cafés at night, where constellations of blue cell phone screens dotted the darkness. The citizens of this unnamed place were engaged in a love affair with these devices (which of course the visitor couldn't comprehend, though it seemed to have a niggling half-memory of them; all sorts of unformed memories tickled at the back of its consciousness). In the day, peering out from its current hiding spot, it would see people squatting on the sidewalks studying their little screens as if trying to divine their futures from them.

It stole a glimpse of a wedding held at an outdoors restaurant, where a red pavilion had been erected over the tables. A huge blown-up photograph of the couple, computer-enhanced to unrealistic perfection, leaned on an easel outside. Undulating up the front steps of the restaurant, a pair of metallic-scaled dragons—teenage dancers crouched inside their skins—represented the bride and groom.

Elsewhere it witnessed an almost identical ceremony: red pavilion, tables, but this time the teenaged dancers portrayed lions, and the occasion was a funeral.

However leery since its accident, the visitor was mesmerized by the unending movement of the streets—motorbikes like shoals of fish, though their shared direction was an illusion. It watched an entire family carried past on a single bike: a father, his wife behind him, a child sandwiched between them, another child behind the mother. And the mother held a chicken in her arms. They swept by in a dull flash of metal, a raw buzz of motor, an ephemeral whiff of exhaust, and then were gone in the anonymous flow of life.

An outdoors marketplace, dazzling at night. The visitor watched two young nuns in gray habits make their way through the current of shoppers. Not far from the market—beside the river, oily black—an equally dazzling carnival for children, open all year round because of the tropical weather. The spinning machines hypnotized the visitor with their bejeweled colors and unknowable functions, seemingly modes of transportation that arrived nowhere.

Though the nuns had stood out to the visitor, as being inexplicably different from those around them, it found itself more fascinated with several monks it observed—for reasons it could only grope at, having no clear memory of its own origin, let alone any concept of spirit versus matter. One day it spied a shaven-headed monk in a robe of sapphire silk walking along the sidewalk holding a covered steel bowl—a donated meal perhaps, probably rice—his eyes looking crazed, as if he might be regretting his vocation, or contemplating the eternal misery of his entire species. But another monk the visitor watched grinned cheerily while conversing into a cell phone. It was all too difficult, too perplexing, for the visitor to put together into any kind of sensible whole.

The visitor did not realize that anywhere it might go upon this globe, no matter how the particulars of a culture might differ slightly from others, it would have been no less perplexed by what it witnessed.

It gradually made its way out of the center of the city, reaching the more rural outskirts, though it had no sense of destination. It became emboldened by the decrease in humanity and sometimes moved by day. On its travels it saw an old man with a bolt-action carbine standing by the side of a country road, aiming at birds perched above him on a telephone wire. When he suddenly looked over and caught sight of the visitor skulking along stealthily, the man shouted a curse and took a shot at it, but the visitor fled swiftly from the loud report and crashed through thick bushes by the side of the road. The birds fluttered up into the air and escaped, as well.

But eventually the visitor's cell growth slowed and halted. Though it had finally formed eyelids and could close its eyes when it chose to rest, it had never grown an upper jaw full of teeth, and had no understanding about how to take nourishment. The visitor weakened, and began to wither. Its vision deteriorated, became unfocused, and its fascinated observation of these alien yet weirdly familiar beings ceased. It dragged itself along at night, laboriously, its tentacles coiling around tree trunks and rocks to help pull it along.

Until at last, one day, it came to rest beside a river, green and opaque, as if some instinct had urged it to slip into the water, which might prove a more appropriate medium for it. Yet it would never learn if this were true or not. It died there in the tall grass by the river bank.

Two young boys, playing, chanced upon the grayish gelatinous mass. One of them suggested they bring their fathers to have a look, but the older of the two said the rotting thing smelled too awful, and he urged his friend to help him push it into the water with long sticks.

Anyway, this boy informed his friend wisely, it was probably just some kind of jellyfish.

CHOLUKAN IN HELL

When Cholukan had subdued the Gold-Scaled Dragon, and turned it to his service—but that is a different story—he directed the beast to thrust its great head through the veil that separates our world from Hell. Squeezing its eyes tightly shut, the Dragon used its horns to pierce through the invisible fabric, and when its head had penetrated the netherworld it disgorged Cholukan—who had ordered the Dragon to swallow him—from its throat. Carefully keeping its eyes shut, the Dragon assured the Holy Monkey that it would honor its promise to return for him when it heard Cholukan play the agreed-upon tune on his enchanted flute, which also served as a walking stick and fighting staff.

"When you return for me," the scribe of the Gods vowed to the Dragon, "I will not be alone."

"I wish you success in that endeavor," the Dragon replied, before withdrawing its head through the tear it had made, which immediately sealed up behind it. Now Cholukan was alone, and he turned to seek out the woman he had ventured into Hell to rescue: the beautiful virgin, Bhi Tu.

But the mission he had set for himself would not be an easy one, and the Dragon itself—though formerly an enemy of Cholukan—had warned him against it. For one thing, the Dragon had advised, if the Gods realized Cholukan was risking his life and very soul journeying into Hell instead of tending to his duties as their scribe among the mortals, they would be displeased—particularly his mistress, the Ruby Empress. But also, as anyone knew, should any creature not of Hell gaze upon that place and its inhabitants, their eyes would be burned right out of their skull. That was the reason why the Dragon had kept its yellow eyes tightly closed, and it was the reason Cholukan had squeezed his own eyes shut before leaping from the Dragon's jaws. If he were to find Bhi Tu in the vastness of Hell, overcome her abductors and return her to the mortal world, he would have to do so as a blind man. Or rather, blind monkey.

He could only assume that Bhi Tu had not been able to keep her own eyes closed all this time; probably her sadistic captors had even forced her to gaze upon them. Though if she had indeed gone blind, then perhaps there was a better chance that she could return the love of a yellow-furred macaque instead of a handsome young man. Cholukan felt guilty for this consideration, but his love for Bhi Tu was that overwhelming.

It was the young mortal girl's uncanny beauty that had so captured his simian heart, but it was this same beauty that had inspired three demon hags to kidnap her.

Every youth in Bhi Tu's village had ached at her beauty since they were even too young to understand what that ache was. By the time Bhi Tu blossomed into womanhood, those same youths now understood their ache all too well, and each young man sought to take the girl as a wife. But Bhi Tu wanted none of them, would not listen to their avowals of love, and spent all her time playing with her friends, to whom she swore one day she would marry a prince or a man of great wealth who could take her far from this too-simple village.

One day while neglecting some chores that her frustrated par-

ents had assigned their day-dreaming daughter, she wandered
out into the grassy hills in search of her silly friends, and along
the way she discovered a lovely flower, the likes of which she
had never seen before, its petals shining like silver hammered
paper thin. No sooner had she plucked the silver flower when
she spied another just ahead, glittering in the tall grass, so she
went to it and plucked it, too. Then another gleamed ahead...
another...until Bhi Tu found herself standing before the mouth
of a cave she had never before encountered, in the side of a familiar hill. Curious, she stole closer, and she could see that an
abundance of the mysterious silver flowers grew in the shadowy
interior, upon the floor of this new-made cavern, which she assumed an earth tremor had opened. Bhi Tu ducked her head
and stepped across the threshold of the cave, and the moment
she did so three sets of strong hands with long talons fell upon
her arms and snatched her hair, dragging her deeper into the
darkness. Behind her, the mouth of the cave rumbled shut as if
it had never existed.

From a distance, just as she was about to call out to Bhi Tu,
one of her friends had seen the beautiful girl step inside the
cavern and had even glimpsed the trio of figures within as they
seized hold of her. She turned away and ran to fetch Bhi Tu's
parents and other villagers, but when they converged at the
hill they could find no trace of the cave. They did not doubt
the friend's story, because she was overwrought with fear and
sorrow, and because at the base of the hill they found several
strange flowers with metallic silver petals, and yet Bhi Tu's parents despaired, not knowing how they could ever claim their
daughter back again.

Cholukan was by chance visiting their village during this time,
charged as he was to walk among humans and relate back their
doings to the Gods. He had grown familiar with Bhi Tu's beauty,

from afar, but he had never approached the girl to speak with her, self conscious about his bestial homeliness. It was because of Bhi Tu that he had been reluctant to leave the area and had lingered longer than he would have otherwise. And so when he heard of the girl's fate, he knew he had to act, even though her captors were undoubtedly demons from Hell. Bhi Tu's friend had seen them only briefly and from a distance, but had said they appeared as grotesque hags. Grotesque hag demons would surely not harbor good intentions for a lovely young virgin girl.

So it was that Cholukan, who had recently bested the Gold-Scaled Dragon, commanded it to vomit him into Hell.

***

As an agent of the Gods, not quite divine but no simple mortal animal, Cholukan possessed marvelous attributes, and one of these was the ability to leap so high and so far that it was as though he were flying. But without being able to use his sense of sight, he was afraid that he might leap straight off a cliff into a lake of molten lava, or onto a field of sharpened knives like countless blades of grass, and so he walked along very carefully, tapping his staff like the cane of a blind man.

Fortunately, another of his attributes was his amazing sense of smell, and his flat monkey's nose sniffed at the air constantly in the hopes of catching a whiff of Bhi Tu to guide him. He had become familiar with Bhi Tu's scent in the village. The virgin's fresh golden skin and glistening obsidian hair formed an odor particular to her, which had nearly driven him mad in close proximity. (As mentioned, however, Cholukan had never dared draw *too* close to her, and wondered if he would have dropped dead of bliss if he had.) But so far, as he tapped his way along rocky paths, the only smells that wafted to Cholukan were the stench of rot and burning flesh, the iron tang of blood, vomit and feces and sulfur.

The Holy Monkey's hearing was uncanny, as well, and he knew by heart the village girl's tinkling giggle, her joyous soaring laughter, her clear and childish voice in song, even her petulant sobs when her parents wouldn't let her have her way. Therefore he tilted his head this way and that as he traveled on, tireless and alone, too driven to admit to exhaustion or loneliness, but the only sounds that were carried to him on the hot breeze that sprinkled him with ash and burning embers were the wailing screams and hysterical weeping of the damned, and the bellowing roars and cackling laughter of demons.

Cholukan knew that it was only a matter of time before he put himself in danger, so he was not surprised when it came. He had followed his current path into a cavern (he could tell by the drop in temperature and the close echoes of his tapping stick), hoping this tunnel might connect with the one from which the three hags had opened a doorway to the mortal world, and he came upon an open chamber in which he heard muffled moaning. He was sure a number of the damned were held prisoner here, no doubt restrained in some form of torture or other, and apparently with their mouths gagged or even stitched shut. But he could not open his eyes to view them...not even when he realized that tending to these prisoners was a demon, which he became aware of when he heard its claws shift on the stone floor and felt its hot, foul breath wash over him.

"Ho! What is this?" the demon growled in a voice like three people speaking all at once: an insane old man, a drowning woman, a shrieking child. "A monkey among the damned? Have you blundered here by some unlucky accident? Animals need not suffer as humans do. You must be a foolish monkey, indeed."

"It is no accident that I am here," Cholukan told the demon, whose form he was actually grateful remained hidden from him, since its voice alone was terrible enough. "I am Cholukan, scribe to the Gods, on a sacred mission, so I would advise you to let me pass." Of course, "sacred mission" was not true, but Cholukan was a monkey and thus a trickster—usually quite gay, filled with laughter and good cheer, always amused by the antics of silly humans, but the severity of his love had made him miserable, since great love is always an affliction like illness, and naturally his journey into Hell had further made him somber and in no mood for play.

"Oh? Well I am Udnet, a murderer in life turned captain of demons, and I have the ability to see into a man's heart and tell when he is lying. I don't know precisely what your lie is, strange monkey, but I can see a lie glowing bright in your heart. How dare you try to trick me, and speak so imperiously to me—you, a mere beast?" The cacophony of blended voices rose in a wild cry. "Prepare to join the Muted on the Wall of Living Nails!"

Cholukan could hear the claws of the demon's feet skittering on the rock floor as it charged him, and he calculated the nearing heat and stink of its breath, so he ducked low and dove into a somersault, rolling under whatever attack the demon threw at him. Above him he heard the demon cutting through the air with its arm or a weapon; he dared not open his eyes to see. But as he came up on his feet again, behind the demon, Cholukan lunged mightily with his staff as if it were a spear. Though the blunt-tipped stick did not pierce the demon's back, it connected solidly. The sharp blow combined with the demon's forward momentum caused it to lose its balance.

Cholukan heard the demon cry out in thwarted rage, followed quickly by pain. There was a heavy thud, mixed with the wet splitting of flesh and the crunch of splintering bone. Then, Cholukan heard nothing more of the demon, besides the faint patter of dripping blood. He knew that whatever the Wall of Living Nails was, it had claimed the demon captain Udnet himself.

Cholukan heard the muffled sounds of the "Muted"—the demon's restrained captives—again, and he felt guilty that he could not free them from their bonds and take them with him out of Hell, but what was he to do? Hell was full of the damned, and he could not save them all. Whether they were sinners who deserved their torments or innocent victims taken into Hell unfairly, like Bhi Tu, it did not matter. Cholukan was here to rescue one soul and one soul only. And so, as badly as he felt, he continued his journey onward, deeper into the labyrinth of stone.

***

Cholukan encountered many more of the damned along his travels through the tunnels, and numerous other demons of apparently multiple breeds and forms, but he was able to defeat or at least escape from all of them. There was the pool in one cavernous chamber, from which a number of yapping, yelping demonic beings emerged. He was able to outrun them, listening to their awkward finned feet slap against the rock floor, and they apparently gave up the chase so as to return to the water, perhaps unable to breathe for long out of their element. In another chamber he had to push his way through a dense forest of hanging bodies, damned prisoners apparently suspended from hooks, who pleaded with him for release, all the while dripping their blood on his yellow-furred head and his blue silk robes.

In one section of tunnel as hot as a furnace, the rock walls of which Cholukan was careful not to touch, another demon burst upon him from out of nowhere and knocked him onto his back on the hot stone floor, almost causing him to open his eyes in surprise. When the demon leapt at him again he thrust out his staff, and as a result of his fighting instincts or just sheer luck the creature impaled its own eye on the end of the stick. Maybe all it had was that one eye, and a huge one at that, for Cholukan was sprayed with its juices. Whatever the case, the dead demon tumbled sideways to the ground, and Cholukan regained his feet, withdrew his staff from the beast's skull, and continued wearily onward…battered and burnt and bloodied.

***

At last, shuffling dejectedly and nearly convinced he would never find his love, nor even find his way out of the infernal maze, Cholukan realized he was inhaling a familiar scent, an intoxicating perfume that did not belong in Hell. He quickened his pace, but no longer tapped his cane, afraid the sound would give him away. Soon enough, he heard faint weeping ahead, in a voice he knew too well. The Holy Monkey found new energy in a powerful surge, his heart filled to bursting with love for the village girl Bhi Tu and hatred for the monsters that had dared spirit her living soul to the netherworld.

Squatting down behind a stalagmite, Cholukan listened to the voices of the demon hags, just ahead in an open room of the cavern's network. In their raspy and croaking voices, they were saying:

"Your great beauty will be ours, maiden!"

"Sip by sip we will take it!"

"We will be more beautiful than any demoness in Hell!"

"More beautiful than once was the Ruby Empress, in Heaven!"

Such blasphemy, Cholukan thought, enraged and ready to burst into the open right then and there, but next he heard the sobbing voice of his beloved:

"No! No, please! Please let me return to my village!"

"Ha! There is no returning from Hell, child!"

"But I came here as no sinner! Through no fault of my own!"

"Oh no? Do you not think vanity is a sin, silly mortal?"

Cholukan heard Bhi Tu spit at the demons. "I can not blame you for wanting to steal my beauty, hag! Look at you...all of you! Like the posterior of an ape, are your faces!"

Ah! thought Cholukan. So Bhi Tu could see them, her eyes not burned out of her head. The demons had obviously cast an enchantment to protect her eyes, then, fearing that her beauty would be disfigured before they could steal it for their own. Once they had done that, what would be left of poor Bhi Tu? A mere husk? No! He would not allow it!

In response to Bhi Tu's angry taunts, the three demon hags screeched in unison. Cholukan feared they would advance upon the virgin girl then, and realized he could no longer delay. And so he jumped out from behind the limestone pillar, and shouted, "Ho, demons! I am the Holy Monkey, Cholukan, scribe of the Gods, and I am here to undo your wicked schemes!"

Now the demon hags wheeled about to face him, for he heard them screech in unison once more, shocked and furious. Then the trio were upon him like three converging whirlwinds.

Never had Cholukan fought so fearsomely, and here he was without benefit of vision. He twirled and swung and thrust his staff, his nimble body spinning and rolling. Claw-tipped hands raked deep grooves in the flesh of his cheeks and tore his blue silk robes to tatters. But one of his fierce jabs caused one of the hags to choke horribly and fall away, her throat crushed. (For demons, having no souls and thus not immortal, could be extinguished like a creature of the mortal world.) He speared another of the hags in one ear and out the other, then planted his sandal on the demon's skull to jerk his staff free again.

The remaining hag fought all the more desperately, leaping upon his back and gouging at his throat with her nails, with the intent of opening his veins. Cholukan dropped his staff and reached up to pull the hag off him. His fingers found her wrinkled face and long fleshy nose, but beneath that he felt something like the mouthparts of a mosquito, including a long quill-tipped proboscis. He took this straw-like growth in his fist, bent forward and threw the hag off his back. Not letting go of her life-stealing proboscis, with his other hand balled into a mighty fist he struck her repeatedly in the throat until the squirming monstrosity went still at his feet.

"Oh monkey! Monkey!" cried Bhi Tu behind him. "You have saved me from those wretched crones! I know you, monkey, from the village where I live."

"Yes, maiden," Cholukan replied as he released the dead hag's weird mouthpiece, his back still turned to Bhi Tu. "I have come to return you to your home."

"Oh monkey," wept Bhi Tu morosely, "look what they have done to my beauty! Poor me...oh look at me!"

What was this? Had the evil hags already begun to sip away Bhi Tu's immeasurable beauty with their greedy mouth-straws? Horrified at the thought, already lamenting, Cholukan whirled around and opened his eyes to gaze upon his beloved Bhi Tu.

In the seconds that his eyes drank in Bhi Tu's beauty for the last time—the seconds before his eyes were burned away like two balls of crumpled paper—Cholukan saw that the girl stood against a rock wall with her shackled wrists connected by chains to two stalactites. She wore a white robe, dirtied and somewhat ripped. And it was true that Bhi Tu had looked better. Her hair was in disarray and in need of washing. Smudges of dirt marred her bared arms and her cheeks and neck. She even sported a few dark bruises here and there, and a number of faint scratches including one across her forehead, but no wounds that would not heal perfectly. The demons had not yet stolen even the tiniest sip of her immense loveliness.

Cholukan dropped to his knees, delirious with agony as his eyes melted away, leaving two empty hollows of bone. He felt around him on the rock floor, searching for his fallen staff which doubled as a flute, so that he might play the special tune that would alert the Gold-Scaled Dragon and summon it to return him and Bhi Tu to the earthly plane...but in his anguish he couldn't locate it. For now was he truly blind.

Helplessly, Cholukan lifted his head and cried into the darkness, "Bhi Tu...tell me, please, and soothe my pain...do you love me now? Will you be the wife of the scribe of the Gods?"

"What?" the Holy Monkey heard the virgin blurt in shock. "Me...the wife of a monkey? Are you mad?"

"But I have saved you! I can bring you back to your parents!"

"Bah!" Bhi Tu spat. "Such a thought! Better I should remain chained to this wall for all eternity than be married to a furry beast!"

Overcome more by the pain in his heart than by the pain of his dissolved eyes, Cholukan pitched forward then onto the stony floor, unconscious.

***

When Cholukan awoke, he found himself cradled in the arms of the Ruby Empress, who sat upon her jewel-encrusted throne in Heaven. Coiled like an obedient dog nearby was the Gold-Scaled Dragon, who had courted the goddess's favor by seeking out Cholukan on its own. Having discovered him, the dragon had swallowed both the Holy Monkey and the screaming, protesting virgin Bhi Tu so as to deliver them to Heaven.

Cholukan gazed up into the Ruby Empress's face in great confusion, thinking at first that he was dreaming. For one thing, he could once again see! Understanding his surprise, the Ruby Empress smiled and explained:

"Foolish child...when the Gold-Scaled Dragon told me of your plan to rescue that mortal girl from Hell, and coughed you up so that I might see your maiming for myself, I wept in great misery. But taking pity on you, despite your rebellious act, I collected two of my ruby tears and placed them into your skull so that you might have sight once again."

"But...but my mistress," Cholukan said in awe, "I believe these new eyes of mine must be enchanted, and enhance the perception of beauty, for you appear more radiant and splendid in your loveliness than any goddess or mortal woman I have ever seen!" Indeed, the ancient Ruby Empress was so youthful and stunning that tears of rapture trickled down the monkey's scarred cheeks.

"Your new eyes do not deceive you, my beloved pet. My beauty has been restored by a spell I have cast upon myself...with the help of a friend of yours. But I must insist, use your new eyes wisely, dear child. You must perceive the earthly world and its denizens more clearly henceforth. Do you promise?"

"Oh yes, yes, heavenly one!" Cholukan wept, embracing his mistress as she held him on her lap. "My love is only for you, from now until the close of eternity!"

"Very good!" said the Ruby Empress. "We shall celebrate your return with tea...and then you can tell me, and the other Gods, of your mischievous adventures in the underworld." The goddess then clapped her hands to summon a new servant girl to bring tea for them.

Into the Ruby Empress's chamber came shambling a bent and hideous hag, with a wrinkled face and long fleshy nose. Whimpering under her breath as she brought forward a tray bearing teapot and cups, Bhi Tu kept her eyes lowered in humility.

And drinking their tea, Cholukan and the Ruby Empress and the Gold-Scaled Dragon laughed in wonderful delight.

AFTERWORD

"We owe more to our illusions than to our knowledge."
— Lafcadio Hearn, *Glimpses of Unfamiliar Japan*

I n 2012, being between jobs, I spent two months in Viet Nam with my ex-wife Hong and our daughter Jade. It was my longest stay there, but not my first. As of the date of this writing I've been to Viet Nam twelve times, beginning in 2004. I fell in love with that vibrant and beautiful country from the first. In 2005 I met Hong there, and though we divorced in 2010, by which time she was living in the States, I have remained close with her and her family.

Hong and her best friend were taking driving lessons during our 2012 visit, so I'd tag along in the backseat, just to enjoy the ride and stare out the window at the world passing by...a world that endlessly fascinated me, a world seemingly other than my own. Beyond the pane of glass that separated me from what I was seeing, there was much beauty and mystery, and occasional pathos. One time we found ourselves in a traffic jam at an intersection, and as our car crawled along I realized why: I saw a pool of blood congealing in the street, standing as thick as nail polish under the hot sun, no doubt the result of a scooter crash. A little purple bag rested in the pool. I would like to think it was just a tiny shopping bag that had blown there, but my imagination told me it was the toy purse of a child. Maybe a child had been the victim. Maybe this child had died. I had no context for the pool of blood.

It was during these rides that it really came home to me how little context I had for so much that I had been seeing for years in Viet Nam. I would see gravestones standing alone or in small clusters in the middle of fields, or even rice paddies, adjacent to rural homes, and I'd wonder how common this was...why the deceased had not been interred in a cemetery. (This inspired the first story I wrote for this collection, "The Uninvited Grave," which I actually began writing on my ex's family's PC.) I saw a tall apartment building draped in green mesh, that was probably under construction but gave the aspect of having been abandoned due to lack of funds; in my imagination, I fancied it might even be under deconstruction. Near the top of this building (or am I conflating it with another building?) I saw huge metallic lettering as some kind of designation. Accurately or not, I later recalled this designation to be *B-2*. If not that, something equally simple but equally impenetrable. Was it an address? If so, why displayed so prominently?

Just as it was that during a car ride with my father in 1980 I came upon the idea to write stories set in a far future city called Punktown, it was as I looked out at this building maybe-going-up/maybe-coming-down that I decided to write a series of stories in which I would supply my *own* context, the context of my imagination, to many of the intriguing sights I was witness to in Viet Nam.

Even with Vietnamese friends and a former Vietnamese wife, too often the real answers and explanations for these sights just didn't come across, either due to our language barrier or our cultural upbringing, or maybe these sights were just too abundant for me to inquire about. What it boiled down to was this: though I had been to weddings and funerals in Viet Nam, divorce court to lend support to a former brother-in-law, had been invited not as a tourist but as a family member to a feast and festival in a local Buddhist temple, and so on, I was still and ever would be a white man, more than a tourist but less than an expat, a stranger in a land that was strange to me but hardly exotic—only too mundane—to those who lived there.

Partly, I decided to set these stories in a fictitious, and nameless, Southeast Asian country out of respect, out of concern for seeming arrogant for writing too far outside my personal background. Even then, I worried my portrayal of people of even a fictitious culture might appear too ugly at times; but then again, without ugly conflicts how involving can fiction be? I've often wondered what Russians feel about all the dark doings Martin Cruz Smith portrays. (All I know is, I love those Arkady Renko novels.) Especially since I wanted only one Western character to appear, who would guide the reader into the Unnamed Country early on before abandoning them there.

But partly, it was simply that to write of Viet Nam, despite my extensive personal experiences, I'd still have to do a tremendous amount of research. I know this because I have, in fact, written of Viet Nam in several short stories, and as of this writing I have a crime thriller novel set in Viet Nam half-finished, but long neglected. Though I'm fond of it and dearly hope to finish it one day, the prospect of delving back into it is daunting indeed.

Lastly, and perhaps most importantly, I simply thought it would be *fun* to translate many of the things I'd encountered in Viet Nam into the stuff of fiction. Worldbuilding could well be my favorite part of fiction writing.

So, I won't tell you here what, in particular, might be a subtle distortion of reality. What might be straight up reality and what might be absolute fantasy, without overlap. I won't reveal what might have been more inspired by Thailand or some other country I'm not personally familiar with. Are two cousins in one story inspired by two cousins in real life, dearly loved nieces of mine? Did the mother of a deformed child in a stroller try to sell me lottery tickets? Have I endured torturous clinic visits to drain blood and pus from a badly infected leg? While suffering this infection, did I have a feverish nightmare about white masks with empty holes for eyes, boiling in a big pot, gradually melting down into the long blanched forelimbs of a crustacean? Did two of the doctors who treated me at this clinic have prominent hairy moles? Did my ex study for a career in nails? For that matter, in the States did I used to work with printed circuit boards? No, no...why reveal the mechanical guts of my fiction to excess? Pay no further attention to the man behind the curtain.

Except, that by way of acknowledgement I'd like to express my eternal love and gratitude to Lan for first introducing me to the culture of Viet Nam, here in the States. Also, to those who showed me Viet Nam firsthand and at length: Thanh Lich, Hong, Quyen, Linh, Thuy, and other friends, lovers, and relatives through marriage. Warts, moles, and all, this is my love letter to you and your gorgeous country, where I will always be an outsider, though it is also my second home.

ABOUT THE AUTHOR

Jeffrey Thomas is the creator of the science fiction setting Punk-town, in which many of his stories are based. His other work includes the novels *Boneland* and *Subject 11*, and the short story collections *The Endless Fall* and *Haunted Worlds*. His novel *Monstrocity* was a finalist for the Bram Stoker Award, and his novel *Deadstock* a finalist for the John W. Campbell Award.

Thomas' stories have been selected for inclusion in *The Year's Best Horror Stories XXII* (editor, Karl Edward Wagner), *The Year's Best Fantasy and Horror #14* (editors, Ellen Datlow and Terri Windling), and *Year's Best Weird Fiction #1* (editor, Laird Barron).

CPSIA information can be obtained
at www.ICGtesting.com
Printed in the USA
LVHW031132120320
649838LV00003B/122